Never Can Say Goodbye

CHERYL BARTON

Copyright © 2025 Cheryl Barton

ISBN: 978-1-948950-75-6

Published by: Pen2Book Publishing House
This book is a work of fiction and any references or similarities to actual events, real people, living or dead, or to real places, are intended to give the novel a sense of reality. Any similarities in names, characters, places and incidents are entirely coincidental.

For permission requests, write to the publisher addressed to: "Attention: Permissions Coordinator," at the email address below.

Pen2Book Publishing House
Email: cheryl@cherylbarton.net

Ordering Information:
Quantity sales.
Special discounts of this novel are available on quantity purchases by corporations, associations, and others. For details, contact the publisher at the address above. For orders by U.S. trade bookstores and wholesalers, please contact cheryl@cherylbarton.net

Dedication

This romantic story is dedicated to my mother, Barbara, who lost the love of her life, my dad, John A. Barton, Jr., to pancreatic cancer. Their 60 years of marriage and endless love from the beginning, when she was fifteen years old and he was seventeen, until his last breath on June 27, 2024, was and will forever be a true testament to what love is all about. Their love is why I love, love and it remains the genre I love writing the most!

Love rules everything around us! I'm blessed to have you; I wouldn't trade you for anything or anyone else. Thanks for being you! Love you, Mom. Miss you, Dad.

About the Author

Cheryl Barton is the author of over sixty romance and inspirational novels. In her spare time, she enjoys traveling, reading crime, espionage and sci-fi novels, watching classic movies and television shows, making wreaths, time spent with family and friends and indulging in Maryland steamed crabs. Connect with Cheryl on Facebook, Instagram, Threads and TikTok. You can find links to her social media accounts at www.cherylbarton.net.

Check out the complete listing of Cheryl's books!

Romance Series'

Island Embers
Hunger for You
Desire for You
Thirst for You

The Brothers of Chi-Town
I Can't Let Go
Swagger and Baggage
Claiming His Child
Always Bet on Black
It Takes Two to Tangle
Crashing into Love
Leaks, Lies, Lust and Love
Love's Gamble

The Sullivans of Montana
Home for Thanksgiving
The Way You Love Me
On the Right Track
Three's a Crowd
The Law of Love

Sister Act
An Unexpected Destiny
For You, I Will
More than Friends

A Lovers' Heart
Heartthrob
Heartbeat
Heartbreaker

Second Chances
Snowbound
Cupid's Arrow
One Wish

Bachelor Series
Bachelor Not for Sale
A Designed Affair
A Perfect Combination
Love at Last

Amorous Occupations
The Artist
The Bookkeeper
The Chef
The Dancer
The Electrician
The Gambler (2026)
The First Baseman (2027)

Sweet Things
The Sweetest Temptation
The Sweetest Revenge

Romance Standalone

Never Can Say Goodbye
The Diner
It Should Have Been You
The Christmas Layover
Love Therapy
Mister Christmas
The Power of Seduction
A Christmas Wish
Being Neighborly
Seize the Moment
Baby, Come Back
Unforgettable
One Moment in Time
Dashing Through the Snow
True Lies or True Love
A Trick and a Treat
When I Think of You
The Lake House

Love at First Sight
Take a Knee
My First Love
Love on Top
His Halloween Promise
Bossy
Holly for Christmas
And Then There Was You
Un-break My Heart
A Better Man
Winter's Wonderland (2025)
His Holiday Wife (Dec. 2025)
Playing for Keeps (2026)
Girls Trippin' (2026)
The Real Deal (2026)

Inspirational Series'

When God Says Yes
Rescue Me
Release Me
Restore Me (July 2026)

Dad's Matter
Girl Dad, 1
Girl Dad, 2 (June 2026)

Encouraging Words from
One Sister to Another
One Sister Away (Vols 1—4)
On Sister Away, Vol. 5

Inspirational Standalone

Breaking Chains: Down, But
Not Out
A Letter to My Mother
Straightening Her Crown

Urban Drama Standalone

*Amerikka: Justice or Revenge
(Dec. 25)*

Urban Drama/Romance Series

Straight Outta Baltimore
Seven Days, book 1 (2026)
Six Relays, book 2 (2026)

2026 New Romance Series

House of Cards
Ace of Spades
King of Clubs
Queen of Diamonds
Jack of Hearts

Family Drama Series

New 12-Book Series
Begins September 2026

Divas of High Hill – The
Series

*Prequel - The Come Up: The
Rise of Tyrus Hill (09/2026)*
Secrets, Book 1 (09/2026)
*Pillow Talk, Book 2
(12/2026)*
*Scandalous, Book 3
(04/2027)*

*Upcoming books italicized

What if I can offer you a lifetime of hellos?

Taryn quickly assessed the weight of what Adrian's devotion to them could and would offer her. Was she ready? Could she live a lifetime of the erotically laced, potent and extremely intense connection between them that caused her body to sizzle with the deepest desire at the mere thought of his touch? His kiss? His...*everything?* At the same time, she also had to consider what his reaction would be if he knew the secret from her past that was now coming back to haunt her thanks to a vindictive ex-boyfriend. Adrian was as close to perfection for her as any man could be. She wanted forever with him and all that it entailed. What she couldn't handle would be his reaction or the way he would look at her if he knew what she'd done. Her fear of that is what gave her pause.

Her eyes rose up from the blank space on the red hardwood floor of his office that she'd been staring at to avoid his gaze. His eyes mesmerized her. She was locked in every time their stares met. When his gallant face came into view, she exhaled at the thought of the millions of questions that plagued her mind.

"No one can offer that with concrete surety. As you can see from my life, I'm always saying goodbye to those I care about the most."

"Baby, there are some instances that are beyond our control. Your aunt once said to me that when your uncle passed away, she didn't see it as a moment of goodbye, but as a time to declare that she would see him later. She never had any regrets because their time together was magical. I'm sorry that you've had so much hurt. I want to be the one to help take as much of that hurt away as I can."

"What if I'm jinxed? What if I'm not supposed to be this happy forever? I'm afraid to say that I love you. Those I love, leave," Taryn sorrowfully declared.

"I can patiently wait for those words to be said to me from you. I know how you make me feel. I know what love looks and feels like. Can you make me a promise?"

Taryn nodded. She would do anything for the man she wanted to love for a lifetime.

"What's that?"

"Focus on saying hello to me every day. When the day comes when your heart wants your mouth to say *love* because no other word will do, you won't fight it. Just let it flow."

"What if I'm afraid?"

"Then my love will be a fence around your heart. My heart will send your fear packing. I'm not going anywhere."

"You don't know everything about me, Adrian. I have a past. I'm not proud of everything I've done in my life."

Taryn wanted to make the promise. Her history of losing her parents and her parental figures, all of whom she loved with everything in her, brought not only fear, but doubt in her ability to have a lifetime of hellos. Most of all, there was her secret. Her past indiscretion was now back in her present. It came with threats against not only her image and her character, but also her relationship with him that could put all that he's built in jeopardy. She cared too much for Adrian to have anything or anyone from her past come for her while also hurting him.

"I don't care. It's who you are now that has me captivated. I'm willing to risk anything. I'm that sure about us."

"What if…"

She paused before telling him her truth. She couldn't; not yet.

"Taryn, baby, no more what ifs. Promise me."

She opened her mouth to say the word and instead, dread over losing him one day was all that her heart and mind could muster up. She couldn't hurt him. She couldn't embarrass him. She'd done something so stupid back in college that she never thought would come back as karma. She couldn't risk it. Her heart loved him, though she couldn't utter the words. Her body loved his and with the way he loved hers, there was no doubt that he was in deep with her. She wanted to get up and run into his arms while screaming yes to anything he asked of her.

Taryn's heart raced. Her palms began to sweat. She knew that she truly loved him with everything in her. She could be left alone in the world if a threat ruined not only their love but any future they could possibly have. She wouldn't be able to live with herself if any part of her past marred Adrian's present and future.

Standing, she walked toward his office door instead of over to him. She opened it and without looking back, she uttered words that she knew were going to cost her everything.

"I…I'm sorry, Adrian. I can't make that promise."

She left, leaving real, true love behind.

1

Paris, France.

Majestic. Enchanting. Artistic. *Romantic.*

This was the place that Taryn Novack called home after years of growing up in the United States, first in California and then in New York City. In Paris, she found the kind of peace that she had been seeking but couldn't quite find until she moved here after graduate school at New York University. Her life was content even on days when she felt that she could be happier someplace else; maybe even with someone? True happiness always seemed to be just out of her reach. What was missing, she didn't know.

She had fallen in love with Paris and its varying yet aromatic smells, its people and its visions of love and romance everywhere she looked. The atmosphere of Paris emitted love in its purest form. That was according to the story her mind fed to her each day. To anyone else looking in on her life, they would think that she was living a dream life. For the most part, she guessed she probably was. Complaining about her life, she would never do. Comparing her life to anyone else's wasn't something she ever did either. There were many people who were less fortunate than her. She gave to charities focused on the arts for that very reason. She couldn't help everyone, but for those that she could give a little of what she had, she happily did just that. Coming from a family that had material things and wealth, she never took any of that for granted. She thought about that and remembered the exception during that rebellious time during undergraduate school. That was when she wanted to be like everyone else. She'd failed at that miserably. Thankfully, there were a few people in her life who refused to give up on her.

At thirty years old, Taryn had taken her time getting to where she was. Dreams were possible; at least when it came to business. When it came to her personal life, not so much. That part had been rocky when it came to her choice of men. Her worst was an ex, Nathaniel Marsden, who just happens to be the son of Eloise Marsden, her boss and the owner of Bridge Tower Publishing House. Located in Paris, the firm hired her right out of graduate school. They had other locations in the United States, even in New York, but she thought change of location was needed.

Nathaniel has been in and out of her life since those early college days. Currently, he was out. She was finally done with the drama of privilege he brought into her space. One thing she knew about herself was that she had commitment issues when it came to relationships with men. She accepted her role in taking an active part in things not working out. Though with Nathaniel, their issues were all him. For now, business would have to suffice when it came to what made her happy.

Her dream job had always been something in the book publishing business. As a senior agent and publisher at one of the largest book publishing companies in the world, she was living a life that made her happy. Not having family close by was a constant hindrance to pure bliss.

The only family member she was close to, on her mother's side of the family was her cousin, Sherita Clayton, who now lived in Boston but grew up in New Rochelle, New York, not too far from her luxury digs in the heart of Manhattan. They spent a lot of time together as kids. There were two others, but now, only her cousin remained. Her favorite aunt and uncle were gone. Other family members detested her due to nothing she'd personally done to them. All she had to do was lose her parents and have her aunt take her in. There were times when she questioned whether she was the drama. She wasn't.

As for her father's side of the family, she never knew them. Her father, Nicholas Novak, had gone no-contact with his family years before he had met and fell in love with her mother, Christine. They had once been living a beautiful life in California; until they weren't. Sudden sadness overtook her. Taryn shook it off and changed her thoughts to happier ones.

Being a romantic at heart, she kept hope that her own prince charming would enter her life one day. Besides, who could live in such a lovely place and not want all things love in their own life? She was just like any other woman with imaginings of love finding her. Her feelings of being alone would hopefully fade with the right man one day. She was ready for more hellos and less goodbyes. Maybe it was her approach to what forever looked like for her; maybe not. Being in Paris never let her forget that love is possible.

Taryn thought back to her last call from her most recent ex-boyfriend, Sean Timpton. Like her on-again and off-again relationship with Nathaniel, Sean, was a reminder that she would not settle for a one-sided relationship just to have someone. She had hoped for something more centered on them instead of what she got, men like Sean who centered on themselves.

Her first mistake once she attempted to have a serious relationship with Nathaniel back at NYU was getting involved with him at all. He was definitely a part of her wild stage in life. She'd grown up following all the rules and doing everything the right way. With him, her wild-child side came out. All that she had done that her aunt finally had to put a stop to, she would take to the grave with her one day. Only her cousin and her best friend, Julianna, knew her absolute truth. Well, them and Nathaniel.

She hated how vulnerable and stupid she'd been with him. Unlike his business-minded mother, Nathaniel was a quick-scheme kind of man. He would have at least one new big money-making plan a week. Not one of them ever panned out. As he had been years ago, he was still living off of his mother's money; unable to make his own way in the world, even at thirty-two. She shook off thoughts of him, Sean and anyone else she didn't want to have living in her head on a day that she was, again, grieving. The last time she grieved this much was when her parents had died back in their California home when she was a little girl.

Today, a bright and sunny day in Paris, her thoughts about them were heavy on her mind. She was old enough when they died to remember them but her memories were fading with each passing year. She thought about them because the closest person to her besides her parents, was her aunt, Misha Horneslow-Rivera. Getting the news that she'd just passed away in her sleep in New York, was devastating. Taryn roamed around her apartment trying to work through what that meant. Her family was getting smaller and smaller.

To begin with, it was official that she was pretty much alone in the world. Her aunt and uncle, Alexander Rivera, who died some years ago, were the bright spot in her life. She missed them more than she thought her heart could stand in order for it to continue to beat.

As she leaned against the glass enclosure of her top floor apartment with a panoramic view of the Seine River and the Eiffel tower, an image in her head turned her frown into a smile. She was thinking of her aunt and uncle, who took her in and raised her as the daughter they were never able to have on their own.

Opening the glass door to her glass-enclosed private balcony, she took in a deep fresh breath of air and closed her eyes against the radiant sun that graced her face. With her aunt on her mind, she found herself already missing all of the adventures she had hoped they would have together. There was so much to enjoy in Paris. She thought about her favorite things to do.

One of her most enjoyable pastimes was having fun on the Bateaux Parisiens Seine River Gourmet Dinner & Sightseeing Cruise. She would love to be doing that with someone, but even alone, the magical moment always exhilarated her.

The view today looked different knowing that she would never get to take another boat ride with her aunt. Their last ride was their final one together almost six months ago. It was one of the few times that she was able to get her aunt on a flight out of the United States. In her later years, she chose to live a quieter life as a best-selling author, writing her popular fiction novels from her top-floor, upscale New York apartment. Memories of life there brought a sudden smile accompanied by a giggle. Those were some amazing days.

Taryn exhaled loudly with a reminder that her last remaining connection to who she was had passed away. There was nothing for her left in New York City now. Talking to her best friend, Julianna Hale, had helped mend her breaking heart. What she had to do next, she was not ready for.

When her thoughts lingered on the past, she rushed back inside of her apartment and picked her cell phone back up. She had left it sitting on her living room sofa, still connected to her call. She was supposed to be grabbing a bottle of water when she'd become distracted by her thoughts and ended up on her balcony.

Plopping down on her medallion yellow velvet sofa, she apologized profusely to Julianna for her forgetfulness of leaving her on the phone, mistakenly forgetting about her. Julianna probably thought she'd left her hanging again, like she's done before; never on purpose though.

"Sorry, bestie. Ugh, I am so, so, so, so sorry. Back to our conversation; I can't go back. I've barely slept after getting the news of Auntie's passing," Taryn explained. She hopped back into their conversation as if she hadn't just ghosted her for a stroll out on her balcony.

Taryn didn't share more just yet. Her nerves have had her up and stressing about her return to New York City. Playing the avoidance game would only take her so far. She knew handling her aunt's affairs was a priority. Truth was, she simply wasn't ready to deal with losing another loved one.

"What do you mean you can't go back? Oh, before I forget, stop leaving me on the phone while you take a stroll around your apartment. I am not that forgettable! I'm your *best* friend," she yelled in a playful tone.

Taryn chuckled to herself at Julianna's fake anger.

"You and Natalie."

"No, chick! I was your friend *before* Natalie came along. Just me. I'm your only best friend. She's a close second. I'll give her that."

"Oh, I am so going to tell her what you said."

Taryn appreciated the friendship of both of her best friends. She and Natalie met at NYU. During their junior year, the Air Force is where Natalie's heart was. She was currently out of the country on a secret assignment. Julianna was able to get word out to her about her aunt's passing. Even though she has yet to hear from her, she knew that Natalie was sending her good vibes and would be in touch when she could.

"You better not. I've seen her take down men twice her size. She would lay me out flat. I digress. I'll be your best friend when we're talking," Julianna kidded.

"I said I was sorry. I promise I won't do it again, today," she joked.

They laughed together.

"Just stop forgetting me when we're on the phone. It's crazy how you do that. Back to what you need to do. You have to go to New York. It's your aunt's final arrangements. She trusted you to take care of everything despite her evil brothers and sister. It's you that she left all the decisions to. This is the woman who raised you. She would go between calling you her niece and then sometimes calling you, daughter. You loved when she did that. I know you don't want the planning of her final arrangements to be left up to her greedy siblings. They will only look out for what would be for them. Who she was wouldn't be considered in whatever outlandish foolishness they would plan. These are siblings who used her as their own personal banks. Your auntie was kind, but not stupid. You can't let her down now. You have to go. I know what you're thinking about. I had a brief image that I'm trying not to bring up."

Taryn exhaled a loud breath again. As soon as she did, she heard a snicker on the other end of the phone. The conversation was about to switch. Leave it to Julianna to make her laugh at a time like this. Taryn threw her head back and gasped out loud. This chick is the only person she would allow to playfully taunt her. She knew her words wouldn't be spoken in any way other than love.

"Jules, do not laugh at me. You know why I'm stressing out over going home. You always do this. What kind of bestie can't stop reminding me of that incident? I wish that I had never told you about it," she grumbled.

"Girl, it's not like you haven't been home since the *big* incident. Should I say big and *long* incident? Should I add in the word, thick? I'm just saying. I need to describe it in the most precise way possible. I wouldn't want to short change anything, as if that were possible! Hey, I'm only quoting your words," she continued with her amusing gibes.

To hear her friend bellowing with outright laughter on the other end of the phone had her chuckling a little to herself. She could never forget that day. At least the thought of day shifted her from a place of sadness over her aunt's death.

Taryn kicked her feet in the air like a child and quietly laughed to herself that they were about to revisit her most embarrassing moment. She hopped up off the chair out of sheer frustration and landed on the black velvet loveseat across from the sofa. She placed her bare feet on the matching ottoman in front of it.

His face appeared and her body tingled at the thought of him.

"I know you're doing the air quotes when you say, *big* incident and all the other words. Don't make what happened sound like a small thing. It was ghastly embarrassing for me. I would hope that you would be more sympathetic."

"Well, according to you, it wasn't a *small* thing at all. In fact, I do believe you used the word big; wait, biggest you've ever seen is also what you said, and so will I."

Taryn tapped her foot and waited through the teasing.

She wasn't ready to entertain that conversation yet again. Before responding to Julianna's outlandish comment, Taryn stood and raced to close her home office door. She had somehow forgotten that one of her assistants, Cordell Howard, was working in there inputting her second round of edits for a novel by one of her latest clients. He was a recent college graduate who was in his sixth month of a paid internship ahead of him going to graduate school soon. She peered through the side glass panel and found Cordell not paying attention to her end of the phone conversation. If he did hear it, he showed no signs. Once a week, she worked from home with one of her assistants in tow. Cordell was today's lucky employee. She had two others, all a major asset to her.

She moved far away from the door before speaking again.

"See? I knew you wouldn't be able to resist bringing that up. Why? Why would someone who claims to be my best friend bring up such a tragic day for me?" Taryn asked, trying her best to whisper and sound serious, though she wasn't.

"*Tragic*? Did you say tragic? Girl, you got a look at the family jewels of one of the finest men either of us has ever seen in our lives. That gorgeous hunk of desire, Adrian Jarreau, according to you, didn't even bat an eye after he realized you'd gotten an eyeful of him; *all* of him. Should I say the best part of him? Tell me again how you ended up face down, eyes peering up under his bath towel? He was naked under there? Hot, sexy New York attorney, Adrian, flashing you like it was a regular day for him to be in the hallway in only a towel, all wet and glistening and sh..."

Taryn stifled a giggle with her hand over her mouth, as she thought back to that day.

"Ugh! Do not complete that sentence. I really hate you. You love rubbing things in my face, don't you?"

Taryn knew when the word left her mouth that she'd made a gigantic mistake. Jules would catch it and make her pay in her torrid response. She loved scorching the earth with her quick comeback.

"I wasn't the one with something in my face that could be rubbed, stroked and all kinds of other naughty things. I would have, you know?"

"Jules!"

"I'm just saying. Not him because he's all yours. Given the opportunity with a fine ass man like him, yeah, I would have. All that and you got up and ran away like you stole something other than a good look at him. I haven't had enough girl chats with you about my antics with men? You have learned nothing from me and my boldness! That was your chance to get a...I would say taste, but not in the hallway," Julianna kidded.

"You are diabolical! I still can't believe I was caught off-guard like that. I didn't mean to snoop at his apartment door. It's just that I could hear him talking to a woman on the other side. I was going to knock. That's why I was at his apartment. Being nosey had me forgetting to knock and do what I had been there to do. He lives one floor below my aunt. He was her attorney. She needed me to drop off a file to him. I wanted to scan the documents in so that I could email them. She insisted that I go deliver them by hand for her. How was I to know that he would open the door with his chest all wet and gleaming with his hips wrapped in a black towel?"

"Whew! Girl! All that chocolate grinning at you from under the towel too? You didn't want just a little?" Julianna joked. "I mean, did you at least wink at it? After all, I bet it was winking at you with that one eye!"

The pure joy of laughter on the other end of the phone had Taryn trying her best to hold a straight face. It was a struggle but she was doing it. She knew Julianna was trying to get a rise out of her over her most embarrassing moment, while also letting her know that it wasn't and still is not that serious. Julianna's plan was working. She was feeling a little less stressed about going back to New York.

She had mourned the day before after receiving the call that forever changed her life. In the midst of that, her thoughts had also turned to Adrian. It was his law firm that had reached out to her about her aunt's death. He'd been on her mind ever since. She would soon have to face that gorgeous rugged face. Adrian was definitely the cause of the warmth currently infusing through her body.

Jules was right that he was number one on the list of fine men. The first time she saw him, there was no doubt that no man could hold a torch to his good looks.

Adrian was tall, over six-feet, sported a close-cut haircut, neatly shaved and a sexy as hell goatee. He had a strong, powerful, confident and more than sensually erotic strut. Just watching that walk was enough to have any woman fanning herself; she included herself in that count. He had legs that made a woman shiver just by looking at them. Along with a behind that could make a woman hum a tune for no reason at all, she was sure he was causing women's legs to twitch and rub together to relieve the pressure of carnal desire. He was the kind of man whose prowess and fierce confidence entered a room before he did. She could attest to that.

"Did you not hear me when I said he was in his apartment with a woman? I could hear her."

"Was she moaning or groaning? Were there sounds that they were getting it in? I'm just saying. You are so short on all the good details."

"Stop it, girl! I tried to race back to the elevator to go back up to my aunt's apartment when his door opened. He poked his head out and called to me."

When she uttered the word, poke, she knew she'd again given Julianna a reason to make yet another crass joke about that word as well.

"If you didn't knock, how did he know you were there? I bet it was that heavy breathing you were doing, right? Go ahead and admit it. I promise I won't tell anyone that you were foaming at the mouth and thinking about sexy, naughty things you'd like to do to and with Adrian. Taryn and Adrian sittin' in a tree, *K.I.S.S.I.N.G*!" Julianna sang.

Taryn waited through another wave of heightened laughter from the other end of the phone.

"A *child!* I am best friends with a thirty-one-year-old child! Can you stop?" she jabbed humorously and found herself laughing too.

Though that day was awkward, it was also hilarious when she thought back on it. At that moment, it wasn't, but months later, she could admit the visual of her tripping over her own feet and landing on the floor at his feet was comical.

"I wish I could, but I can't. You're talking about how you can't go back to New York to handle family business. I know it's because you don't want to run into Adrian. That makes no sense. His firm has been representing your aunt since you were a little girl. If I thought that you were serious about being nervous in your return home, I would catch the first flight from Australia and beat you over the head until you stopped talking like you're not a beautiful, sexy woman. I'm sure Adrian has the hots for you just like you have for him."

"Whatever. You weren't there. I was channeling you when I turned back around and walked toward him. You're the one in this friendship who has no boundaries when it comes to being bold with a man. I'm not like you. I'm more reserved. I was devastated after that fall played out. I was so close to getting away. Why did he have to call my name? Why oh, why, oh why?"

Julianna sneezed on the other end of the phone.

"Sorry about that."

"Bless you. You're still a little under the weather? What are you taking for that cold?" Taryn asked, hoping to change the subject.

"Don't even try it. I peep what you're doing. I'm taking everything that's legal and over the counter. Back to the story. I know you, remember? Your distraction techniques work on others but not your best friend since undergraduate school at New York University. Spill it. You channeled me?"

"You and your favorite TikTok challenge of '*all the pretty girls walk like this*'. When I turned around, that song played in my head. I tried to do a pretty girl walk back to his apartment door after he called out to me. I was doing good until I got a step or two in front of him and my two left feet kicked into high gear. I started humming that song in order to stay in step. The next thing I knew, I tripped and fell right at his feet. When I tell you I hit the floor face first and right onto his bare feet, I'm not joking. My skirt flew up and I could feel a cool breeze on my behind. I looked up and his hand was reaching down to help me up."

"Oh, oh, wait. This is the part of the story that I love. I'm enjoying revisiting this. Do you mean like the scene in our favorite movie, *Mahogany?*"

Taryn cut her off, knowing what was coming next.

"Don't you dare, Jules," she yelled.

Her plea was ignored when she heard the beginnings of the famous line from the movie.

"You want my arm to fall off," Julianna quoted from the movie.

"You had to do it."

"It was that movie kind of moment. I'm saying, just priceless. All the good stuff happens to you. The jewels – you got an eyeful, huh?"

Taryn shivered remembering exactly when she lifted her head and her eyes landed on that part of him under his towel that was uncovered, long, and thick and pointing at her.

"I've never seen anything like it. It was big, Jules. I mean, bigger than any I've ever seen in person. Not that I have as much experience as you. Still, I've seen a few. He was more than what you would call, hung like a horse. Just, damn! I was *shooketh*. I couldn't speak. I couldn't move. I tried to look away and when I did, it was to look up in his face. The look he had said he knew what'd I'd seen. I would say it was a cocky look, a slight grin, but it wasn't. He earned that self-assured look. He knows what he has in that department."

"As he should. Not all men can say they have that. All I need to know is, did you secretly wish for the towel to fall?"

"No. I was too stunned that I'd fallen face down and ass up in front of him."

"Please tell me you didn't have on granny panties. You had on something cute, sexy and lacy, right? If you're going to be embarrassed, it's all about the sexy and wowing him at the same time."

Taryn grunted her annoyance.

"I do *not* own granny panties of any kind. You know how I am about lingerie. The amount of money I spend on it because I love how I look in them and how they make me feel, should be illegal. I love that sexy, barely-there stuff, so no granny panties. The only relief I got was that I had on a red-laced thong. He got a view of nothing but cheeks."

"Girl, with all that you have back there, I would say that he was probably well pleased. I say it was all fair game. You saw his, and he semi saw yours. Get your behind back to New York and fake a fall in front of him again. This time, when he reaches down to help you up, reach up under that towel, girl."

"Now, if the tables were turned, it would be considered a crime for him to reach out and touch me. I can't just do that without being invited."

Taryn shook her had no, as if Julianna could see her. They usually video chat, but not today.

"Oh, I get it. You want an invitation."

"Can we end this conversation now? Of course, I'm going home. I'm having a moment about being there knowing that now, my uncle and my aunt are gone. I'll be there for about six weeks to take care of my aunt's affairs before returning to Paris. Maybe a little longer. I don't know yet. I'll need to get her apartment ready to sell. I'll do some work in the last week or so that I'm there. The book editing and publishing business will continue on while I'm in the United States."

"I hear sales of your aunt's books are through the roof since her passing was announced," Julianna said.

"I just received word that all of her mystery novels are flying off of the shelves. The publishing company has put in for an emergency order of all of her books. Downloadable and audio versions have sent all of her books to the top ten lists overnight again; not that being in the top ten is new for her books. Every one of her novels lived there at one time or another."

"What's Eloise putting in place to celebrate your aunt's life and legacy?"

"They are also sad and mourning her passing. She has them preparing a huge media campaign of her career long achievements. Social media is already buzzing like crazy with condolences. Her fans, I hear, have been leaving flowers, balloons and other mementos at her New York apartment as well as at book stores across the country. She was a big deal in the writing world. Once I began working for the firm and my aunt switched from her old publishing company to us, we have moved from being one of the top ten publishing houses in the world to one of the top five. Her books have done wonders for us, like a Stephen King novel does for his. Her latest was already sitting at number one for the past five months with over seven hundred thousand copies of her latest mystery novel sold in the first week of its release. The writing world just loss a major player in the game. Twenty-five years of writing some of the best mystery novels made my aunt a household name."

Sadness replaced her feelings of anxiety about going to New York the next day. Taryn needed a little time to make sure everything at the office was covered while she was away. She was planning on doing work while away, but not as much as she usually would. Everyone understood what was ahead of her. She was being given the room she needed to take care of wrapping up her aunt's life in New York. What she wasn't prepared for was dealing with her aunt's two brothers and one sister, along with their kids when it came to the millions of dollars they knew she had coming to her. Her aunt's wealth was well-known. Whether it was true or not, an estimate could easily be found on the internet.

"Your aunt was the best. I swear, every time I was at her apartment and she cooked those soul food meals, I didn't want to leave. When she would send me meals where all I had to do was heat them up in the microwave, I ate every single one of them. Trust, I never left even a crumb. My cat even scowled at me for not dropping anything for her on the floor."

"Molly will forever hate you for that. Your cat is precious. My aunt was an amazing creative writer but more than that, she could hurt something in the kitchen. I loved her meal care packages too."

"I am that typical Caucasian who did not come from a family that knew how to use seasonings. She sure could cook. She loved me like I was a daughter to her. I will miss her. Once arrangements are made, you know I will be there on the first plane smoking to New York. I'll be back home in Los Angeles in a few days. Call me if you need me. Don't you let your uncles and aunt get under your skin. They've always been jealous of the love and financial support your aunt has always given you, even before your parents died. Your relationship with her was priceless. Hold your head up and ignore your family if you need to. Do you think they dislike you because your mother and your aunt had different fathers than your uncles and aunt? I mean they are Maxwell's while your mother and aunt were Horneslow women."

"Those Maxwell men, my uncles Antony and James, are the biggest thorns in my side. Both have been calling me nonstop about money just since yesterday. That could be why. My aunt never really said. No hint of condolence in their voices. My aunt has only been gone for one day. She died a day ago! They are relentless. They barely speak or talk to me, yet they hound me about what they feel they deserve from her estate."

Taryne exhaled in frustration. She had to make herself stop answering their calls. She didn't want to block them, not yet, but she wasn't ready to handle conversations about money until she knew what the estate was all about. She would soon find out.

"I don't like them. They look creepy, anyway. I still wish your uncle Antony would spend his time looking for that *"h"* missing from his name," Julianna joked.

Taryn stood and reached for the letter she had received early in the morning from her aunt's law firm. She had skimmed it but now, she wanted to read it more thoroughly.

The minute she stood and laughed at the running joke about that letter missing from her uncle's name, she almost tripped over her feet that often didn't want to cooperate with her brain.

"I almost fell I'm laughing so hard. He still tells the story about how their mother misspelled his name on his birth certificate. He went eighteen years spelling it with the 'h', only to find that there was no 'h'. That was discovered when he applied for his first job and needed his birth certificate. It's the family joke that won't die."

"Your uncle is so weird. He tells everybody that story."

"He's a clown for sure. I'm actually ready to deal with all of them. They've treated me like I was a virus ever since my aunt took me in. There is no love loss at all. I will abide by whatever my aunt put in her will. If she didn't give them much, I don't owe them anything. I need to get off the phone. I still need to finish packing for my trip tomorrow. Wish me luck."

Taryn knew it wasn't luck that she needed. Truth was, she needed a fairy godmother to help her get in and out of New York without too much interaction with Adrian. That was a lie and she knew it. She wanted to see him while also, not. She still wondered what he and the woman in his apartment had been doing when she walked up to his door. Had they just finished something or were they on their way to doing something? She didn't know. What she did know was whoever the woman was, she was lucky at how blessed Adrian was in all arenas. He was fine, intelligent and wealthy. Yeah, he checked the boxes of most, if not all women.

"I'm wishing you luck for another chance to be head down and tail up but in an entirely different setting!" Julianna screamed in the phone.

"I hate you!" Taryn laughed.

"I love you too! Text me later and when you land tomorrow. I'm sure we'll hear from Natalie soon. Tell Adrian I said, *heyyyyyyyyyyy*!"

Taryn ended the call, dropped her cell into the pocket of her sweat suit and raced off to her Zoom meeting. Cordell was already waving her to hurry. It was clear he had already logged them onto the meeting.

With Adrian and her aunt on her mind, if she didn't slow down, for sure she would topple over her feet again. Thankfully, if she fell today, she had on pants. She could save face with Cordell.

That day in the hall with Adrian did delight her desires and her dreams. Every night, she dreamt a dream of a different scenario that day. All of the dreams began with him welcoming her into his apartment. She would find that there was no other woman inside. Instead, he had his television on. From there, each dream started out differently but ended the same way; with her satisfied beyond her wildest and most wickedly, erotic dreams.

Adrian is that man. In another day, he would no longer be a star in just her dreams when she went to sleep at night. He would be the star in her waking hours as well; no doubt. With his firm representing her aunt, she would have to face him. What happens after that, she could still only imagine.

2

Adrian Jarreau stood at the floor-to-ceiling window in his fifteenth-floor office located in downtown Manhattan looking through the electronic file of the client who'd just left his office. His plan for the meeting was to transfer the case to a junior partner in his law firm, Jarreau, Gerard and Associates.

The firm was situated on the top three floors of building. They were at the top of prime real estate in the heart of New York City. With the partners and senior attorneys occupying the top two floors, everyone else sat on the ninth, tenth, eleventh and twelfth floors.

The offices were easily accessible either by the spiral staircase that went from the eighth to the twelfth floor. The eighth floor was full of conference rooms where most of their meetings with clients took place that were outside of their individual offices. There was also an elevator that serviced the entire building. Not just residing in the building, the law firm now owned the entire building; an acquisition he oversaw a year ago. He and his best friend and partner in the law firm, Zacarious "Zac" Gerard, leased out the rest of the building to various companies that occupied the remaining floors.

The firm that their fathers, William Jarreau and Armand Gerard, had started when he and Zac were little boys was flourishing beyond where most thought it would be, including their fathers who were both retired.

Looking down at the file again, he was glad that Zac had agreed with him that the case could go to one of their junior associates with the proper oversight from one of them. They grew up as sons of partners in the firm. He and Zac went to separate schools but remained close. After attending the same law school, they realized it was a given that they would join the firm. The plan all along had been that they would take over once their fathers were done with the heavy load that partners carried. It was an easy transition from the fathers to the sons without even needing to change the name of the firm.

The letters declaring their partnership stood in big, black and bold letters on the wall of the eighth-floor entry level of their firm. There were sixteen other junior partners but their names were not on the wall. It had been decided years ago, long before he'd even started undergraduate school that the name of the firm would never change as long as a Jarreau and a Gerard sat on the board as senior partners. Another one of Zac's brothers, Tomarious was also employed by the firm as a junior partner. They were absolutely keeping it all in their families.

Adrian thought about his younger twin sisters, Adore and Amira who were twenty-six years old. Adore, who decided going into the family business was not for her decided on a career in dance. Loving dance and theater since she was a child, she was already a star on Broadway who had recently made the transition from theater to the movie screen in an upcoming movie with a musical touch to it. According to early reviews, that was certain to be a blockbuster. He couldn't wait to be in the front row supporting.

Adore was so sure of her career that she was making a move from her New York apartment to a new place that she'd recently purchased in Los Angeles. They remained close, not just as brother and sister, but the firm also represented her in all legal matters. He was looking forward to meeting her for a quick bite to eat in a few hours before her plane flew out to the west coast. His father had already flown out to California ahead of his sister declaring that he wanted to do a thorough check of where she and another friend of hers would be living. He was happy knowing that she wasn't giving up on Broadway. She was planning on flying back and forth depending on the project. If his father hadn't volunteered to go, Adrian was going to make plans to accompany her. He loved his sisters and watched over them closely as a big brother should.

Amira was an entirely different story. He and his father had to watch her and her finances closely. She was, what they considered, the wild child of the family. She likes to flaunt the family wealth and often drew the wrong attention, especially across her many popular social media accounts. Because of her still not knowing what she wanted to do with her life, his father made it his mission to watch all of Amira's spending.

After she agreed to go to college after much negotiating years ago, he was happy when she graduated with honors in fashion with a minor in interior design. Since then, even though he tried to get her to continue on to get her master's degree, she decided to be a social media influencer. That included many ups downs and questionable boyfriends of all types. Luckily, she was still tapping into her degree in interior design by working for a friend, Loren Bailey, as a favor to him. Loren had recently opened a New York location for her firm.

Adore was the only reason he'd driven his own car to the office today. He parked in their underground garage, reserved only for partners and senior attorneys. Most used the company car service, so the garage wasn't utilized often. He rarely drove himself. He preferred his exclusive use of one of their company cars the majority of the time. That way, he could be free to look over work or handle business calls in the back seat as his driver weaved in and out of traffic like a typical New York City driver would do. Zac had exclusive use of a vehicle just as he did. The other four were available for other junior partners and attorneys to use for work purposes only.

Today, he'd sent one of the cars to bring his client, Otis Jones, to the office for a sit-down meeting. That wasn't his usual action, but today, outside of their monthly appointment, he needed to discuss a change in his representation. The talk needed to be held in-person. Suffice it to say, Otis didn't take to the change very well.

Adrian had been his lawyer since acquiring the case from his father a few years after Otis had won large in the New York lottery. The senior Jarreau had helped Otis with all of his legal matters, including pointing him in the right direction for financial help with an accountant and a financial advisor. Otis didn't want to be pawned off on a junior associate and fought hard against the change. Adrian's plate was fuller than usual with a lot of new business they'd acquired over the last year.

Most recently, he became the lead attorney for Tellum, Byrum and Callum Blackstone out of Detroit, Michigan. The brothers own a very profitable company, *Blackstone Real Estate Investment Trust Corporation*. The popularity of the resorts they own have skyrocketed to wealth that not many others attained as fast as they have. With their newest resort ventures, three hugely popular resorts, *Secret Whisper, Silent Whisper* and *Quiet Whisper*, along with big revitalization plans of several Detroit neighborhoods, his firm being their new lawyers would see great things in the business world for them all. He had promised more dedicated time for them which meant moving some of his cases to other associates. He was starting with Otis'.

Recently, Otis had begun to be a problem for him. He wanted someone who could spend time keeping him out of trouble more than anything else. Besides that, Otis was being hit with a bogus lawsuit, something he warned his client to be on the lookout for. People often targeted the newly wealthy in schemes to get a quick come-up for themselves. It wasn't until he guaranteed Otis that he would keep a close watch over the case and would step in if he was needed, that the man agreed to let a junior associate handle his case on a temporary basis.

Flipping from one electronic folder to the other, he smiled when he clicked on the folder and the first file was that of a beautiful woman. While his mind focused on her case, his eyes focused on her beauty. It was Taryn Novack.

Adrian couldn't help but smile knowing that even though Taryn did her best to avoid him her last few visits to her aunt, there was no way she would be able to do that going forward. He looked over the context of the last will and testament of her aunt who had passed away in her sleep a few days ago.

Misha's housekeeper had found her still in bed on her side, her body cold to the touch. After making the call to emergency services, who confirmed Misha's death after arriving, her housekeeper made a late-night call to the law firm, knowing that's what Misha had always instructed her and others close to her to do if that time came. The firm had a phone service that employed live customer service agents around the clock. The call from the housekeeper was immediately forwarded to him. He reached out to his father who wanted to make the call to Taryn. Adrian had no problem with his father's request. He had been a longtime friend of the Rivera's. He had always treated Taryn like family. At this time of great sorrow for her, he didn't want anyone else talking to her except him. Adrian gave him that.

As for Misha's representation, Adrian had been handling everything and would continue to do so until the work on her will and various trusts was done. He would make sure everything she wanted would be done according to her specific instructions. The first of those was that he be the one to handle everything exclusively. Misha had been very clear that under no circumstances was he to pass off or allow another lawyer in the firm to handle her business. He found it odd that she was clear that the overseer would be him and no one else; not even his father.

While she was alive, even after his father retired, she would reach to the elder Jarreau for all of her legal needs. His father stayed on for three of four of his clients who agreed to stay with the firm as long as they could count on him to stay abreast of any and all legal issues. Misha was one of those clients. It was a shock to him and his father that her wish was no one but him. He would do exactly that.

As for Taryn, he was told that she took the news extremely hard, as he expected she would. He'd had a rough night of sleep that night himself knowing that he could do nothing for the pain she was going through. There was something about her that he'd kept only to himself. He felt drawn to her for more than just the connection through her aunt. He genuinely felt like they could have something special. There was an innocence in how she responded to him while at the same time, there was a sexy woman with electric eyes that reeled him in like a moth to a flame. That is, if she would stop avoiding him every time she was in town. He cared about her. She seemed like the kind of person who had resigned to walk through this life alone. He knew what that looked like and it was all her.

He spent the evening before going over all of Misha's assets to be sure he had a full record of everything. She had been one of his father's longest running clients, for her and her husband. Their investments and business wealth had made them a very wealthy couple. Alexander, who had passed some years ago, had become one of his father's closest friends. It was due to clients like them that kept the firm in the green with record profits each year. They also represented some of the most affluent around the country. Most lived whole or part-time in New York City. The law firm went back over thirty years and was well-known. Giving his full attention to Misha's estate was going to be his priority until everything was settled.

What he remembered reading in the file was how she was estranged from her family, specifically her brothers Antony and James and her sister, Valencia Clayton. She was close with her nieces and nephews but her siblings felt entitled, something she had dealt with most of her adult life. Not only were her novels extremely profitable, but her husband had been a self-made millionaire several times over. They had no children of their own and enjoyed splurging on Taryn.

They had raised her since she was made an orphan when her parents died when she was a small child. That child would turn into a beautiful young woman whom he'd been infatuated with for a few years. That was a long time before they'd had the most awkward interaction in the hallway outside of his apartment. That was actually the day that his desire for her awakened in a way that no woman had made him feel more alive before. He was excited to see Taryn again. He chuckled to himself when he thought back to the last time he'd seen her three months ago on the street outside of the building where he and her aunt lived. Misha had the top two floors of the apartment building that overlooked central park. He lived one floor below her.

Three years ago, he'd bought the apartment from one of the firm's clients after he had the chance to see Misha's apartment when he accompanied his father to a meeting with her. He loved where the building was located and the views were the best he'd ever seen. He didn't have two floors but he had a corner lot and could see his favorite view of central park. His parents owned an apartment on the other side of the park that also overlooked the view of the entire park.

On that day a few months ago when he saw Taryn in New York, she must have seen him get out of his car when his driver dropped him off in front of the apartment building. Most times, he would have him drive into the garage and take him right to the elevator that would take him to his floor. Only those he gave the passcode to could get off of the elevator on his floor. He'd given that passcode to Misha and a few others in his building that he'd befriended. That had been how Taryn was able to get access to his floor that day that she'd tripped and fell at his feet. The vision of desire of her that day lived permanently in his head. His body had reacted that day and did again on the day he caught her trying to avoid him. He was hoping to get to a place with her where she no longer did that.

He had caught sight of Taryn as he exited his car. He was on his phone, but he sensed her presence. He often did when she was around. It was kismet. Taryn had been walking in the direction of the building. At a call he'd had with Misha earlier that day, she mentioned that Taryn was in town to visit her. In fact, every time Taryn was in town over the past year, Misha made a point of dropping that information to him in a conversation. If he hadn't known any better, he would have thought that her aunt wanted the two of them to connect on a level that wasn't business. He would like nothing more than that if it wasn't for the fact that Taryn stayed as far away from him as she could since that day in the hall.

Out of the side of his eye, he caught sight of her headed toward the building entrance. When she saw him, he watched her pivot and race back in the direction she was coming from. She probably thought that he as preoccupied with his phone call. He wasn't. He was preoccupied with everything about her. Before she disappeared hurriedly around the corner, she tripped and almost fell. He reached for her from a block away as if he could catch her if she had fallen. He was happy that she hadn't. He was saddened that she had once again, ran from interacting with him. It wasn't his plan to open his door in only a towel after a shower. While in the midst of a conversation with a woman friend he'd had over ahead of them going out on a date, he heard footsteps outside of his door. Only someone with the passcode could be on his floor. He was curious as to who it could be. He then looked into the camera next to the door and saw her on the other side. After that, the rest of his evening was a blur. The way she looked up at him with her big, beautiful, bright light brown eyes, he was a goner.

Taryn was beyond what the word beautiful would describe. She was irresistibly alluring. In a way, he would describe her as bewitching because of the spell she'd cast over his entire being. He didn't want to think about her body. The part of her that he'd seen that evening was more than he knew she wanted him to see. He couldn't look away. No red, hot-blooded man would be able to do so. Still, he tried to give her grace by helping her up. He was so taken by her that he actually forgot that he was naked under the towel. His concern was in helping her after her fall. He remembered when she saw how naked he was underneath of his towel. That's when he tried to swiftly lift her up beyond where her eyes could see. Before he could say more than a few words of apology once she was standing, she pushed a folder into his chest and raced off. He wanted to go after her but knew that the time for that wasn't that day. Since then, he'd seen sights of her but each time, she made sure she dodged even a simple hello. Her swift greeting was more of a goodbye because she was always heading in a different direction if she spotted him.

Taryn was heading back to New York. He had been expecting her a day ago but she had called the firm to leave a message that she was delayed. Her message had been left for his father. She would soon find out that he was the attorney who was handling her aunt's estate. If she had plans to continue to sidestep him, that would no longer be likely. He'd had one of the executive assistants reach out to her to schedule a meeting with the firm, but not mention who the meeting was with. He assumed that Taryn would think she was meeting with his father. Being hopeful that the awkwardness could soon be put to rest, he was hoping a meeting in the office to talk only about business could assuage any odd feelings between them. As the trustee over her aunt's estate, he wanted to have a preliminary talk with her about everything that was included in the three separate trusts in his firm's hands. One of direct finances, or money, another over property and the last over all stocks and investments. A completely separate trust was set up to be distributed to charities. Her portfolio was worth over a hundred million dollars. Most of that was headed in Taryn's direction. The New York apartment alone was worth over twenty million dollars.

Flipping back to the first page in the folder, he looked over the note Misha left for him that could only be opened after her death. In it, she warned him about her family and to be on the lookout for their schemes to get their hands on her money and property. Adrian wasn't worried. Everything his father and he had worked out with her was iron clad. Anything her family got their hands on beyond what was left to them would only come by way of Taryn, if that's what she chose to do.

"Adrian, Melvin Tribble is on the phone for you," his assistant, Jocelyn Fox said, entering his office and invading his thoughts. He cleared his throat in hopes it would clear his mind as well.

"The office phone?" he asked.

"Yes. He said he dialed your personal cell and your business cell a few times and you didn't pick up. He has some questions about the updates to the trusts for his daughters."

Adrian looked to his cell phones on his desk and saw the missed calls. His phones must still be on silent from the evening before. At least once a week, he promised himself that he would either turn his phones off or put them on silent for an entire evening. There wasn't a person around him who didn't remind him that he spent too much time on business and not enough of anything not work related. Last night was that night of stepping away from business. He took the time to finish reading the latest Stephen King novel and chowed down on pizza and nachos, the opposite from his usual healthy eating. Staying in shape was a priority for him. He loved that his apartment building had an entire floor dedicated to a gym for the residents only. Once a month, he put eating healthy aside and just indulged himself with whatever he wanted. Good food and a great novel relaxed him. He'd fallen asleep with the book on his chest. Invitations from friends, some who were women he deemed friends-with benefits, had bombarded his phone, but he turned them all down. Even Zac tried to get him to hit up a private party being thrown by one of the top actors in the business. His emphatic no had him pleased with himself. He just wanted some time to himself. He could hang out another time. A night like that was few when it came to his schedule. He was learning.

He reached for the speaker button on his office phone before selecting the line that was lit up.

"Mel! What's going on, man? It's been a minute. What can I do for you?" he asked.

"What's got you bogged down today? I've been calling you for the past hour or so."

"Looking over a client's file for a meeting I have coming up. Problems with the trusts?"

"Not really a problem. I want to raise the age of when my daughters will receive their trust funds. This isn't about the trusts they'll get when I pass one day. It's about making sure that the additional money they were going to get at twenty-five won't come to them until they're thirty. I want them to have a stipend distributed monthly, but not the full amount until five years later than what we have in the original documents. My wife and I believe neither is mature enough to handle the kind of money coming their way at twenty-five. Age thirty would be better. Can we meet and take a look at that? I've already spoken to my money guy, Jimmy. I told him I would like to have you in on any discussions about the trusts. I don't want any legal issues with them. These girls are meeting some of the most outlandish type guys who we believe are all about their money. I used to think social media was a good thing until my daughters started meeting fools," he quipped.

"Did you take my advice and talk to them about not telling anyone about the kind of wealth coming to them? With your popularity, I know people can read about it, but who believes those numbers. It's a given that one day, they will be rich. No one needs to know what that day is."

Adrian often asked his clients with teenage and young adult children to set up an appointment with them and him so that he can share how important it is for them to protect the knowledge of what they have or will get financially. Every schemer will come out from the depths of hell on earth to get their hands on the money even if they have to make them think they're the best thing since popcorn. He'd spoken to Mel's twins. Apparently, the chat hadn't worked.

"I tried talking to them. They are twenty years old now and are already out of control."

"Don't tell me one of your girl's has met such a guy."

"You got it. Maia has. Mia, not yet, but she's just like Maia. It's some law student she's dating at her school. Every week she calls me with some reason of why she should and could be entitled to her trust fund now. I'm tired of hearing it. She meets people who know they're the daughters of a former professional quarterback."

"That must be interesting."

"I thought my boys would be bad. It's the girls I'm having issues with."

Adrian understood that. His mind turned to his own sisters and the plight with them, money and men.

"Okay, let's set something up. We can use my office or I can come to you. You know my schedule is brutal but I'll make time for you."

"Can you and I get together first about something else? I have another legal problem I need to talk about in private."

The minute Melvin started whispering, Adrian knew it meant he must have slipped and fallen into yet another woman.

Adrian exasperated an air of disappointment. He knew what was coming.

"Tell me you didn't?" he asked.

"Man, I don't know why I can't stop," Melvin admitted.

Adrian shook his head and slammed his body back into his large leather office chair. He spun it around to face the window as they talked. He was glad his assistant had closed his door on her way out. This sounded like it was going to be a heavy talk.

"You cheated on Sabrina again? How far along is this one?"

"A couple of months. I'm sure Sabrina is going to leave me this time. I have too much time on my hands after retiring."

"We talked about this. I'm not only your lawyer but I'm your friend. You will forever be a target for those out looking for their come up. You give your kids the same advice but you don't listen to it or me for your own actions. Was this another strip club honey?"

"You know it. We've had a thing going for about six months. It kind of happened," Melvin tried to explain.

"No, it didn't. It happened to you because she wanted it to. I know it's how you met Sabrina. You actually married her after meeting her at the same kind of spot. You have four adult children with your ex and two kids with Sabrina. She forgave you after the last slip up that's now a beautiful five-year-old little princess. I think you're right that she's not going to let this one slide. Do you remember what I told you about how much of your money she will get if she divorces you behind this one? I warned you about this. I'm pissed that your old attorney, before you moved to me, didn't give you a stern warning about not having a prenuptial agreement. You didn't learn from your ex?"

"I want to get ahead of what she's going to do. I know it's going to cost me plenty."

Costing him plenty was the least of Adrian's thoughts. If his wife decides to leave him, due to the prenuptial agreement they signed, she will get half of everything.

"Half, Mel. She will get half. That's over two-hundred million dollars in money and assets. Geez, man. Let's get together over a few beers tomorrow evening. I'm meeting my sister tonight before she heads to L.A. I'd like to have this conversation sooner rather than later. This new girl? She's going to keep it or is she looking for a big pay day to get out of it?"

"She wants to keep the baby. Of course, she wants eighteen years' worth of pay days. How have you escaped populating New York all of these years? I've seen the women you've been connected to. I mean, you've had some serious beauties. No slip ups? Not even close?" Melvin asked him.

"Not even close. I don't play like that. I love women. There has been no shortage of them in my bed. I'm purposeful about there being no babies until I'm ready. I'm as careful as any man can be. I'm selective. No disrespect to you, but a strip club isn't where I would find a woman to slide into. I love a cute face and a sexy body. Most of all, I love brains and a plan on top of all of that. I also don't plan to have any kids until I find the right one. No kids with women I'm just having a good time with. I make sure I'm clear about that. Sure, some have plans of a wedding and babies. That has to be a two-way street for me."

"How do you plan to ever do that unless you come out from under all the legal books every day? You're more dedicated to your career than I was as a quarterback."

Adrian thought of Taryn and the possibility. She was his perfect woman. He knew everything about her from her aunt. She was the kind of equal that he wanted and needed in his life. He'd met other women that could fulfill him for a lifetime of great sex. He could even see that with Taryn, if she would give him a chance at that. With her, he was treading lighter than he usually would with a woman he found attractive. There was something about Taryn that told him she was the one. He didn't want to mess up an option to have her in his life for more than just sex.

"Believe it or not, I have someone in mind. I have to work on my swag in order to see if she's as interested in me as I am in her."

"What? I'm intrigued. There is a woman out here in the world that has turned the great Adrian Jarreau's head and heart? I'm jealous. You got it, bro. I've seen you with celebrities of all types, especially some of the hottest models.

There have been actresses, women big in business and even a talk show queen. Not once have I ever heard you say that there is someone beyond the benefits alone. I will believe it when I meet her. She has to be some kind of woman. As for tomorrow, let's do it. I need all of the help I can get. If that includes a brick up the side of my head, bring one with you. I'm an idiot. I didn't learn the lesson when I cheated on Maia, Mia, Kenny and Damon's mother. Now, Sabrina will leave me and take my two I have with her away. Seven kids, man. I've got seven kids, not counting the one on the way. I guess money doesn't buy common sense," Melvin admitted.

Adrian chuckled, not out of ridiculing his friend but because they have been having this kind of conversation for many years.

"Let's meet at our favorite spot in Brooklyn," Adrian offered.

"Eight?" Melvin asked.

"Eight is fine."

"Come prepared to tell me about this mysterious woman. I have to know the woman who is about to turn the world of single women everywhere upside down," Melvin joked.

"Yeah, whatever. I'll see you at eight."

"Wait. This isn't someone who'll be out for your money, is she? You're worth what now, about fifty-million dollars? Who knew that lawyers actually had that kind of worth?"

Adrian snickered. He's seen all kinds of articles on his net worth on the internet. None of it was true.

"A few million more than that. All due to my pops and his penchant for investing in us and providing trusts for my sisters and I when we were young. He invested well and our accounts reflected his good choices and decisions. About half comes from that. The other comes from my own investments and clients like you who keep me busy and in the green. As for this woman, she wouldn't need to be after my money. She has her own. Believe it or not, it's more than what I have, so it's all good. I hope she feels that way. I'm not a man who has ever been the type to be after a woman's money. I've dated a few who have been better-off than me. I like a woman that has her own. I am a man who has my own. I see that as the makings of a great power couple in any arena. That way, money isn't a factor when it comes to love," Adrian explained.

"Love? You're in love with this woman?"

"I didn't say all of that. I'm just explaining my thoughts when it comes to money and relationships."

"See, that's what I'm talking about. My first wife had money coming into the marriage. I messed that up by not keeping it in my pants. Don't get me wrong, I love Sabrina but she's about the money and I knew that. I let the wrong head lead me down a path that had me two kids in with her in three years. Now this new chick. I keep getting in my own way. Well, I can't cry a river now. It's happening. Catch you tomorrow?"

"You bet. Can you try to keep it in your pants at least until tomorrow night?" Adrian playfully chided one of his best friends in the world.

"Yeah, yeah. If I could find someone to snip it today, I'd make an appointment."

"All your kids and then this new one? Yeah, do that. I'll buy the scissors. See you tomorrow."

Turning back to his file, Adrian stood and placed it in the cabinet where only he, Jocelyn and Zac had the access code. He had meetings to get to before wrapping up just in time to meet Adore. Oddly enough, something told him that she would also ask about Taryn. He'd let it slip one day when she was at his apartment, that he had a thing for a client's niece. He didn't know how Adore did it, but she was able to pry the information out of him. He looked forward to the chat. With Taryn being in town for her aunt's business before heading back home to Paris, he may not have enough time to get to know her on a more personal level. He didn't want to be in a rush. He'd missed the opportunity so many times in the past. He was hoping for another chance before he had to say goodbye to her for perhaps the last time now that her aunt was gone. Taryn would have no reason to return to New York again. That would mean he would miss out. He wanted a gracious and forever hello.

3

Taryn navigated her way through the many rooms of the top floor, penthouse level five-bedroom, seven bath, two-floor apartment that had once been her home growing up. Her heels clicked on the black and white marble floors, creating an echo throughout the apartment. The sound bounced off of the high-ceilings and rang in her ears like loud cymbals. She smiled at the remembrance of that sound as a child growing up in these very halls. The décor had changed significantly over the years, but the full design, that remained the same, brought on that nostalgic feeling. What she hadn't expected was the loneliness she felt as she slowly walked around taking in the sight and smell of each room. She was overwhelmed with the feeling of home that surged through her. She pushed thoughts out of her mind of the day she would put the place up for sale. She would soon have to let go of the three or four times a year that she would travel to New York to visit her aunt.

Her aunt took her in when she was seven-years-old after her mother and father perished in a fire in their California Hills home. Her parents had tried to stay there to save their home when a major fire suddenly changed paths and headed in the direction of their home. She had been with her aunt for the summer in New York when the call of the catastrophe came in. That was the day New York City became her permanent home.

The year before, her aunt had met and married her uncle, an older and very much financially secure man. He acquired his wealth first from money invested in him by his father, Herman, in what turned out to be a very lucrative real estate investment. Then his wealth increased from his own investments and business deals. He had also become the owner of a textile mill along with other major investments, making the family extremely wealthy.

Their wealth sent her to the best in private schools from elementary all the way through college. They were happy when she decided on the job in Paris. They didn't want her sheltered New York life to be the norm for her. At one point, when she showed her wild side, her aunt told her that part of that had been that she hadn't had a chance to explore life more to see that fun didn't have to mean indulging in things that weren't good for her just to prove a point to anyone else. She had learned that lesson and never looked back. They drilled into her that there was so much more to see.

During her last year of undergrad, she had started to travel and loved it. Her girls' trips with her friends each year were the highlight of her life. Over the years when she dated, there had been travels with men that she also enjoyed. Nothing serious came out of those in the way she'd hoped. She lent that to what she was looking for. No one had made her heart skip a beat in the way she wanted. She believed such a man was out here in the world. Sure, she'd had fun, but she wanted more. She wanted a connection she couldn't shake. In fact, the man she was thinking of lived one floor below where she stood.

She ran her hands along the walls and shelves as she walked. She touched a chair that was her aunt's favorite. In front of it, the maid had left her aunt's slippers where she loved for them to be. She felt the desire to slip out of her own shoes and to put her feet into the slippers, but she didn't. She enjoyed seeing them where they were; undisturbed. The apartment was in immaculate shape. She wouldn't have to do anything to it in order to sell it. The place had always been given the best of care.

As an only child, her aunt and uncle made sure she had the best of everything. She loved them with everything in her. When she first moved to Paris, the year before her uncle died, they flew with her and enjoyed helping her get settled into her first home. She had standard week and sometimes two-week visits to see them in New York. There were also times when she took quick trips for a day or two just to set eyes on them and to get the best hugs, which both of them gave.

Being in their home alone made her feel lonelier than she'd ever felt before. When she had arrived in New York earlier in the day, her aunt's doctor had called and said he couldn't find a medical reason of why she passed in her sleep. To him, she simply slept away. Taryn knew how much her aunt missed her uncle. They spoke of that often. She tried to encourage her aunt to get out more often and spend time with her friends. She even asked her to come to France to stay for a few months. She offered the idea that they could work on her next book together. Being part of her aunt's publishing team was a joy for her. She had declined saying she loved the beauty of looking out over the New York skyline from her apartment as she sat down to write. Taryn remembered many days as a young child of running around and playing in her aunt's office while she wrote.

She turned and walked into the office. It was as if everything about the space had stopped in time. Nothing was disturbed. Even though she never wrote using a typewriter anymore, something they went back and forth about for years, the old typewriter still sat in the middle of her desk, toward the back. In front of it sat the computer where her aunt penned all of her masterpieces, her last arriving in France just two weeks ago. Taryn patted the backpack that was slung over her shoulder. She had her assistant print out the manuscript for her before she boarded her flight to the United States. Her plan was to begin reading it on the flight. That was before she opened the package to the dedication page and saw that her aunt had dedicated the book to her. She had read the passage on the flight:

'My darling, Taryn. You have been the biggest and brightest light of my life. May you live and love deeply. May you find the kind of happiness with someone as I did with your uncle. I know you struggle with relationships because of your feelings that all things die when you least expect them. I encourage you to not focus on the death but on the life that is and can be lived before then. Don't live this life alone once I'm gone. You have so much love to give. Be open to that kind of love if it crosses your path; especially if it already has and you aren't paying attention or simply out of fear of the unknown. I said hello and yes to love once and it lasted a lifetime. Don't worry about the goodbyes you have to say when I pass on. Let the kind of love find you that will never have you saying goodbye again. Live, love and then live your best life. I love you, Aunt Misha, your second momma.'

Taryn cried again just as she had done on the plane. This was her confirmation that her aunt knew that her time was coming to an end. She never did get to the manuscript. She would gather the strength to get back to it during her stay in New York.

She walked around the large office with book shelves full of books on all sides, except for the large wall of windows that ran from the floor to the ceiling. She ran her fingers across every surface, remembering what it felt like to be in this home and in this space that her aunt loved so much.

Leaving that room, she pulled the door closed behind her and walked into what had been her uncle's home office. In his later years, after his second heart attack, he'd begun working from home. To this day, the office had not changed since the last time he was in it. Her aunt was clear about not wanting anything in it touched. The only people allowed to move anything, besides her, was the cleaning crew who kept the room spotless. There was so much she would have to go through.

Walking down the long hallway beyond the first bathroom on the first floor, she walked into her favorite room of them all; the oversized family room. Growing up, she'd had many sleepovers with her friends in this very space. During quiet family times, the three of them would gather here to relax over their favorite foods while enjoying movies that they always allowed her to pick out.

Her aunt never had children of her own due to a medical issue that was never discussed in full with her. After her parents died, making a new life in New York was as natural as breathing. The room she always stayed in when she visited was transformed into the kind of bedroom any little girl would want with a closet full of princess dresses and the best in designer wear. Until she reached high school, her aunt would decorate her room in the best Black Barbie décor she could find. She was always told that she would have the kind of life her parents would have wanted her to have. As surrogate parents, they had certainly done that. She'd never lacked for anything including support of her studying English and Journalism, just as her father had done. He was an evening, nightly news host and anchor. He had actually been at work the night before in Los Angeles where he had done a story on the California wild fire that had taken their home and them.

Taryn hadn't been in the apartment alone in years. There were times when her aunt and uncle were on vacation that she's been home by herself as an adult. She felt like yelling for her aunt in hopes that her death hadn't happened. She longed to hear her soft voice saying nothing was wrong with her hearing so there was no need to shout. She smiled at the memory of arriving and her aunt would rush, in her own slow manner, to pull her into a tight hug. She inhaled and closed her eyes, still able to smell the perfume her aunt loved to wear. Not yet ready to venture upstairs, she grabbed her phone when it rang and sat in her favorite spot, the navy chaise lounge in front of the large television on the wall.

"Jules, I was waiting to hear from you. It's two in the afternoon here. What time is it in Australia where you are?"

"It's five in the morning."

"What are you doing up? You should still be asleep."

"I haven't been to sleep yet. I'm just getting in from a party. I've really been living it up these last few days here now that I'm feeling better."

"You're not missing your life in Los Angeles? You've been gone for three weeks on that project for the publishing house."

"I miss my life there. It's been a lot of fun hanging out around Australia. I know you've been here a few times to visit our office. This is my first time. I've been trying to see everything. I'm not calling to talk about me. I'm heading home soon. I want to hear how you're doing. I checked your flight so I know you arrived. What's going on? What are you doing?"

"Walking through the apartment. Oh, I heard from Natalie today. She could only talk briefly. She's going to try and slip into New York to see me. She may only get a day, maybe two so she wants to plan it around the funeral service. I can't wait to see her."

"I'm glad. I was hoping word would get to her. Are you walking around being all sad or are you using memories to brighten your spirit a little bit? I know you're feeling nostalgic."

"I was home three months ago and it looks like it did then except she's not here. It's so quiet. She was such a large force in my life. Her presence and her voice were massive even as she became frailer as she aged. She loved playing music. Whenever I came home, there would be some kind of gospel or jazz music playing. I miss her so much. She was supposed to come and visit me for Christmas this year. We had plans for her to spend the whole month and through the day after New Year's Day with me. I was setting up a few book signings and everything. I was making plans for a lot of fun things to do while she was there. How can she be gone already? This is nightmarish for sure," Taryn bemoaned.

She sniffled and worked hard to hold back tears she'd been shedding since she walked into the building.

"You'll get through this. You know I'm coming for the memorial service. If you need me before that, I can make it happen. I don't want you to go through this alone. What about your cousin, Sherita? I know how close the two of you are. You've also got a bunch of friends that still live in New York. Don't go through this alone. What about the family? Have you heard from them yet? They have to know you are in New York by now. I'm sure they are pissed that you haven't been returning their calls."

"Not one word. A received a few calls before I left home but I still didn't answer any. I guess they got tired of calling because there has not been any today. You also know how they feel about me. They hate the relationship I had with her, especially after I became an adult and she grew older. The only person I've heard from is Sherita. The fact that she and I are the same age helped us stay close all these years. She also loved my aunt and my aunt loved her. She called a few times to check on me. When I got off the plane and turned my phone on, she had left a message that she would be making her way to New York from Pennsylvania soon. I'm so glad she's coming. You're right. I have friends here. With them and Sherita, I'll be fine until you arrive. We spent a lot of time together when I was young. We still stay in touch. I'll call her in a little while. I want to get settled in first."

"I met her once at a dinner party you hosted for your aunt. She was very nice to me."

"She's good people. Sherita mentioned that they hadn't received a call about my aunt's passing. They saw it on the national news. My aunt is big news in the writing world. Her death has been on all the news channels. I'm not sure what my aunt put into place as far as communication if something happened to her. When I got the call, I tried calling Sherita but I got her voicemail. She said she had been traveling and was glad that I had called. She saw the story on a social media site. She was about to call me when she saw that I had left her a message."

"The world is mourning with you. Her millions of fans are with you too."

"Thanks, Jules. My aunt's assistant left me a message that she's been receiving hundreds of calls of condolences a day. I knew they were coming in, but I had no idea just how much. Thousands of emails and letter. Millions of social media posts and photos. When I got to the apartment building, there is a memorial of so many flowers and other things along the entire street. New York City had to block off some space in order to allow her fans to mourn her publicly in front of where she lived her life. When I reached the lobby, I was taken to a large conference room where flower deliveries were placed since no one has been here at the apartment to accept them. I saw them and lost count at two hundred arrangements. I'll have some of those brought up here later. Others, I'll have delivered to patients at local hospitals. The apartment does not have the space for all of them. I'm sure more are coming. It's only been a few days so far. I did bring one big, pretty red and yellow rose arrangement to the apartment with me. Those were her two favorite colors. I'll ask Sherita to help with them when she gets here. Tawny and Lisa have also already reached out. I got a message from Natalie. I'm feeling better about being here. There is a lot to do."

"Oh, good. You've been friends with them since high school. I'm glad Natalie reached you. I know as cousins, you've always seen Sherita as more of a sister. I'm glad your local friends will be around you. I know you will need their support. I'll be there soon."

"I can't wait for Sherita to get here. I haven't seen her in almost a year. She came to visit me about nine months ago. We had the best time in Paris."

"Then your aunt was right about one thing; she told you that if anyone reached out if something happened to her, it would be Sherita."

"She sure did. I remember telling you that. I don't expect that kind of help from the rest of them unless it involves something monetary for their help. My other cousins, by way of my uncles, are cool – somewhat. We'll see what kind of reception I get from them."

"Don't worry about them too much. You will have enough to focus on including Adrian. Have you seen him yet? Any part of him?"

Taryn smiled for the first time all day. She was waiting for his name to come up.

"Ah, I've been waiting for you to drop his name. Don't start with me again," she joked. "No, I haven't. I have a meeting at the law firm tomorrow morning. I doubt it's with him. His father was my aunt's attorney. I think Adrian worked on some part of her estate planning but his father is who I remember being her attorney. She often mentioned his name. I assume my meeting is with him. Besides, he's the one that called with the news that she passed away."

"Didn't he turn the firm over to Adrian and another guy, the son of the other partner?"

"He did, but his father is still involved. My aunt was still talking to him all the time about stuff. He was the one who helped keep my family at bay. They've been trying to get their hands on her money ever since my uncle died. One of her brothers tried, at one point, to have her declared incompetent in handling her own affairs. My aunt ended up in court and wowed the judge with how in control of her faculties that she was. My uncle James apologized for hauling her into court right before asking her for a few hundred thousand dollars to buy a boat."

"Try your best to not let your family get to you. I know how they can get under your skin. I don't want that for you along with everything else you're going through. Your aunt wouldn't want you focused on them."

"She poured that reality into my brain often. They made me feel like an outsider every chance they got. She was the only one of my mother's siblings that even cared about me after my mother died. I'm assuming I'll hear from one or all of them soon. There will be a reading of the will. If they are included, I'll have to be in the same room as them."

"Are you ready for that drama?"

"I'm dreading it. Maybe there won't be any drama. Perhaps she left them enough that they'll leave me alone. I don't even know what she's left me, if anything at all."

"Nonsense. I'm betting she left you everything. You were her daughter-figure. I should just say you were her daughter because that's how she saw you. The way she loved you is unmatched. The way you loved and cared for her, even from out of the country, is what every aunt or mother-like figure would hope a niece or daughter-like person in her life would do. You found her the perfect caregiver in your absence. Your meeting tomorrow should clear up a lot of things for you."

"I hope so. The law firm left a message for me on my cell while I was on the plane. They wanted to confirm the appointment for tomorrow morning. I'll call them after I finish talking to you."

"Did you see that news story on the Today Show? It was from about two weeks ago. I caught it on YouTube™. Adrian was a guest. They invited him on to talk about the new rise in the popularity of the firm after he took it over from his father. Of course, the show spent little time on that and a lot of time on his personal life. The brother is fine. After he shared that he was single, knowing the world knew of his last break up with that actress, can't remember her name, they asked about his perfect woman. At first, he tried to talk around the questions, but then gave a few hints. I swear, if I didn't know any better – I would have believed he was talking about you."

Taryn stopped moving about the apartment. She then brushed off the idea.

"Jules, that's nonsense. We don't know each other like that."

"I'm telling you the truth. Look it up on Instagram. Those eyes of yours don't see well. I think you like him a lot too. If you didn't, you wouldn't avoid running into him whenever you go home. Don't let your history with the serial dater, Nathaniel, keep you from being receptive to a good man like Adrian. You certainly wouldn't need to worry about him being interested in you for your money. He has millions on top of millions. He's a great catch. Nathaniel was and is still a snake. He'll sliver out soon now that you'll come into money. I think Adrian is fantastic. He has all the qualities that every woman would want in a man. You've already seen on very big quality. I promise, I won't reference that again."

"Yeah, right. I don't believe you. If he's so great, then why don't you go for him? Huh? Tell me that."

"Girl, if you weren't my best friend, I would fall at his feet in a second. He's only got eyes for you. I love him for you. You are the only one of the two of us who has blinders on. I may need to take you to have your vision checked. The two of you would make some beautiful babies with your beauty, those eyes and his strikingly handsome looks and features. Look, text me after you meet up with him. I know it's him; it has to be. She did leave the apartment to you, correct?"

"I believe so. What she told me was that the apartment was put in a separate trust from everything else, along with some other property that she has. She once told me that the other houses she owns are one in Florida, which was a summer place we went to every year. The other one is in Maryland in Ocean City. That's one of my favorite ones. I loved going there. In fact, Sherita and I were there last summer. Remember, you couldn't make it to go with us? I won't really know what she left me until the reading of the will."

"I regret not being able to get away for that trip."

"There is also the lake house on Snake Road on Lake Geneva in Wisconsin. I love that place. The air is so different there. It's actually a fresh air smell, unlike big cities like New York or Chicago. She once told me that if something happened to her, she wanted me to decide what to do with all of the properties. She wanted to give me the option to keep them or sell them. I would love the house in Maryland and the lake house, if that's the case. It's so quiet and peaceful there. It's a great place to go to write. There is so much to get through. That's what the law firm is for."

"What about the apartment?"

"I'm probably going to sell it if it's left to me. I love New York. It's a lonely place for me. I don't know what I will do about anything. You know I will confide in you once I talk with the law firm. Since my life is in France, I will sell it eventually, again, if it's mine. Timing depends on the cost of upkeep until I can get that done. I don't believe it will happen in the month or so that I'll be here. I need to focus on the memorial service. I'm not sure when that will be. I need to wait and see if her family is going to work together or not. Since I just arrived, I haven't done much other than come straight here."

Taryn yawned. She was more tired than she thought she would be after she landed.

"Get unpacked and relax tonight. Rome wasn't built in a day, as the saying goes. You don't have to do anything today or even tomorrow, if you don't want to. If you're not ready, push your meeting with the law firm out an extra day. Take it all in and take your time. I'm here if you need me. I'm glad you made it there safe. Once you have arrangements confirmed, let me know. I'll be there. We're not besties just for the sake of calling each other bestie. You have always been here for me. No matter what I needed, I could always count on you to be the friend I needed; it's actually beyond friendship. You're more like family. If no one else is there for you at a time like this, you know I am. Life is *lifing* for me right now, but that doesn't matter. Work is crazy. Everyone at the publishing house knows we are friends. They wouldn't try stopping me from being there with you even if they tried; which they would never. Whatever I need to do to get to you, I'm there."

"I know and I appreciate you and love you! You are the greatest friend I've ever had. Thanks for always being there for me. I'll call you later when it's a more decent hour where you are. Get some sleep. Go ahead and party enough for me too."

"I'm all over that! Talk to you later."

Taryn stood and went back to the door to grab her luggage. This would be a perfect time to head up to the bedroom level to take a look around before ordering something to eat. She'd had a nervous stomach ever since she received the call that her aunt had passed. That had been when she'd had her last meal. All she'd been doing was snacking since then. She was in New York. She was home. It was the place that she knew had some of the best food in the world. She was ready for something good. Maybe good food will help elevate her mood. Her new reality had finally hit her as she stood looking down at her bags. Her world was getting smaller and quieter.

4

Adrian checked the time on his watch again. He shook his head realizing he'd done so at least five times in the last thirty minutes. Time was winding down. He smiled through the embarrassment of a woman making him so nervous that he could barely focus on the discussion he was having with a new client, a very high-profile client.

"What do you think, Adrian?"

Klaus Marta, the father of the firm's new client had explained how his son, Cary, had formed a legal business using illegally obtained funds. At least, that's what the accusation was. While he didn't know how true the story the father was wielding actually was, he could ascertain the level of explanation that would be needed when they got to court.

Adrian snapped back into the conversation just as Zac appeared in the doorway of one of their four glass enclosed conference rooms. He scrolled through one document after the other on his laptop as they talked, trying to absorb as much information as he could with the time they had left to talk.

"Well, I don't think that this case will be too complicated if you're sure you can prove that Cary actually received the funds from a legal source. Whoever this person is who claims to have proof that he didn't is who we need to be leery of. Is there any truth to that claim?"

Adrian turned his attention to Cary and away from the father. Though the father was the client paying the bills, it was Cary that he needed to hear from.

"He's lying. We went into business together but what I brought to the table was all legal money. He's the one who is connected to a bank robbery. It hasn't been proven that I was involved in that. I wasn't even in town when that happened."

Adrian knew the story. It had been all over the news because bank robberies were not as prevalent as they had been years ago. Banks made it harder and harder for thieves to rob them and get away with anything. According to the sources quoted in the news story, the robbery had to have been an inside job. The person in question, was no doubt, someone that Cary knew by way of the friend who claims to have proof that they were both in on the scheme. He looked up from the witness statement that he'd been sent and locked eyes again with Cary.

"Where were you?" he asked.

"Uh. Um. Let me think. The time is a little blurry for me."

"He was with me and his mother out of the country," the father offered.

Adrian looked to Zac who gave him a questionable look.

"I looked at the manifest for the flight and Cary isn't listed on it. How did you pull that off?"

"Oh, well, you know how it is when you have money. We left from a private hangar. The pilot didn't question that Cary was with us since he's traveled with us many times."

Zac then entered the conversation.

"When you arrived at your destination, no one asked for his passport or anything? You're going to live on this hill that he was with you? Mister Marta, you are willing to die on this hill even if we end up with proof that you're both lying? I'm not saying that will happen I'm saying the prosecutor is already checking and rechecking your stories. If there is a thin hair of discrepancy, we will find it and so will they. I'm a little less trusting than my partner, Adrian here. That's why we work together so well; we balance out each other with our varying personalities. I will say, unless you come up with hard proof that disparages what this guy is saying, Cary is going to be in a lot of trouble. Not just with the bank robbery but the funds that the claimant is saying came from that robbery that your son used. I understand when you say that you have more than enough money to fund any business your son wants to set up. You have no proof that you did that either, other than to say you keep large amounts of money in your home safe. Telling us that's where it came from is fine but will it work in a court? I'm not so sure. There is a lot of secrecy around this. I'm not saying he's guilty or not. I'm saying, and so is Adrian, that if we represent Cary, we will need the honest truth. He hasn't been arrested for the bank robbery that occurred; at least not yet. I believe that will happen in a matter of days. We need as much information as you can give us outside of what you wanted us to have and not what we need to have. Are we clear here?" Zac asked.

"My partner is right. I've looked through everything you sent. This can't be it. I need a timeline. I need pictures or any other information that Cary was out of town when all of this went down almost a year ago. Someone is coming after your son. If it's not just his friend who is no longer a friend, then there is more to this. I'm going to assign this to another attorney for now. She will dive as deep as she needs to go to uncover all that we'll need. When the law comes for Cary, and they will or you wouldn't be here, say nothing. In fact, do nothing other than call the office line, even if it's after hours. Someone will meet you and take care of everything. For now, Zac, get Theresa. She's one of the best junior partners we have here. She's tough. She hates liars. She will know if you're one. We have your retainer, so the firm officially represents Cary as well. I will handle everything else and Theresa will take care of the criminal aspect; that's her specialty."

Zac walked over to the phone in the middle of the conference room table and pressed the red button in the center.

"Jocelyn, can you get Theresa to meet the client in the Gerard conference room? I have a staff meeting here in the Jarreau conference room in a few minutes. Adrian has a meeting coming up in his office. Send someone in to escort Klaus and Cary to meet with Theresa."

"Yes, sir. I'm on it," Jocelyn exclaimed.

Klaus and Cary stood when Adrian did.

"Thank you both for helping with this. I'll talk to my son tonight about truth. I apologize for my role in what may be a serious level of untruth here. He was with my wife and me on a trip, but...it, uh, wasn't until the next day after that event happened. I promise from this point on that every word will be the truth. Cary really didn't take part in the robbery. I promise you that this is the truth. What I don't know for a fact is whether he got any of the money from it."

Adrian wished that Cary would speak up more, but he got it. The kid was trying to outsmart the smartest men in the room. He was losing. He definitely was not believable to anyone other than his father. His own father would have his back if he were in trouble. Still, he would also expect the truth.

"I appreciate your honesty. Come clean with Theresa. We can only represent the truth. Our firm stands ten toes down on that. I hope you understand the lengths we will go to represent you or the short stay on our roster if we find you're keeping us in the dark," Adrian shared, looking to Cary and his father. "You could impact your father's stance with our firm if we find that you're bringing us a bunch of lies.

"Yes, sir, I understand," Cary replied.

When an associate showed up at the conference room door, Adrian walked them out before coming back in, closing the office door behind him and sitting across from Zac who was now seated at the table. He took a moment to check his watch yet again.

"I'm sure Theresa will get the absolute truth out of him. That's why we call her the hammer; she loves that! This kind of case is right up her alley," Zac said.

"Right."

His mind was on his next meeting. He worried about how it would turn out when Taryn realized who she was meeting with. He didn't want it to appear that he was purposely deceiving her. He wanted her response to him to be authentic and not rehearsed. She seemed to always be nervous around him. He didn't want her prepared to be nervous.

"I kissed your secretary this morning," Zac said.

"Right," Adrian replied again and continued gathering up his things to head to his office.

Zac slammed his hand on the table, drawing his attention.

"Bro! What the hell? Did you hear what I just said? I know you're distracted but damn! She got you like this?"

Adrian looked at Zac unsure of what part of their conversation he missed.

"What? Who?"

"Yeah, okay. I'll let that slide. You weren't at the gym working out this morning. This is your usual day to be at the one here in the office. Otherwise, you work out at your place or at the gym in your apartment building. I thought I'd catch you here. The fellas are thinking of going to Chicago to check out that casino that Torrence Allen and Horace Grant just opened; their second location. Since they are new clients, I thought that this would be a good time to go for a few days and check things out. Do you want the details or would you like to check your watch again?"

"What?"

He heard Zac breathe an air of loud frustration. He looked over at him.

"Adrian, if you don't start paying attention to me! Stop it already. She'll be here in a few minutes. I hope you get some brain cells back after the meeting because right now, you are toast. Have you spoken with her at all?"

"Uh, no. Not at all. My dad spoke to her. Jocelyn also called to confirm her appointment for today."

"You didn't call to offer condolences? I understand that Jocelyn sent an arrangement of beautiful flowers to the apartment this morning."

"As far as speaking to her to offer my condolences, no. I was planning on offering that when she got here today. I did send a floral arrangement from me personally to her. I was up late going over everything in the trusts. The hour got so late that I didn't want to buzz her at that hour. I wanted to make sure, one last time, that there were no holes in the case for her family to come at Taryn. Her aunt was very clear any time we talked. The priority is to protect Taryn at this point."

"You have looked at those files a million times. You even had me go over them. Like your father said, everything is iron-clad and lawsuit proof. Her family can try whatever they want. They will not succeed. Ms. Misha took care of that. You worked hard, along with your father, to make sure there would be no surprises."

Adrian stopped moving.

"There was one surprise," he said.

"Oh?" Zac responded and leaned over the long glass table.

"Ms. Misha left a letter for me. I've looked over everything quite a few times. Apparently, upon her death, she gave my father a letter that he was to give to me. He left it with Jocelyn to give to me yesterday before I headed out to meet my sister for dinner. His note said for me to read it when I got home. He made sure I knew that he didn't know what was inside. She wanted the contents to be read by me only and done so when I was alone."

"Can you share what it said or is it private?"

Adrian opened the red folder that was filled with papers. On top of them was a manila folder. He took out the note and handed it to Zac to read. He stood and paced as his friend began to read.

'My dearest Adrian. If you're reading this, we've had our last impromptu visit and our last conversation. You won't have to worry about any more calls out of the blue asking you to come sit with me in my apartment. I want to thank you for never hesitating to make time for me. Your generation is always in such a rush, hustling and bustling about while not taking time to really smell the roses. Wealth and prosperity don't have to be chased twenty-four hours a day. Find time to stand and be in awe of all that you have

accomplished. Focus on all that you still want in life. I know you were wondering why would this old lady keep asking you to come see her to share tea and cupcakes. It was because I saw a lot in you that I saw in my husband. You have a heart of gold. I wanted to get to know everything about you, especially who you were outside of the office. You are a hard worker and a dedicated friend and family member. Still, there is something missing from your life that you continue to overlook, as again, most in your generation do. You're missing out on love. Now, I'm not telling you how to live your life. I'm simply saying don't focus so much on work that you don't concentrate on what else there is in life. Trust me, there is a lot. I want you to make a promise to me and to yourself. Stop fixating so much on all the things you have and can have with your kind of financial wealth. Instead, look for what you truly want. All that love, commitment and good nature you have in you should not go to waste on all those pretty ladies I see you with. Take the time to nestle in with the one. I know she's out there for you. In fact, I'm quite sure she's already crossed your path. Remember the conversations we had about how my husband courted me and how special it made me feel? We didn't have the internet and all this texting mess that takes away from person-to-person interaction. He came for me daily. I knew he wanted me and he knew I wanted him. We saw that in each other not by phone, text, email or video chat. We sat together, got to know each other and fell in love. I don't usually meddle. That's not my nature. I see something in you as I see in my niece. You are both missing out as if you're passing each other with blinders on. But me? I can see. I want you both to now see. I need you to see from within you. When I speak of her, your entire body lights up and not just your face. You love hearing stories of how she's doing in Paris. I see it. I know it. Let me say right now, that you have my blessing. I may not have lived to see what the two of you will become, but I go to my rest knowing that it will come to pass just as I have dreamed so many times. Stop fighting what you feel. What you feel for Taryn only comes around once in life. Trust me, I know. I had mine for many years. I wouldn't change anything other than having a little more time with my Alexander. Right now, I am with him again. Grab onto life and don't let go. You are truly like a son to me. If I could have had the chance to pick someone for my sweet Taryn, it is you and no one else. Take care of her. She has many friends in the world but not much family or those who love her unconditionally. Make sure the world does right by her. I know I'm asking a lot. I also believe that you understand. Am I correct? I'm smiling right now as I write this knowing that I am. The question is, what are you going to do about it? If I'm wrong, I still wish everything for you that life has to offer. You deserve that. I thank you for every second you spent with me without hesitation. You made this old woman happy. Thank you for giving me your time with your visits and all the times you listened to me rattle on about life and happiness. In it, there are many stories. They were as much for me as I hope they were for you. Love, Misha.'

"Wow! Should I start looking for my best man tuxedo because, damn!" he shouted.

When Adrian looked over at Zac, he found his friend's mouth and eyes wide open.

"Say less, bro. That can't be all you got out of that note."

"This woman was an amazing person, and quite diabolical. She could read how much you want her niece. Just wow! I love her honesty and her spunk. Well?" Zac asked, handing him back the letter.

Adrian put it back in the envelope and placed it back in the folder, closing it.

"I was just as shocked as you are."

"Does she know that you are the poster boy for bachelorhood?"

"She knew. Despite what I thought was my ability to hide my attraction to Taryn, she knew. For over a year, I've been interested in Taryn. After that night in the hall, I gave up on having a chance. I could tell she was embarrassed and there was nothing I could do about it. I can't say I was embarrassed because that would be a rarity for me. I just wished that it hadn't happened. I really wasn't thinking when I opened the door."

"I get that. It happened. You've barely said much about her since that night."

"What could I say? First, I was in my apartment with a woman and I was pretty much naked. Then I appear in front of Taryn pretty much naked and she saw..."

"I don't need that image. I get what she saw. That's no reason to assume you wouldn't have a chance with her. Unless the woman came out of the apartment that you were with that night, how would she know someone was there?"

"She did. Ms. Misha mentioned something to me about the files in the folder that Taryn handed to me. She wanted to know if I had any questions. She also apologized if Taryn had interrupted me and my guest. That let me now that Taryn somehow knew."

"So what? Look, she's about to be here. What you do from this point on is up to you. Ms. Misha's letter to you was on point. You haven't been able to get Taryn out of your head. Your dating life has pretty much been non-existent except for sex buddies. As a man of similar proclivities when it comes to women, I understand. This thing you have for Taryn is far beyond that. Don't let her leave New York without seeing if there is something more than saying hello when she arrives and goodbye when she finally leaves."

"That's pretty much been the bane of my existence around her; hello and goodbye."

"Doesn't have to stay that way. You're not one to hold back when it comes to a woman. Why now? Why with her?"

"Did I ever tell you the details of when I realized I wanted her? I'm not talking about sex, though, hell yeah, I would give up all other women if I could have her. That's saying a lot and I know it."

"That is a lot. What happened?"

Adrian gathered everything in his arms.

"One night, way before that day at my apartment, Taryn accompanied her aunt to the gala the law firm hosted to honor our fathers. You were out of the country and missed it. I happened to be near the entrance when she arrived. It was like she was floating on air. She had on a gold and black gown that brought out the hazel in her light brown eyes even more. Her hair was up in a tight bun. She glided more than she walked. She was gorgeous. All eyes were on her, including mine. I've never told you this but I was so taken by her that night that I avoided asking her to dance. I wanted to, but I couldn't get up the nerve. Have you ever known a woman to make me that nervous?"

"Hell no. I knew you were far gone for her."

"I was. I still am. We did talk some that night. Remarkably, we were seated next to each other throughout dinner. When she laughed for one reason or another, my world lit up. The night was shorter than I wanted it to be. When I finally got up the nerve to ask her to dance, I looked around for her but she'd already left to take her aunt home."

"That may have been a lost opportunity. Today is a new day."

"I've seen her but haven't talked to her since that night at my apartment. I know she's been in town since then. I was naked under the towel. She looked up. I don't know how to get beyond that fatal flaw in my judgment when I opened the door. I wish it had been anyone else on this planet except for her."

Zac put up has hand and stopped him from continuing. His other hand remained in the pocket of the pants of his suit.

"You flashed her. I got it. It wasn't on purpose. Who expected her to fall and do so right at your feet?"

"Man, I was so focused on her not being hurt that I forgot the family jewels were swinging free under the towel. Her skirt flew up. I tried not to look but damn. She had on the cutest red thong, from the part of it that I could see. It was a crazy moment that I believe neither of us have been able to get beyond it in order to get to anything else. I actually went out on a date that night and couldn't focus on my date. All I could think about was Taryn and that gorgeous body, mesmerizing eyes and luscious, kissable lips like Gail Bean. You know who that is?"

"Yes, I know who she is. She's that actress that you believe doesn't get the acting credit that she should. Ever since you saw her in John Singleton's show, *Snowfall*, she's been in a lot of your conversations. You're obsessed with her beauty."

"Not as much as I am with Taryn's beauty."

"So, she's showing up today for the first time seeing you and she doesn't know it? Boy, if I didn't have to be in court in a few hours after the staff meeting that you'll miss, I would stay around for the show in your office just to say I was there. Good luck with that. I've never heard you express an interest in a woman outside of, you know, planting the family jewels in someone."

Adrian smiled and walked to the conference room door and stopped.

"I still can't figure out how your mind works. You say the wildest things," Adrian kidded.

Before Zac could respond, Adrian's cell phone rang. It was his assistant."

"Hey, Jocelyn."

"Taryn Novack is here to see you. Are you on your way back to your office?" she asked.

"Yes, I am. Zac and I are just wrapping up. The staff are showing up for his meeting. Can you make her comfortable in my office and I'll be right there?"

"I sure will."

"Alright. It's on!" Zac said.

Adrian started to respond when Zac walked further back into the conference room as some of the members of their staff walked around him and into the room now that he'd opened the door. He nodded to Zac who saluted him using their usual sign off for each other. He would catch up with him later. Right now, he had a beautiful woman in his office waiting for him. Zac was right. It was on.

5

Taryn saw the name of the glass office door before she heard his voice when he entered. When his assistant walked her into his office and offered her water or coffee, she didn't accept either. She was too stunned about who she was here to meet. All she knew from the call the day before was that she was meeting with Mr. Jarreau. She didn't think to ask which Mr. Jarreau. Nothing had her thinking that it would be Adrian.

Before she could ask about the confusion over which attorney, his assistant offered condolences and spoke of the about her interactions with her aunt. She appreciated it. For a few minutes, she'd forgotten about Adrian as she sat down on one of the most comfortable leather sofas she'd ever been on.

The three-seat sofa in a black and gray was beautiful. It was all male. Her eyes took in one of the largest glass desks she'd ever seen. It was dynamic with its gold trim and black and gold desk accessories. Her eyes landed on Adrian's name all over the various awards and plagues on the walls on either side of his desk. After his assistant finished talking, Taryn thanked her for her kindness while she sat nervously awaiting Adrian's arrival. She didn't have to wait long. Her eyes lifted when he entered the office and thanked Jocelyn for getting her settled.

As she shifted her eyes from Jocelyn to a very tall Adrian, her mouth forgot how to talk. She couldn't form any words.

Adrian appeared to be just as stunned. It wasn't until Jocelyn cleared her throat that the two of them realized someone else was still in the room with them.

"Oh, uh, Jocelyn, thanks again."

When Jocelyn looked between her and Adrian a few more times, the level of weirdness entered the space. The silence was even wilder. Taryn didn't know if she should say something, stand, and give him a friendly hug or something else. She remained seated. Her heart was beating so fast, she hoped that neither of them could hear it. After not seeing him for a while, she was reminded at just how damn fine he was. It wasn't like she didn't know it. Being in his presence again reminded her of the impact his sexiness had on her. She thought of that night outside of his apartment. Today he was impeccably dressed in a dark gray suit with a matching tie and a crisp light gray shirt. He had on gold jewelry, a ring, not on his marriage hand, a thick gold link chain on one wrist and a sleek gold watch on the other. The man looked good fully dressed. She crossed and uncrossed her legs as she remembered how mouth-watering he looked shirtless, in a towel with his body covered in water. She liked him both ways; she would love him both ways.

Shaking off her thought, she remembered to thank Jocelyn.

"Thank you for your hospitality. I appreciate it," she finally said.

Her words broke the stance and sexy glances she and Adrian were giving each other.

"Should I stay to capture any part of your discussion?" Jocelyn asked Adrian.

"Right. No, I'm good for now. Let me talk to Ms. Novack."

Once Jocelyn was gone, Taryn crossed her legs at the ankles and leaned forward in her seat. Her eyes followed Adrian as he walked to his desk to place the items in his hands on it. She sat straight back when he walked back toward her. She was again mystified about whether to stand, remain seated or something else besides sitting still, barely letting air escape from her mouth. When he said nothing, she finally got up the nerve to do so.

"It's nice to see you again," she said.

"I'm sorry. I don't know where my mind is. It's wonderful seeing you as well. It's been some time. I'm sorry that we're meeting under these circumstances. I am so sorry about your aunt's passing. She was a wonderful woman. We spent a lot of time together. We shared a lot. She loved you, I do know that. She spoke of you often."

"I loved her too. Thank you so much for the beautiful floral arrangement in her favorite colors. I took that one up to the apartment. I sat it right on the entry table. She loved placing lovely floral arrangements there. I miss her so much and it's only been a few days. I can't imagine what life will be like for me now that she's gone. She was my connection to life. Life without her is going to be hard."

"I don't doubt it. She was special."

"I can tell by all of the calls, messages, flowers and other expressions of sympathy from people."

"That's wonderful."

"It is. I had no idea she knew all of these big-time celebrities."

"Let me know if the firm can help you triage any calls or anything. I can have someone help you go through cards, letters, messages, and proclamations. We've been getting them here as well. Many of our clients knew her and have been reaching out to let us know to tell you that if you need anything, let them know. Celebrities are offering to speak and sing at her service."

"I can imagine. She knew a lot of people. She and my uncle both did. The publishing company I work for, which is also where my aunt's books were published, have been overwhelmed with calls, emails and gifts of all kinds. They've assigned an additional assistant, along with my normal assistants, to handle the influx of well wishes received at our home office in Paris and our U.S. locations."

"Have you thought about any kind of service? We can help with that."

"When she did go to church, there is one on Merrick Boulevard. I was going to reach out to them this week to see if a memorial service could be held sometime next week. I know my aunt didn't want any big fanfare. I want to stick to what I know she would want. I may change my mind. Her fans deserve more than doing things quietly. I'm meeting with my cousin, Sherita, a little later after I leave here. She's arriving in a few hours. I'm taking her up on her offer to help me plan the service."

"I'm glad you have family to help. Your aunt often spoke of the strain with some of them. Just remember, we are here if you need anything. We will need to schedule the reading of her will. There are a few things I'm sure you already know are yours the minute she passed away. Other things are noted in her will. I want to be sure you know what things are outside of the will. We won't bring them up at the reading. You do need to be aware since they are in her full portfolio. You will get a copy of everything. If the family that are invited to the reading bring up these few things, I'll direct them to focus only one what's in the will."

"I know some of that. If you can go over that with me that would be great."

Adrian reached behind him to his desk and opened a red folder. He moved closer and sat in a matching chair across from her.

"I have that right here. Also, while we have been your aunt's representatives, we can also represent you, if you would like. I can also refer you to another firm if you would like."

"Oh, no. If it can be arranged for your firm to represent me and my interest in everything, I would appreciate that. There is a lot that you're already familiar with. I don't want to start all over with a firm that is unfamiliar with what my aunt had that will shift to me."

"Okay, I'll have Jocelyn get everything in order for you to look over. I'll have her set up another meeting soon to go over that. We don't have to talk about what that entails right now. We'll have you sign a retainer agreement. That will lay out the legal services you would like for us to provide for you. Again, no rush on anything other than signing that agreement. We will take a little time to go over what you need to know today. Just important things for now. In this folder is a legal document that is a completely separate trust from the others that I'll go over at the reading of her will. This one is just for you. There is a substantial monetary amount that was separate from everything. This is only for you. I am required to reveal the amount at the reading. No worries about your family, though. This is iron-clad. She has been making deposits into that account you see highlighted ever since you came to live with her and your uncle as a child. She wanted me to share this with you before the reading."

Adrian handed her a piece of paper. She looked at the amount and almost coughed up her breakfast.

"What?" she struggled to say before another coughing spell overtook her.

Adrian stood and went to his office door.

"Jocelyn, can you bring Ms. Novak a bottle of water, please?" he called out.

He waited the few seconds for her to do so before closing his office door again. Handing Taryn the water, she took several gulps before thanking him once she could catch her breath.

"Thank you. If I had known that I would have needed this drink of water, I would have accepted it when she offered. Are you sure this is correct? There is an account with this much money in it just for me? This isn't what's in her will?"

"No, it's not included. Full disclosure, I have to mention it. This account was a deposit only account. She never wanted anyone to be able to dispute this. I believe she actually started the account when you were nine. That means that she's been making monthly deposits for about twenty-four years. You're thirty-three, right? I'm sorry for asking your age. I promise, this is only between you and I. Jocelyn will come in to note things that are for the record. This isn't a part of that."

"Wow. That's a mighty long time. Yes, thirty-three. No worries about asking. I'm not one of those women who walk around thinking it's impolite to ask a woman's age. It's all good," she relayed.

"As you can see, as of today, that account has just short of three million dollars in it. It's untouchable by anyone other than you. The funds can be released to you as soon as you would like. I have the paperwork for that. Do you have a financial manager, accountant or an investment advisor? You will want to have one help you with making sure your money is managed well. There is this account along with what you will get out of the will and the various trust accounts."

"Oh, I have just a regular accountant who lives in Paris. I don't have anyone here in the states. I still have my U.S. citizenship. I'd like for the money to stay in this country in the bank."

"Okay. We have several investment and money managers that we work closely with that I can recommend to you. Also, the penthouse apartment is yours outright. You can do whatever you like with it. I take it that you would want to sell it since your life is in Paris?"

Taryn couldn't seem to think straight. Every time Adrian spoke, her eyes went to his lips. She couldn't help but think of all the ways women probably derived pleasure from him. She hadn't thought such salacious thoughts about any man like this in a very long time.

"Yes. I do plan to sell it. I will eventually get around to that."

"Okay. Again, we can make some recommendations in that area as well. Everything else is tied to the will. Those things I noted already were already in your name only."

"Even the apartment?" she asked.

"Yes. She changed ownership from her to you about a year ago and placed it in a trust for you."

Taryn couldn't believe her ears. Her aunt was preparing for her departure from this world. As she had done in life, she was making sure she took care of the niece she loved even after her death.

"My aunt was the forever planner," she said smiling.

"She definitely had the know-how to be a lawyer. I will need to schedule the reading of the will. Jocelyn will check with you on your availability. I apologize now for all that may seem overwhelming. We do have to have the reading done within the next few weeks," Adrian explained.

"I understand that. I will make myself available at any time."

"Have you heard from your family other than your cousin? I have the names of all of the family who are mentioned in the will. Everyone will need to be in attendance. There will be one reading only."

"No. Well, actually, yes. They have left a few voice messages. I need to call them back. That was my two uncles, her brothers. Maybe one or two from her sister, who is Sherita's mother. Between me and you, she's the meanest of them all. I wasn't expecting a call or anything from her. She's the most bitter."

"Well, you won't have to deal with any of them directly. In fact, the three siblings have already reached out to the firm to inquire about your aunt's will. I told them I would connect with them after you and I talked about some things. Are you okay if I schedule the reading for Thursday? That's in three days. We need to get it out of the way so that everything is on the table."

"That sounds good."

"I also want to release you from having to worry about that as you are planning her services."

Taryn thought about all that she still needed to do. Was she even ready to sit across from her family?

"Will it take place here?" she asked.

She felt safe in his presence and here in his office.

"Yes, it will. It will be in one of our conference rooms. Jocelyn will be there along with another lawyer in the firm. We do that so that there are witnesses to what is said and done. Is that okay with you?"

"Of course, and thank you for that. I'm comfortable with the reading being here. I'm glad we're doing it before her services. I want everything out in the open to give everyone a chance to take it all in."

"I'll have one of my assistants reach out to each one of them before the end of the day today and set that up."

"Wonderful. I was hoping I wouldn't have to reach out to them about all of this."

"Just remember that we will be representing you as soon as you sign the retainer agreement. Whatever you need, just call the office at any time. Are you staying at the apartment?"

Taryn's eyes widened when he mentioned the apartment. When her eyes landed on his, she knew that he knew what she was thinking. He closed the folder and relaxed in his chair.

"I am."

"Okay. That means you know where I live. You can stop down, text or call me with any questions at any time. Listen, I think we need to talk. I saw the expression on your face when I mentioned the apartment."

"You saw that?"

"Yes. Can we talk about that? Are you okay if we do?" he asked.

Taryn was more than okay with it. There was an elephant in the room. It was wearing a towel and completely naked underneath. She smiled slightly at the image.

"I guess we should. We haven't seen each other since...then," she noted.

"I've seen you purposely avoid me since then. I get it. That day was an uncomfortable one; not just for you either."

"It's hard to forget."

Taryn hung her head as that one word slipped out of her mouth; *hard*. Why did she have to say it out loud?

When Adrian chuckled, she looked up and smiled at him. Then they laughed together.

"I promise you, it's okay. I get it. Taryn, that day has been something between us for a while now. It's time we talked about it. You're thinking about that night and so am I. Again, I want to profusely apologize for coming to my door dressed like that; or rather, not dressed. I wanted to apologize that night but you ran out of there so fast. Since then, the few times I did see you, I watched you run away like a thief in the night.

"I didn't..."

Taryn stopped before she finished her statement. She was about to lie.

Adrian tilted his head to the side and rested his chin on his hand. He sensed her attempt at lying too. He humorously gave her the floor and lightened the intensity between them.

"Really, Taryn?"

"Okay, you're right. I did a few times. I didn't know what to say after that."

"Like I said, I get it. Can we admit that we were both embarrassed; red-faced in fact? I saw you outside my door through my camera. You'd never come to my apartment before. I thought perhaps something was wrong with your aunt. I just reacted and opened the door right away. I didn't mean for you to see...that part of me; or any part of me. I'm truly sorry. Is there any way that we can move past that moment and into the present?"

Taryn exhaled loudly. She was glad for the reprieve of walking around with that night in her head every time she thought of him. She was ready to put that night behind her.

"Yes, please. Let's do exactly that. I know it was a mistake that was caused by my two left feet."

"We're two adults. I often wondered if you were hurt in any way when you fell."

"Oh, no, not at all. I was fine."

"Good. Now that we've gotten that out of the way, I have a few other things to go over with you. Let me get Jocelyn started on the paperwork for the retainer agreement and some connections to financial and investment professionals that I think will serve you the best. Give me a few seconds to talk to her and then we can finish up. I don't want to make you late for your time with your cousin. Does she live here?"

"She lives in Boston. She took two weeks off from work at the hospital where she works as a head nurse to come here and help me out. Of course, her mother lives here and so do my uncles. They all followed my aunt here after she got married. I guess they had expectations that she would take care of them. She did her best until they started treating her like a bank. Sherita was never like that. My aunt cherished her. Like my apartment in Paris that they paid for, they also paid for the house that Sherita lives in. My aunt wanted her to focus on school and not on how to pay rent or a mortgage."

"Your aunt was a generous woman. I found that out when I started working directly as one of her attorneys. She donated to a lot of causes, especially schools."

"She's been doing that since before I came to live with them. She has tons of recognitions on the walls of the apartment from a lot of schools and kids, thanking her for her donations. I will really miss her. I plan to carry on her legacy by setting up a legacy fund to send donations out. She would want that."

"You're a lot like her. You have a big heart. We need more people like you and your aunt in this world. If we did, it wouldn't be so out of control. Anyway, make yourself comfortable. I'll be right back so that we can finish up."

Taryn nodded and smiled in his direction when he stood and headed for his office door.

"I'll be right here," she said to herself because he was already out of ear range.

**

"Jocelyn, can you get a retainer agreement package together for Ms. Novak? She would like to have our firm represent her. Also, pull out our contacts for financial services. Start with Taye Epps for investments and Curtis Moore for financial planning in general. The two of them work well together and will be able to help Taryn manage all that's coming her way."

"I'm on it," Jocelyn acknowledged. "You like her," she whispered so that only he could hear her.

Adrian looked around the busy outer office and found that no one was paying their conversation any mind. He leaned over in her direction.

"I do."

"I like the sound of that."

"Yeah."

"She isn't the kind of woman that you would call and ask me to send flowers or little gifts to after a date, is she?"

"Hell no. If I get the chance, I'll do my own shopping."

"Oh, she's special like that?"

Adrian looked toward his office where he could see Taryn relax back against the sofa. With the tension between them eliminated, they could both relax. He was hoping for a little more, but not today. Today, they are talking business. He was hoping for much more when the time was right.

"Yes. She is special like that."

"I'm not mad at you, boss. You know, Ms. Misha would stop by my desk when she was here so that she could keep up on your dating life. She would ask if you were seeing anyone seriously, she wanted me to alert her right away. Do you know why?" she asked.

Adrian was curious. He was learning a lot about Ms. Misha's intentions.

"I don't."

"One day, she told me that she may not live to see it, but she saw you and Taryn married and living a happy life. Can you believe that? Anything to her insinuation?"

Adrian shook that off. He would keep his inner most thoughts to himself.

"I believe she believed it. If she had that thought on her mind when she left this world, I'm happy that the idea of it made her happy."

Adrian turned back toward his office. The idea didn't scare him one bit. For the first time in his life, he found a woman who had him thinking about the future on a personal level. He whistled as he entered his office.

6

Sherita wished her phone would stop buzzing. She didn't want to completely turn it off while she waited for Taryn to show up for their early evening dinner. The plan was to meet earlier but Taryn had a meeting with their aunt's attorney. She was arriving late in New York, so they agreed to meet later. The traffic had been heavier than she expected from her home in Pennsylvania. She expected several hours on the road, but the extra two hours did her in. She arrived in town and went straight to the restaurant. Her luggage was still in the trunk of her car. Her plan was to get a hotel because staying with her mother was not the answer. The fact that her mother called her phone every thirty minutes to pass along what she wanted her to say to Taryn was annoying. All her mother had to do was pick up the phone and talk to her own niece. Instead, she wanted her own daughter to pry into Taryn's life now that her last sister had passed away.

When her phone buzzed again, she didn't want to check it but was forced to do so just in case Taryn was calling. This time, like the last ten calls, it wasn't Taryn, but her mother. Valencia Clayton was a forced to be reckoned with. Sherita wasn't in the mood for dealing with her persistence today. As soon as they were aware of her aunt's death, her mother had pushed her to get to New York to be her eyes and ears with Taryn. Sherita appeased her mother most times; this wasn't one of those times. She and Taryn had always been close. She would never take sides, even for her mother's sake. Still, she answered her call in hopes that she would stop harassing her.

"Hi, mom. You're ringing again?" she asked

Sherita signaled for the waitress.

"That's not a proper greeting from a daughter to her mother," Valencia declared.

"Can I have a glass of Chardonnay?" she asked the waitress in a voice that was a little over a whisper. "Mom, you keep calling. Even when I was driving and I told you I was driving, you kept calling with something else you wanted me to talk to Taryn about without her knowing it's coming from you. Some of what you've brought up would be clear that it's coming from you and not me. Taryn knows the kind of things I would and wouldn't ask her. Why don't you call her?"

"Have you ever known me to call her? If I do so now, she'll know it's about money and what's in the will. I haven't heard anything about when the reading of it will take place. Your uncles and I were talking about that earlier. We have each reached out to her attorney and so far, we haven't gotten a response other than that they will get back to us after speaking with Taryn. The princess is in charge, I guess," her mother huffed loudly.

"Mom, don't be mean. It's not her fault that she lost her parents and aunt Misha took her in when no one else would; not even you. I don't mean any disrespect but the things you want me to pry out of her are unreal."

"Have you seen her yet?" Valencia asked.

"No. I'm waiting at the restaurant that she chose. I arrived later than I had planned, so instead of a late lunch, we're doing an early dinner. She should be here any minute. I am not asking her all of those things. She's mourning aunt Misha. I want to be here to support her. We have always supported each other; you know that."

"Yes, I know. It's just that my sister has probably left her everything. None of us will get anything."

Sherita didn't want to tell her mother that she knew her aunt left her something. She and her aunt had talked about that several times over the years. She'd been getting a yearly stipend from her aunt for about ten years. After she graduated from college, which her aunt had paid for, that was when she released the funds that she'd been saving for her. If she got nothing else from her aunt's estate, she would be fine. She'd been given enough to make all of her own dreams come true. Her aunt's one ask was that she not tell her mother about the money. She didn't want anyone to talk her out of even a cent of it. Upon her aunt's death, her mother would get something; what, she didn't know.

"Mom, I don't know anything about that. Once the reading is scheduled, I'm sure you'll be told about that. You and uncle Antony and Uncle James will hear something soon, I'm sure. Can you let me call you after I get settled later this evening?"

"Why can't you stay here with me? I'm only an hour outside of the city. Why would you come to New York and not stay with me and your father?"

"I already spoke to daddy and he said he understood. I told him I'll be here about two weeks. I will come out to the house. I wouldn't come this far without coming home. I'll get settled into my hotel, spend some time with Taryn to see what help she needs and then I'll call you with when I'll come home."

"Okay, sweetheart. I just miss you."

"Mom, you were just at my place two weeks ago for a visit. I miss you too. Listen, Taryn is walking into the restaurant. I'll call you later?" she asked.

"You better. Try and ask some of the questions I gave you. Taryn won't know they're from me."

"Okay. I will try," she lied to get her mother to stop asking.

Sherita ended the call even though she had lied to her mother. Taryn wasn't coming in the restaurant door. There is so much animosity in her family when it came to her mother and Taryn. She wasn't in the mood to deal with it.

"You look deep in thought."

Sherita looked up at the sound of Taryn's voice. She stood immediately and was pulled into a strong, tight hug.

"I was watching for you. I didn't see you come in," Sherita said near Taryn's ear.

"I've missed you. I'm sorry I'm late. My meeting with auntie's lawyer went over. Then I had to make a few stops. I forgot how awful New York traffic is, even with speed racer for a driver. I've actually retained them, from this moment on, as my attorneys as well. I spent some time going over that and getting the contract signed."

Taryn released her and they took their seats across from each other.

"Thanks for meeting me. I wanted to lay eyes on you. My heart was hurting for you. I know how much auntie loved you and how much you loved her. Oh, my goodness. You look amazing. I bet you don't even work out."

"Thank you. I work out some. Hitting thirty was no joke. Auntie loved you too. You were more like a daughter than a niece to her just like me."

Sherita nodded.

"I can't believe she's gone. I was just with her two weeks ago when you called and asked me to go with her to see her doctor. That appointment went well. I can't imagine what happened. She was fine when I left to go back to Boston."

Taryn picked up her menu and glanced over it.

"I'm supposed to get a copy of the report on her death. It was natural causes is all I know right now. Her doctor, working with the medical examiner, couldn't find anything specific to point to her death. He said she went to sleep and didn't wake up. I will say, if I am to go, I want it to be just like that."

Taryn had often thought about that considering how her parents died. From what she was told, it wasn't short or painless. She dared think about it.

"I agree, cuz. I'm having a glass of wine. I see the waitress coming this way. Do you want anything?" Sherita questioned.

"No alcohol for me tonight. Perhaps another time. I'll have a lemonade," Taryn told the waitress.

"How are you? I take it your flight from Paris was fine?"

"It was great. I had been so worked up over auntie's death that I hadn't been sleeping. I slept just about the whole way on the plane ride."

"You look rested. I was worried."

"Thanks for coming all this way to see about me. Are you staying with your parents? I'm sure your mom is pressing you to stay with them. No doubt she misses you when you're home in Boston."

"No, I've decided to stay in the city. I'm going to get a room at the Marquis so that I'm close enough to help you out with whatever you need."

Taryn placed her menu down and eyed her up and down the way they used to do as kids.

"A hotel? You're staying at a hotel? No way. Stay at the apartment with me. There is plenty of room. Besides, it's so lonely there. I still see Auntie in every room. I love that, but still, I could use the company if that's okay with you. That is, unless you were getting a hotel because you want your space."

"I was doing that to give you your space. If you don't mind the company, I would love to stay at the apartment. I love that place. When I was here for her doctor's appointment, I stayed in your room. She cooked for me every day even though I begged her not to."

She and Taryn laughed together over their combined memories of their aunt.

"She loved cooking for us all the time. When she knew I was flying in, she would prepare a feast. I will miss that."

"We both will. How did things go with the lawyer? I hope they were able to give you a little clarity."

"Adrian was great. He laid a lot of things out for me that I was unsure of."

"Adrian? That's who your meeting was with? The hunk that every hot-blooded woman in the world lusts over? Wait, he's the one that you saw his..."

Taryn raised her hand and ended the rest of her comment, causing them both to laugh again.

"He and I talked about that. It was time we swept that under a rug. I've been avoiding him ever since it happened. He called me to the table on that today."

"Did he?"

"Yes. We are officially moving on from that."

"Ah, what are you moving on to? I know you like him. You would be insane not to."

"I'm not insane, trust me. That brother is gorgeous. I'm sure he's involved with someone, even though my best friend, Jules, said she saw an interview with him on the Today Show where he declared he was single. That doesn't mean he isn't seeing anyone or a few someone's. Can you imagine a man that fine not being involved with anyone?"

"That's what a lot of people say about the most handsome and prettiest people in the world. Everybody think because they are so good looking that there is no way they would ever be single. I'm sure he dates but is he serious about anyone? If not, are you interested?"

The waitress reappeared before Taryn could answer her. They gave her their orders and relaxed and talked.

"I like him, but now, he is my attorney. There has to be some rule against that."

"I doubt that. You once confided in me about how much you desired him. That was before the day of the great fall at his feet. You've been attracted to him since you first met him. What about how the two of you vibed at that gala? A few days later when we talked, you referred to him as mister perfect. Is that still your assessment of him?"

"It is."

"Okay. Well?"

"I don't know. He makes me nervous. When I'm around him I lose all train of thought. I've never encountered a man as virile and magnetic as him. I look at him and the first word that comes to mind is perfect. Not just because of his looks."

"Are you and Sean still involved? I won't even ask about Nathaniel who likes to pop back up in your life with love devotions. Sean was okay, but Nathaniel will forever leave a bad taste in my mouth. I can even tolerate that guy you dated for a minute that looked like Rick Fox in his younger days."

She'd lived through her own wrong choices in men, so she never judged.

"No. Sean and I are officially done; have been for a while. We broke up months ago. As for Nathaniel, he still lingers around trying to find his way back into my heart, but that's not happening. I haven't heard from him or seen him in a very long time, though, surprisingly. That's a great thing."

"He'll probably reach out now that auntie has died. I see him trying to console you with dreams of the two of you getting back together."

"I hope not. The unlucky part for me is that his mother owns the firm. I have to run into him every time he comes through. He's still out in the world trying to chase the next, big quick-money scheme. He didn't cheat or anything, at least I don't think so. We just weren't going anywhere in any direction. The relationship had become stale. He was fun back in college. I've grown. He's still that college playboy. I've been giving the dating scene a break. What about you? Are you seeing anyone?"

Sherita shrugged her shoulders. She had been but things seemed to be up in the air.

"I was or maybe still am. I don't know. I met someone but there is no real spark; just a strong like for him. He works at a government building near where I work. He's a numbers guy. We can be relaxing together and watching a movie and all of a sudden, he would start talking about math, science and just numbers in general. It's getting annoying. This break with me being in New York is needed. I'm working on how to break things off. I want a man who has me dreaming about him when I go to sleep. I want to melt when I talk about him like you do when you mention Adrian. I'm just saying, that spark between the two of you is more than a spark; it's more like a lightning bolt; it's like fireworks. I hope if you get the chance, you'll see what Adrian is all about."

"I just may do that. What are you having for dinner? I think I'm going to have the stuffed flounder. First, I'm going to start with dessert. I see a piece of chocolate pudding cake on that cart right there that is calling my name. My appetite has been null and void. I swear, after I left Adrian's office, I was completely famished. I'm starving."

Sherita knew what that was all about even if her cousin didn't. Taryn was in heat over Adrian. A man that good looking could do that for a woman just by being in his presence.

"Hungry for more than food?" she asked Taryn.

When her cousin winked at her over the menu, Sherita knew she'd hit it on the head.

Her thoughts turned to her mother and her millions of prying questions. She had no plans of asking any of them. If and when the time came for the reading of the will, everyone would find out what they're getting at that time. For now, she wanted to enjoy connecting with Taryn again.

"When are you coming to visit me in Paris again? You've only been one time."

"All I was waiting for was an invitation. I could in a few months. I would love that. My visit with you was amazing. Who knew they had such an electric night-life? Are the men still fine? I may need to find me one because I have a dud. I need more fire!"

"Don't we all!" Taryn said, agreeing with her. "Yes, we do."

7

"If I had known that you would be this distracted all night, I would have canceled the date before it happened. You know, the way you're known to cancel on me? You're here with me physically tonight but not in any other way. If it wasn't for the play where we couldn't talk, what would we have had to say? You've been unusually quiet. Even over dinner you only responded to questions or statements I had. That was unlike you. What is it this time? An important case? A new client? A new woman?"

Adrian's head snapped to the side and then back to the road since he was driving. He knew he'd been off all evening even before he picked Kelly up for their evening out. Cancelling their last two dates was beyond his control. He was working with a client on a major merger and he needed to put in the extra time. He was making it up to her tonight and still, she was complaining.

"I've apologized a million times about cancelling on you. It's not like you don't know what I do for a living. My life can be unpredictable."

"Adrian, I'm only in town a few times a month. I make you aware of my schedule weeks ahead of time. I don't mind you being a hard, driven attorney. I get that. It's you making plans, showing up and then not really showing up. I'm assuming tonight will end the way our nights usually end. We'll go back to my place, have amazing sex and then it's sayonara until the next time. Dates with us seem forced. You are more distant tonight than you've ever been. What? Have I lost the appeal of what drew you to me?"

"No, no. Please don't think that."

"I know running a law firm is major. Your head has to stay on a swivel at all times. You have to stay ready for clients who demand your attention around the clock. You don't deal with your run of the mill issues, but you have big clients with big money and even bigger problems."

"All true, Kelly. I have a lot on my plate and on my mind these days."

"I get that I'm not the only woman you're seeing. Don't leave that out. You've made your lifestyle clear to me. You don't want to be tied down to one woman. You're not ready for a committed relationship. We had that conversation six months ago. Nothing about our time together has had you reconsidering that? I thought we were good together; that we could really have something. For a man not ready for a relationship, when you can, you put your all into us. Then there are times like tonight when I feel like I can't reach you. There is more to life than working. Don't you want more than this?"

Adrian thought about her words. He also thought of how Ms. Misha said pretty much the same thing to him in her letter to him.

Since Taryn came to town a few days ago, he'd been thinking of nothing but what could be next for him on a personal level. He wasn't sure how to broach the subject with Kelly that it wasn't her that he was thinking about having more in life with.

They'd been dating for a while. As a flight attendant he met while on business travel, they had gotten into hooking up anytime her flights brought her to New York. When she called last week to give him an update on her schedule, he was more than ready to spend some time with her the way they had comfortably been doing. Sometimes, they would go out like tonight. Other times, they went right to a bed. They were always fiery hot for each other. Tonight was different. That flame for her had burned out. It wasn't that she wasn't an amazing woman because she was definitely that. She just happened to be perfect for the non-relationship way he liked to engage with women. He wasn't afraid of investing in a serious relationship. He just hadn't found that woman that made him want to think about stepping away from how he's always been; that is until he and Taryn cleared the air. The rest of the week, he had been on cloud nine. He thought about her at night when he was at home knowing she was in the apartment above him. He was tempted to pay her a visit, but didn't. He wanted to respect her time with her cousin. They had a lot to do.

Tomorrow was the reading of the will. They had been in contact throughout the week on different topics. He hadn't seen her at the apartment building nor in person again since that first day in his office. Though he'd been desiring to have an excuse to see her again, he didn't tread on the time she needed to focus on her aunt's arrangements,

"Right now, I don't know what I want. I also don't want to lead you on."

"Lead me on? Do you realize how amazing you are? Not just as a professional but in how you deal with women. Even though we are surface dating, I can't complain about how you hold your heart behind a steel wall. I enjoy our time together. I can see more happening between us. You can't? I've had men that I've been involved with who haven't treated me as good as you have and we're not in a serious relationship. Listen, I have a friend who is planning a couple's trip to Tulum. I was hoping you could be my date for the week."

This was not the conversation he was interested in having tonight. Maybe now was a good time before he ended up hurting her. He never, ever wanted to do that. They were having fun when time permitted. He screwed up by not paying attention to the fact that she was moving in a lane ahead of him. He had been convinced that they were on the same page. That was no longer clear. He didn't mind a trip here and there. What he wasn't going to do was a couple's trip. That would give her and those around them the wrong idea.

"We aren't that kind of couple, Kelly. Yes, we've been to events as a couple and have even hung out with my friends and your friends. Going away on a couple's trip is more like going to the next level."

She gasped out her frustration. He heard her suck her teeth to show her unhappiness with where he was about to take the relationship.

"We're also not getting any younger; at least I'm not. You seem to age in the other direction as if you're staying forever young. Me? I'm thirty-five. I know I agreed to friends with benefits when I'm in town or when you're traveling and we can hook up if it's near where I am. I got that. I guess it's just me who feels like we're more than that. How can I be in this alone? You don't have any serious feelings for me? I'm not talking about love, but don't you want that?"

Adrian darted in and out of traffic on his way to her hotel. He'd driven tonight instead of taking his usual car service because he wanted to take her on a car ride outside of the city. That wasn't going to happen. It's clear that the air between them needed to be refreshed. No matter how his mind tried to play out what the end of the night would be, it hadn't involved him bringing her down when she requested the flight that would bring her to him for the next few days. He just couldn't shake Taryn. His mind was playing tricks on him in the way that had him feeling like if he moved forward with anything with Kelly tonight, he would be cheating on Taryn; a woman he wasn't even involved with on any level outside of a business one. That's how much he wanted her. Taryn is that woman that even Kelly spoke of and didn't know it. He hated that he felt this way. He had to be honest.

Turning one last corner, he stopped short of her hotel so that they could spend a few minutes talking in the car. He would not be going up to her room.

"I'm sorry, Kelly. I'm not heading in the direction that you are when it comes to us. I could be one of those guys who would string you along until I've had enough of getting my needs met and then walked away. That's not who I am. I think you are an extraordinary person. Every guy would be lucky to have you to want a life with them. I don't think it's going to be me. No, that's not right. I know it's not going to be me. We've had some good times. You absolutely deserve better. I have been distracted a lot more lately than any other time. My firm has had a plethora of new clients. We're hiring new team members."

"That's great."

"It is. We'll also be adding two new partners in about six months. A lot is happening at work. That's where my head is."

"Oh, and not on a woman? I know you. Are you telling other women the same story? I get it, you're not ready. Are you saying you never will be?"

"I'm not saying that. I don't want this to continue between us if what you're looking for is something other than hot times when you're in town. I don't want to sound or seem crass like I was using you. We agreed to what we had. I assumed that's all there was going to be."

"You mean forever or until we got tired of bouncing between the sheets together? Which describes you? I guess now is a good time to end things then, huh? Your timing sucks but I get it. I've turned down man after man who expressed their interest in me. I did that because if there was more for us, I wanted to be available for that; to you."

Adrian had to be honest. He didn't want a gray area or any confusion.

"I want for you what makes you happy. Yes, work is busy. Life is crazy and most of all, yes, there is a woman. I didn't expect it. I don't mean to hurt you in any way. You're beautiful, sexy as hell and a very good woman."

When he looked her way, Kelly was smiling a soft smile. She turned to him and placed one hand lovingly on his cheek.

"You know what, I understand. I really do. I mean, I would love for your heart to recognize me but Black love should be where you find it. There was something different in you tonight. I'm glad you've shared what it was. I'm selfish enough to say that I didn't want it to be something negative about me. Whoever this woman is, I hope she realizes what a true gem she will have in you. I want to be so angry with you right now for not choosing me. I can't because I know what it feels like to want someone. The fact is, want has to be a two-way street for it to work. We said we would have fun and we did. Yes, I would like more but I want that with someone who wants more with me. I so want to be downright disgusted with you but I can't. You are one hell of a catch."

"Our time wasn't wasted. I hope you agree."

"I do."

She kissed his cheek and then wiped off the lipstick he assumed she saw when she pulled her lips away.

"Thank you," he said.

"I wouldn't want her to see lipstick on your face. She is a lucky woman. One day, if you can, please tell her that a woman who cares deeply for you said that. She had better treat you right or I'm coming for her. Thanks for being honest with me. You're right that men who string women along for their own desires aren't good men. It's the ones who can speak and live their truth that will end up the happiest. I wish that for you."

"And I for you. I really do. I hope you can find some downtime while you're in town."

"One of the other attendant's is laying over as well. I'll connect with her so that we can take the city by storm. If you see me out in these streets being wild and crazy, don't tell anyone. I have an image to uphold. Well, I'm going to get out and go inside. The play and dinner were great. So are you, Adrian. I know telling me that you have an interest in another direction wasn't hard. You're that kind of good man. You do look good tonight. I guess a cold shower is in store for me because I had plans for us," she boasted.

"I'm sure you did. I know what your plans include."

Adrian laughed along with her. He put the car in drive and pulled closer to the front of the hotel so that she could get out and go inside. He started to get out after stopping. Kelly's hand on his arm stopped him.

"Do you want me to walk you up? I can have the doorman watch my car to be sure you get to your room safe."

"Baby, not unless you're coming inside. I mean that in the sexiest way, just in case you didn't catch that double meaning. Since we both know that's not going to happen, I'll be fine. I'll text you when I'm in my room with the door locked. Good luck Adrian. I really mean that."

"I wish the same for you. That will be one lucky man who will one day give you everything you want and need."

The doorman walked up to the car. Adrian rolled the window down on his black Jaguar and gave the man the thumbs up to open the door. Kelly got out and blew him a kiss before she walked inside of the hotel. When she was out of sight, he leaned his head back on the headrest and closed his eyes while he sat idling. That was hard to do. His mind had been on how to have that talk with her once he picked her up after leaving the office. He had hoped that a talk wouldn't end badly. He was glad it didn't. He'd told Kelly about Taryn without saying her name. He had no clue if Taryn was even interested in him. He needed to free himself up just in case he had a chance. If not, he would join the dating game again. Something told him that there was more for him when it came to her. He had to find out.

There was the reading of the will in the morning. Perhaps he could convince her to sit and talk with him on a more personal level after. Passing up a night with Kelly was saying something loud to him. No doubt she was not the type to want a man who wasn't all about her. Could he be that after vowing to never be that kind of guy? He didn't know. He is discovering that Taryn is worth the try and the wait.

When his phone pinged, he checked it and found two thumbs-up from Kelly. He pulled away from the curb and entered traffic. It was close to ten at night. He thought about heading into the office to catch up on a few cases, but not tonight. Making a right turn, then another right turn, and then another right turn, he turned left and headed home to his apartment. He didn't need to go over the will before tomorrow, but it wouldn't hurt to get more prepared for any response the family would levy on him. He would protect Taryn at all costs.

**

"Cousin, you know that man at the restaurant who kept staring at you wanted to take you home and do all kinds of naughty things to you. Have you ever been to that restaurant before? He kept saying he knew you from somewhere. Clearly, it was a line from a very old play book," Sherita said.

She and Taryn walked the last block to get to the apartment. As they had done each night since Sherita arrived in New York, they were heading home from another nice restaurant where they had dinner and had dined sufficiently, as her aunt would say on many occasions. The rideshare they had come home in had dropped them off a block before the building. They wanted to get some snacks for their scheduled late-night gab fest. The last few days of them being in the apartment together were going great.

She and Taryn had begun going through their aunt's things, especially her office. They would continue that tonight while fake watching anything on the television.

They laughed as they walked arm-in-arm through the dark New York night.

"He was trying extra hard. I felt sorry for him when I had to let him down easy."

"He wasn't bad looking."

"True, but he smelled like smoke and not just regular smoke. He was smoking on something else within the minutes before he walked up to us at the bar. I don't do men that smoke anything. I can't stand the smell. It makes me sick to my stomach. Besides, the way he was stumbling, he'd already had too much to drink. I don't' want to judge but I like what I like in men."

"Oh, like Adrian?" Sherita questioned.

"You like to bring up his name, don't you? Why is that? You are Jules are alike. She does the same thing."

"Oh, please. Don't act like you don't like talking about him. I see how the idea of him has you lighting up and biting that lower lip of yours. I know the signs. What are you waiting for?"

"Waiting for? I'm not waiting for anything. I have a job to do and I'm focusing on that."

"You can't multi-task? If I remember correctly, you are an expert at that."

"Why are you pushing us together?"

"Am I really doing that?" Sherita asked.

"Have a good night," the doorman said behind them where he stood after being sure that they were safely at the elevator.

Sherita nodded and then pulled Taryn inside of it.

"Hello," Adrian said.

They were stoic hearing the familiar low sexy voice.

"Wow. Fancy seeing you here. We were just talking about you," Sherita offered right before she felt a nudge to her side by Taryn.

Taryn inserted her key for their floor. The doors closed encasing them in a small space.

"Oh? I hope all good stuff," he said.

"Good stuff, Taryn?" Sherita said and winked at her.

Taryn cleared her throat and looked toward Adrian.

"Hello. We were just talking about the reading of the will tomorrow. I'm a little nervous. How are you? I haven't seen you since earlier this week."

"Tomorrow will be fine. I'll be there to support you one hundred percent. I'm doing well. It's been a busy week."

"No big plans for working into the wee hours of the night for you tonight?" Taryn asked.

"I had planned to look over some files. Instead, I'm going to relax and catch up on some missed shows; perhaps my favorite ice cream with some unhealthy syrup on top," Adrian laughed.

"Sounds delicious," Taryn added.

"Yes. It does."

The elevator landed on Adrian's floor and he stepped out, holding the door to keep it from closing.

"It was a pleasure running into you. You as well, Sherita. Your family has very strong genes. The two of you could almost be taken for sisters instead of cousins."

"It was great seeing you again, Adrian. I think the last time was at my aunt's place for one of her impromptu luncheons about a year ago," Sherita said.

"I believe that's correct. Taryn, don't forget. I'm available anytime you need me. I'm one floor below or stop by the office anytime, especially after tomorrow. You will never need an appointment. I've already alerted Jocelyn about that. I'm here to help in any way. Have a good night, ladies."

Sherita waved and Taryn nodded her head as the door closed.

Taryn exhaled the breath she'd been holding in.

"Why the hell is he so fine?"

"He and all that fineness can be all yours for the right price of just stepping out on faith. That man is yours, honey."

"From your lips to...well, you know the rest."

"Yeah. What are you going to do? Hmm?" Sherita asked as the elevator rose to the next floor.

Taryn didn't respond. She had no idea. Her only thought was that each time she saw Adrian, her attraction to him grew more intense.

8

Taryn walked into her aunt's home office and shook her finger at Sherita while shaking her head from right to left over and over again. Sherita sat on the floor in front of several already put together boxes that she was filling with books.

"I thought you were going to wait for me to finish my shower before we tackle more of the office. There is still so much to go through. Have you boxed up all that you know you want? I hope you're thinking of letting me ship those boxes instead of you packing them in your car."

"I agree. I'll call a service to pick up and ship my boxes. What about everything that you're not taking back to Paris with you? I know you're not going to try and focus on doing anything with all that's here. There is over twenty-five years or so of stuff here."

Taryn looked around the room and realized that even though they've done a good job of going through the contents of the apartment, there is so much more to go.

"I'm going to get a storage unit; a really big one. Probably more than one. There will be a lot even after I don't some of it. When the apartment goes on the market, I want to have all of auntie's things out. I'll have it staged with things that I have no connection with. I still can't imagine her not being here or not being in this apartment anymore. I've never been through anything this hard other than the passing of my parents and my uncle. A lot of that is still a blur for me because it's been so long ago. I'm going to miss this place."

"Why not keep it? Do you think you'll never come back to New York again simply because auntie is gone? This is still your hometown. You have friends here. I would say family but they're all being asses."

Taryn giggled. They both shared the same sentiment. It wasn't that they treated Sherita as bad as they treated her, but Sherita saw first-hand how their uncles and sometimes her mother, treated her. She hated it too.

"I don't know. I'm waiting until after the reading of the will tomorrow. That will give me some time to unwind and think. I love my life in Paris. Without auntie here, I don't know if I need to keep the apartment if I come back to New York to visit friends. That would make this an expensive hotel. She would want someone living here. I don't want to leave it vacant. Before you ask, I know one of the uncles are going to ask about living here. They won't want to buy it. They'll feel entitled to it, which they are not. The last thing she would want is for either of them living here."

"She would love for you to live here. Imagine raising your own family here one day."

Taryn grabbed a box and moved to the bookcase.

"That's a lot of wishful thinking. I have to have a man first before there is a family."

"Oh, there is a man. You just won't make that move. He sure looked good tonight. Did you feel the heat of his eyes piercing right through you? The two of you are getting on my nerves. Two people who want each other and neither of you are making any kind of moves. Anyone around you two for more than a minute can see and feel the attraction, except the two of you? That's wild!"

Taryn started her defense and was cut off.

"But..." she tried to say.

"But what? But you have a lot to deal with? But you're going back to Paris when this is all over? But you saw parts of him that you can't forget about every time you see him? That doesn't make you want him even more? But you've dealt with womanizers like Nathaniel? I'm glad he's dust. You deserve better. You deserve Adrian. I think you should at least talk to him. You can even go do it now. You know he's home, all relaxed and stuff with cold ice cream and hot syrup. Okay, he didn't say it like that, but I bet you were thinking it. You have questions about the reading of the will tomorrow. Go talk about that with him in person."

"But I don't have questions."

Taryn dropped two books in the box."

Sherita tapped on a box to get her attention. She turned in her direction.

"Yes, you do."

"I really don't."

"Taryn, don't be that person. You know what I'm saying. Go see that man. I don't care if you go to ask him for a recipe to make lasagna. Hell, go ask if you can borrow some ice cream. Go talk to him. You know you want to. I want you to. He probably does too. You said auntie wrote something to you telling you to live life with gusto and don't hold back. Not her exact words, I'm sure, but the sentiment is the same. There is something about the two of you that can't be denied. I feel it."

"I don't know."

"Auntie felt it and knew it. Why don't you? What are you afraid of?"

Taryn paused loading books to the box and leaned forward on the floor to ceiling bookcase. She lowered her head and questioned why she would deny herself a chance to get to know Adrian. If he was as attracted to her as she was to him, was she wasting valuable time she could have with a great man?

"Sherita, I'm afraid of having to say goodbye when I go back to my life. I know he's special. I can see myself getting all wrapped up in him, for what? For it to end in a month and a half? I have not had the best of luck in the man department; you know that. I'm not used to making the first move with a guy. If you think he's so interested, why hasn't he?"

"Perhaps because of the ice-cold, stoic posture you tend to have in his presence. It's like you told me before, I think a year ago, that he makes you nervous to the point that you're in a hurry to move away from him so that you can breathe? How many more times will you hide behind walls and buildings to avoid him?"

"I told you about that?"

"Yes, you did. You even wondered if he saw you. I bet he did and that's why he hasn't made a move. He doesn't appear to be a man who doesn't go for what he wants and that includes a woman. You know they are probably dropping panties at his feet like flowers were done in that *Coming to America* movie. You won't know if you don't talk to him. Have you talked about that day?"

"Yes. The first day when I met with him about auntie's passing. That's in the past. We agreed it was awkward and we laughed about it."

"Okay, then now you have nothing preventing you from clearing the air even more. I believe all you need to do is give him one little sign that you won't flee when you see him. He'll take it from there. Listen, I got this. Go talk to him before the hour gets too late."

"No! I can't just show up at his apartment unannounced."

"He made the offer. He said that you could contact him night or day. He even noted that he is right downstairs. I'm a big girl. I can work on this a little longer. After that, I'm going to grab my slice of Junior's Cheesecake. I can't believe you bought an entire pie just for the two of us. I may eat a piece and a half. You, on the other hand, should get on the phone and call Adrian. Go see him. Talk. No more hesitation. Him being your lawyer or not, I don't care. That man is yours, girl!"

Taryn grabbed her bottom lip between her teeth, nervous about making such a move. Could she really do it?

"What if..."

"No what ifs. Gone are the days of women waiting for men to start the conversation. We go for what we want as well. Right now, you, my dear favorite cousin, want that man."

Dropping her last book in the box, Taryn took her phone out of the front pocket of the pink sweat pants she'd put on along with a white cropped t-shirt. She stepped out of the office and walked into the large family room as she dialed.

"Hi, Taryn," Adrian's deep voice sexily boomed in her ear before the phone barely rang. Had he been holding it in his hand waiting for her to reach out? Was he going to call her? Just hearing him say her name sent sensual chills through her body.

"Hi. Did I catch you at a bad time? I know it's late," she said, pacing around as she spoke.

To say that she was out of her element wouldn't give her current stance any justice.

"I told you that you can reach out to me anytime. Is everything okay? You have questions about something?" he asked.

"Actually, I was wondering if I could stop by to talk. I don't want to interrupt your planned evening of relaxation. Trust me, after dealing with my uncles and my aunt tomorrow, you need this evening before to relax and prepare. They can be a lot," she kidded.

"Come on down. I'm not doing anything other than eating some fresh fruit and watching ESPN. I'm a night owl which means I'm wide awake. See you in a few minutes or do you need some time?"

"I'll be right down. Thanks, Adrian. I appreciate it."

"Anytime. I'll be waiting."

Taryn ended the call and kept her eyes on her phone.

"Did his voice deepen at the end of the call?" she said to herself. That strong powerful, yet soft and stimulating voice of his absolutely matched his handsome looks. She made her way back to the office.

"So?" Sherita asked before she could share.

"I'll be back in a little bit. I'm going to go down to talk to Adrian. I don't know what I'm going to say, so don't ask me that. Don't eat all of the cheesecake. I'll want some when I get back. You're sure you're okay here by yourself?"

Sherita laughed at her.

"How old am I? I live alone. I drove all the way here to New York from Boston. I'm of drinking age, and yes, over thirty. In fact, a year older than you. I think I can handle being by myself. Just text me if I shouldn't expect you back tonight. You know what I mean."

Sherita hopped up and danced around the room.

"You are so full of yourself. I'll see you in a little bit, like I said."

"If you say so. Have fun."

Taryn turned and waved over her shoulder. She slipped her feet into her pink Crocs, which were at the door. Waiting for the soft-close door to shut and lock behind her, she made her way to the elevator. She didn't know what this trip to Adrian's apartment would turn out to be. At this point, she didn't care. All she knew was that she wasn't backing down. She wasn't going to get any rest tonight if she didn't get to see him again. It was now or not at all. She was choosing now.

9

Adrian opened his apartment door the minute he heard the elevator open at the end of the hall. He knew Taryn was on her way. He didn't want her to walk the hall alone to get to his door. Even though the only other apartment on the floor was occupied by two New York University students who shared the place owned by one of their fathers, he still wanted to be sure he was able to keep his eye on her. He was anxious. He was excited. He was mesmerized by the mere thought of her. Most of all, he was happy that she was coming to see him, even if her visit was about business. Any interaction he could get with her, he would take.

The minute his eyes landed on her, his body, especially his heart came to life. He was looking at her as if it were his first time taking in a gorgeous sight. He wondered if Taryn knew how amazing she really was. He watched her confidently and with a bright smile walk toward him.

"Hello," he happily said when she walked right up to him. They stood on opposite sides of the door frame. Instead of replying to him with a greeting, Taryn started laughing, leaving him mystified. His eyes landed on her lips. Timing may be bad, but damn, he wanted to kiss her.

"I'm sorry. I didn't mean to laugh like that. I was remembering what happened the last time I was here at your door."

Adrian relaxed and laughed with her.

"I'm glad that's so far behind us that you're not hesitant about being here tonight. Come on in."

He moved to the side to give her room to walk past him."

"I get to see the inside of your place. Very nice."

Taryn was calm and cool but he could see that she was still a little nervous. He was actually feeling a bit nervous around her. There was so much on his mind that he wanted to say. They were alone and not at his office. He wanted to address the strong vibe between them. Instead, he wanted her to gain a level of comfort with being in his place.

"Thank you. I'm glad you like it. You look very nice; relaxed, in fact. The few times I've seen you, you are usually dressed up and in high heels. Crocs and a sweat suit are definitely a style for you too. I bet you rock well in anything you wear."

"I do. I could say the same for you. Gone are the suit, tie and dress shoes. You look very relaxed in black sweat pants and a blank t-shirt. I like this version of you. I see you were serious about relaxing for the evening."

"It was needed. My week has been quite busy."

"I have never seen a man with bare feet that were as perfect as yours," she said.

Adrian was enjoying how hard she was working at lightening the mood.

"The answer to that is bi-weekly pedicures. I know some men shy away from that, but I like my feet to look and feel good. I run several miles during the week. I also work out. There is wear and tear on the feet. I don't do polish or anything, but taking care of the full body is a priority. For me, that includes the feet."

"Yeah, I get it. I see that," she said and then looked away.

He clasped his hands behind his back while Taryn looked around.

"Deep purple, gold and black everywhere. Wow, I have never seen décor this magnificent before. Why this color scheme?"

"I'm a Que who hails from Howard University. I pledged in undergrad."

"Ah, I get it. Fraternity colors. I should have known by the gold boots right there against the wall. I think I saw these same boots in your office. Now it makes sense. Then there is the framed fraternity shirt in the glass frame above them. Nice."

The entryway lit up when Adrian turned the light on to give her a better view of the large open space. To the right was his entertainment room, where he had been sitting before she arrived.

"That's my favorite space. It's got everything in it that I need after a long day at the office or in court. It's definitely my man-cave."

"I have a room like this back in Paris. I don't call it a man-cave, but it's my inside she-shed."

"I like the idea of that."

"Are you a video game enthusiast? I see this gigantic television in the center of the wall with two smaller television underneath. Looks like a gaming center."

"I do sometimes, but it's not a big thing for me. I'm usually working all the time. When I get to relax, it's to catch up on the news or my latest shows. That's the reason behind the 83-inch television."

"Can I go further?" she asked, pointing to the rooms beyond the entry area where they stood.

"Absolutely. Take it all in. I will give you a tour."

"Okay. Are you sure I'm not keeping you from your planned night? I've seen you in action at work. I'm like that when I'm home. I like to unwind without interruption."

"Taryn, you're not an interruption. To the right, beyond the family room is my living room. Across form that is my dining room – yes, I still believe in having that space. I love having family and friends over for dinner."

"Same color scheme. Purple is one of my favorite colors," she acknowledged.

"That's good to know. Come take a look at my colors anytime you want."

"I may do that," she alluded. "Your place is incredible. Is the entire place like this?" she asked, walking ahead of Adrian, moving further into space.

"No, just these three rooms and the entryway. My kitchen, which is off of the dining room, the four bathrooms and three bedrooms have their own color schemes, thanks to one of my sisters who I let decorate."

"She has a great eye for details. Twin sisters, right? My aunt mentioned that once."

"Yes. Amira and Adore. Amira is the one who decorated my place. She has a minor degree in design. She knows me well. I loved everything she came up with. She knows what my fraternity means to me, so this area was an easy undertaking for her. The bedrooms are all to the back. I turned one of them into a home gym, the other two are guest rooms. The master suite is separated from those rooms by a large office; my home office."

Adrian turned on even more lighting and invited her with a swipe of his hand, to join him in his entertainment room. They sat together on the deep purple leather sofa.

"This is the softest leather I've ever sat on. Well, that is except for the couch in your office."

"I'm glad you like it. Can I get you anything? Water? A glass of wine?" he asked.

"No, thank you."

When both remained silent for a few seconds, Adrian decided to break the quietness. He saw her wringing her hands. There was something on her mind.

"You had questions? I have your file right here and other information here on my iPad. Does something have you troubled?"

"You mean besides how to handle my crazy family tomorrow? I, uh, didn't really come to talk about them or tomorrow, if that's okay with you."

Adrian closed the folder on the table in front of them and placed his iPad on top of it. He turned toward her like she had done when she sat down.

"I'm all ears. Is something wrong?" he questioned.

"No, nothing is wrong. Can I ask you a question? It's pretty much out of left field."

"Taryn, you have the floor to talk about anything you want. Hit me with it."

"Okay. Um..."

She paused. She appeared to be working on finding her words. Because he truly believed they were always thinking the same thing when it came to each other, he decided to give her a reprieve.

"Can I say something first?" he asked.

"Yes, please do. As you can probably see, I was, for some reason, at a loss for what I wanted to say. I thought it was simple until I got here."

"Your eyes? They're hazel with a speck of blue right now. I've also seen them in a light brown and semi-dark brown. The way your eyes change colors is beautiful."

"Yes. I get that all of the time. I'm told I get my eyes from my father. Not many people know this but my father was white. I get everything about me from my mother except my eyes."

"They are so beautiful. I don't want to put you off or overstep, but looking into them is pretty spellbinding. I can't be the first person to tell you that."

"You're not but the way you said it is different."

"Oh?" he asked.

"Let me explain. Everything you say to me sounds and feels different than when I engage with other men. There is a stern, rough, yet soft and gallant tone to your voice. No one has ever used the word spellbinding when speaking of my eyes. Still, I got it when you said it because that word has been in my head ever since I met you. When you look at me, I feel under some kind of spell. There are others who seem to see something in you when it comes to me that I, apparently, have been overlooking."

"That's so crazy. I could actually say the same thing. People seem to know more about what I'm thinking and feeling when it comes to you, except for me. I know we're jumping right into this. Please let me know if I'm being too much. I don't mean to be. When you called and asked to come see me, I was hoping it wasn't about work. I've been dying to talk to you about any and everything except work."

Adrian didn't take his eyes from hers even when he felt her soft hand land on his. Her eyes didn't move away from his either.

"I didn't call about work. I wanted to see you. I wanted to talk to you; really talk to you. I'm not usually forward when it comes to a man. You, are different."

"We've been missing something, haven't we? You feel it? You see it? Like me, you've been hesitant about it."

"Yes," she quickly replied.

"I like you, Taryn. I don't know if the timing is awful. I don't know if I should even say anything at this time. We are in a weird space with the legal matters at hand. I'm attracted to you. This didn't just happen within the past few days. It's been...well, over a year, perhaps longer when I first realized I was attracted to you."

"Adrian, it's been about that long for me too. My aunt wrote something to me in a book that she was planning to publish. In that, and another letter I found in an envelope addressed to me that was on her desk, she said some things that I haven't been able to stop thinking about. That's what I wanted to talk to you about. I really thought I missed the opportunity with all that's going on."

"Same for me. Your aunt was always throwing out little hints to me about you. I knew she wanted me to ask you out to get to know you better. I have been wanting to do that for a long time. I felt like the opportunity for me to do that kept escaping me. Then she passed away. I knew we would see each other again. What I didn't know was whether or not my attraction, my desire for you had a place in what you're going through right now. I'm not after anything from you other than, well, you."

Taryn nodded. That's when he knew that they were on the same page. What had been plaguing him was if he approached her now, would she think that he had an ulterior motive.

"I've had a single thought about you since my aunt passed. I knew we would see each other again," she said.

"And that would be?"

"If you would ever ask me out or in or anything without wondering if I felt like you were doing it because of what I will soon come into. Before you react in any way, my response would be, no. My aunt spoke so highly of you all the time; I do mean, all the time, Adrian. It was like she was losing patience with how complicated you and I were about finding a way to each other to see if there was anything there or not. I've always relied on discernment to help me make the right choices. Money or wealth of any kind is not a factor here. You have your own. There isn't an article that's written about you that speaks to the growth of your firm and what you're worth. You would have no reason to want mine just as I would have no reason to come after you for yours. That means..."

He finished her thought for her.

"That means that my desire I have had for you all of this time is as real as you sitting here in my home, making the first move that I never made. It wasn't that I didn't have plans to do so. I swear, you are a slippery one. All the ducking and dodging me that you were doing," he kidded.

Taryn bellowed over with laughter.

"I know. I'm pretty good with that. I have never had a man have me as nervous as I was any time I saw you."

"I missed a lot of chances. Truth is, I could have reached out by phone, email, text – a lot of ways. I didn't think you were interested, especially after the hallway thing. Also, the fact that yes, there was a woman here that night. Being transparent, even she said that after what happened in the hallway, I was different for the rest of the evening. She asked me who you were. Something about my reaction to you that night triggered questions in her brain. I didn't address it, but I knew it was there."

"All this time, Adrian. I thought about you a lot. I still think about you all the time."

"Getting you off of my mind was never going to happen. I wish we could have had a chat like this while your aunt was still alive. She knew it."

"She knew things about people before they knew things about themselves. My aunt was special that way. She could tell you about you and have you wondering how."

"Taryn, your aunt wrote me a letter too."

"She did? What did she say?"

Adrian stood and reached for the envelope inside of his briefcase on the floor next to the chair. He handed it to her.

"Before you read that, let me just say, whew!"

Adrian faked wiping his brow and then winked at her.

"What are you doing?" Taryn laughed.

"I have been in some sort of prison not knowing what to say or do about my attraction to you. It's blowing my mind that you're here. Whatever your aunt said to you, it's probably similar to what she said in her letter to me."

"She actually wrote you about me?" Taryn asked.

"Read it," he suggested.

Anxiety over sharing the letter was stressing.

Taryn opened the envelope and took her time reading the contents. By the time she was finished, she was overwhelmed.

"What did you think about what she said?"

"I think that, though I appreciated her letter, I already had my eyes set on you. I needed the time to be right. I told you, I was on a date that night when you fell in front of me. It didn't go well because I couldn't stop thinking about you. That wasn't the first time I felt something between us," he admitted.

Taryn shook her head in agreement. She knew when that first time happened. There truly was something special between them. There was no doubt that they had to explore it further.

"The gala," she boldly declared.

Adrian's eyes brightened.

"Yes. The gala. You knew? We connected that night. And then, nothing. Every time I think about that night, I realized I had a chance. I let it and you slip through my fingers. By the time I got up the nerve, because yes, I was nervous for the first time around a woman, you and your aunt were gone. Not long after, the incident happened. I assumed after that, I would never have a chance. Do I?" he asked.

"Do you what?"

"Do I have a chance with you? Can we get to know each other better? I mean, you know a lot about me, you know," he said and didn't finish.

"You know more about me too," she said, making reference to him getting an eyeful of her ass.

"That I do. You're gorgeous; every part of you. What do you think? I know we're connected on a business front. Does that overshadow you having dinner with me after tomorrow happens? I know how to be business when I need to be. I'm hoping to be relaxed with you. There is more to me than what you saw that night. I promise you that what you started to learn about me the night of the gala is only a small part of who I am."

Taryn thought about where they were right now. She didn't have to make the first move; not really. She only needed to show up and she did. It seems, that was all Adrian needed. He had to confirm that the night in the hall didn't ruin any chance of them perhaps dating. He needed her to know that he wanted her and nothing else from her. She already knew that.

"I believe that."

"Any reservations about joining me for dinner? I know you have a lot to do. I don't want to be a hindrance to that. I am a patient man; that has to be obvious. I've never waited to be with a woman. I was going to continue to wait."

"Yes, it is and no, I don't have any reservation at all. I would like that."

"Cards on the table?" he asked.

"All of them."

"Are you seeing anyone?"

"No. I'm currently not even dating. I was in a relationship with a man that seemed like it was always going south. That's over with."

Adrian exhaled deeply. He was happy to hear that. Realizing her hand was still on his, he placed his other hand on top of her hand that was still resting on his. He held her hand tight.

"I was seeing a few women; nothing serious. That was just easier for me with my busy life. Tonight, when you and your cousin saw me in the elevator, I was coming home from a date. This was with a woman that I've been hooking up with for quite some time. Whenever she was in town, we hung out. I ended that even before I saw you in the elevator. I told her that there was a woman. Surprisingly, she wasn't angry like I thought she would be. She wanted more from me. That was something I knew I couldn't give her. I was determined to see if there was anything between us. My plan was to give it a few days. I was then going to ask you out. I want to have a clean slate when it comes to being available in every way for you; for us, if there was going to be an us."

"An us? I'd like that very much. I didn't know how coming down here to talk to you would turn out. I'm glad that we're here now. No more being uncomfortable around each other."

"No more running away from me."

Taryn smiled brightly. She took her hand from between his and placed it softly against the side of his face. Adrian closed his eyes and focused on the feel of her hand on him. He dreamt of being able to touch her; hold her; kiss her. It was on his mind. He was ready.

"After coming all this way without falling in the floor to see you? Not on your life."

"Do you know what? I've been dying to do something since the night of the gala."

Taryn looked over at him with her head turned sideways with a question of what he was thinking.

"What's that?" she asked.

Her question wasn't answered with words. His eyes, smoldering and dropping down to her lips was all she needed to see to know what his intent was. Her body was ready. It had been for a very long time. Perhaps that was why she never had a desire for another man. She was waiting for Adrian. Her mind was screaming with yearning for him to relieve her longing to be kissed by him; to be touched by him. She didn't have to wait long.

Adrian moved closer, placing his hand on her neck, moving it around to the back of her head. He allowed his fingers to lock within her hair. He loved how her natural, silky tresses flowed down and around her shoulders. When her eyes landed on his lips, his body came to life, hardening like never before. He pulled her closer to him. There was no doubt that they both wanted this kiss that had been in the making for a long time. When Taryn slid closer to him, he moaned his pleasure at having her this close to him; to his heart, to his raging need. After not having her all this time, they had taken a major leap forward.

"Though we were not together all of this time, I feel like time stood still to allow us this time to get here. Thank you for coming down here tonight. You are a fantasy come true for me."

With their lips just a whisper away from each other, he joined them together as one. He took his time loving her mouth. He gave Taryn, who breathed out her pleasure against his lips, a few moments before he took the kiss a little higher. He didn't have to encourage her mouth to open for his entry. Taryn was with him in every way possible. They were one. The vibe that kept his faith in what they could be stoked an already burning flame of heated desire. She felt like heaven to him.

She reached her hand up and caressed his face when his lips kissed her deeply when he connected their lips again and then again, unable to move away from the feeling of love that was driving their need.

Taryn was experiencing a moment of perfect bliss. She was in Adrian's arms, his mouth kissing hers like a confession of forever. She needed him to know how much she has longed for a moment like this. She was an equal participant in their lip locking, giving as good as she was getting.

"Sweet," Adrian said against her lips before diving deeper yet again.

The minute she opened her mouth to take his tongue in, Taryn's world spun out of control with desire on a level that she'd never known before. This is what she could have been living through with him all this time? The idea of that made her kiss him amorously, barely getting in much needed breaths. She didn't care. Breathing wasn't a priority. The feel of being with Adrian was all that mattered.

Taryn closed her eyes and went willingly into Adrian's arms when he lifted her body and placed her across his lap, straddling his hips. He pulled her body snug against his and now their mouths dueled with pent-up longing that had been on the surface for a long time. They were giving into what they'd both been needing from each other but not speaking into existence.

She found herself loving on his mouth with zest, with gusto, with fervor. She's been kissed before but this thoroughly? Never.

All of Adrian was hard and as manly as they come, but the way in which he was kissing her and holding her like she was as precious as porcelain increased her yearning for him to never release her lips. He smelled good. His lips felt good. His tongue tasted like everything sweet.

Her heartbeat quickened. She knew this kiss could mean a lot for them going forward. The way he felt loving on her mouth, everyone who said that they had a connection knew something she hadn't before this very moment. She was ready to learn and be more with him.

Adrian deepened the kiss that had turned wild, heated and damn near out of control with an intensity giving her a raging taste of passion that stirred her body to life on an exquisite level.

The quiet in the room allowed her to hear every moan coming from her mouth and every groan coming from his.

Before she was ready, Adrian broke the kiss and leaned his forehead against hers as they equally attempted to control their breathing.

"Damn. I knew kissing you would be like this; exactly what I need and desire with a woman I've been thinking about nonstop for months. Perhaps we should stop?" Adrian asked before moving back so that they could read each other's eyes.

Taryn suddenly felt the boldest and bravest she's ever been. She wasn't going to give up on what could be next for them tonight. Her body was on fire. From the feel of his, so was his.

She finally found her breath.

"Do you want to? You really want to stop?"

Adrian shook his head fast from side to side like a cartoon character. Did he hear what he just heard?

"Whew! Sweet goodness. Don't tempt me to tell you what I really want. I'm really trying hard to be a gentleman here. The way you feel and taste is testing my boundaries of control. What I want, I don't want to push us into until we're ready."

"We? You're not ready?"

Taryn answering him breathlessly was breaking through every barrier he had put up in order to take things slow.

Before he could respond, Adrian kissed her again, lingering on her lips, sharing how in sync they were; how perfect they were together. If the kiss was an early factor, she was all in. She can't remember the last time she was this into a man just from kissing. Adrian had her, hook, line and sinker.

"That was my answer. Am I moving too fast if I ask if you could stay?"

Taryn leaned back and placed her hands behind her, bracing her body on his knees.

"What does stay entail? More kissing? More touching?"

"It could be that and so much more. I know neither of us planned for even the kissing. Is anything else moving too fast? I will say I've thought about getting you naked."

"Mmm, is that so? As naked as I've seen you?"

"Sweetheart, you are really killing me right now. I have never wanted a woman as much as I have and do want you. I'm almost afraid to be inside of you because I know I'll never want to be anywhere else ever again. I think the not knowing all this time has reached its peak. The way in which I deeply want you is immeasurable."

"Damn. If that's your desire for me. I'm all in. I want to stay. This is fast, I agree. I don't think it's too fast."

Adrian loved how this reality is so much better than buildup of images of being with her.

"It can't be. We've been building up to this moment and didn't know it. Would you like to see how the bedroom is decorated?" Adrian asked.

He couldn't resist touching her. He stroked the side of her face with his finger; moving it slowly up and down her cheek and then down to cup her chin, bringing her lips to his again. This kiss was slow and methodical. He stroked her lips with pure risqué imagery. He wanted no doubt between them anymore. When he pulled back, the only sound in the room was of their mutual excited breaths that spoke of more to come. Neither of them could look away as both took in huge excited breaths. Before he could make another move to prove his desire, Taryn leaned in and initiated the kiss this time. The way she loved on his lips and stroked his tongue, they were absolutely ready. It's true that they were on the same page. It put a stamp need between them that words could not express. Only their searing kissing would do. Her kissing him this way spoke volumes.

He knew that the time of making either of them wait anymore had passed. He lifted her body up, bringing their bodies flush. She wrapped her legs around his waist when he moved and walked them toward the bedroom. The wait was over. No longer caring that he had an early day in the morning, he would survive on coffee all day as long as nothing stopped him from having the only woman he wanted. It was time that they forgot about all the avoidance that has happened. They needed to let desire rule what happens this night. They would deal with tomorrow and any residual feelings when they arrived.

10

"You've got this," Taryn said to herself the minute she stepped off of the elevator at the law firm. She wasn't sure how she would feel knowing that after the night she'd spent with Adrian, words like sexy, desirable, wanton and needy crossed her mind. It was the word, needy, that had her thinking of another word; *more*. Well, two words, *much more*.

Her head was completely filled with images of Adrian both clothed and to her delight and desire, *unclothed*. Both options were the biggest turn-on that she'd ever experienced.

Being in his presence was enough to have her thinking of being alone with him in the most zealous of ways. She smiled to herself with lips that turned up into a sexy curve. Her body vibrated with joy that she got the opportunity to experience him. All of him filled her, and then some, throughout the night, again and again and then again.

A short wave of sadness caused her smile to relax knowing that she'd wasted time knowing they could have been together earlier than last night if she hadn't played the avoidance game every time she came home to New York for a visit.

What would be her reaction to seeing him today? She was both hesitant and excited to the point that her flesh zinged with unadulterated desire. The feeling caused her to blush, unable to forget the feel of his hands all over her body. The things that they had done together was nothing short of out of this world. Her thoughts were on her response to every touch, every kiss, and every surge into her body. Adrian made sure her needs were met in every way. She loved that he consistently showered her with praise when she returned his loving with her own eagerness to not just get what she wanted, but exploring every part of his gorgeous body along the way. A shyness she knew as her usual character was nowhere in sight last night. She let go and gave her all to their time together. She wanted him too long to let a night in bed with him go to waste. Reality was, the night wasn't long enough. That's where the word, more, came into play once again.

Looking in several directions as throngs of people milled about and rushed past her, she turned in the direction of the conference room where the reading of her aunt's will was about to take place. After taking three steps down the hall, she raised her hand to smother the yawn that escaped her lips. Since leaving Adrian's apartment in the wee hours of the morning, she'd lost count of the number of times she has tried to suppress yawns this morning. Each one reminded her of the lack of sleep neither of them had gotten.

She woke up to her body tingling in places that she forgot could get aroused by just the thought of a man. The minute he'd touched her in the slightest way, she came to life like never before. That occurred even before she experienced the best marathon sex of her life. Her legs still felt like rubber. Even after an early morning soak in her bathtub to ease the soreness, her body could still feel the remnants of the many times he'd rolled over or rolled her over to join their bodies again and again. Neither could seem to get enough of the other. She wasn't a virgin, but Adrian gave her an experience between the sheets that she thought only existed in the words of those steamy romance novels she loved to read. Her times with other men had been missing something. Her night with Adrian proved that. She enjoyed more than any book could ever express in paperback or digital. As a book publisher, she'd encountered many books of authors that were hot and steamy. Experiencing in real-time for herself was so much better. Her own imagination couldn't make last night any better. Adrian went above and beyond. The way he kept telling her much he wanted to be inside of her was proved by the way he loved her deep, hard, slow, wild – in every way that she barely got the words out to express before he read her mind and completed her desire.

"Are you okay?" a voice behind her asked.

Taryn shook off her thoughts from the night before and turned around. She was suddenly made aware that she'd been standing in place and not moving for what was probably to others, a weird amount of time. Behind her was one of Adrian's assistants that she'd met the first day she had arrived to meet him to discuss her aunt.

"Oh, I'm sorry. I didn't realize I had stopped moving. My mind was all over the place. I was just about to walk up to the receptionist desk to ask about the meeting I'm here for this morning," she explained. "The receptionist on the eighth floor told me someone would be up here when I got off the elevator who could make sure I went to the correct room.

"No worries about that. I can walk you over. I was heading in myself. I believe your family members are already there. Adrian will be here in a few minutes. He's on a last-minute call."

Hearing his name stirred her sexual demon. She already wanted him again. Clearly, one time wasn't enough.

"No problem. I'm a little early," she replied.

"Would you like to follow me? I'm Jocelyn. You're Miss Novack?"

"Yes, but please call me, Taryn. I remember you from my visit earlier this week. I'm terrible with names, but I'm an expert on faces," Taryn smiled as they walked.

"It's good to see you again. Can I just say you look amazing in red? This red suit says you are ready for the day; for whatever it brings. Matching heals and Louis bag says confidence all day, every day!" Jocelyn declared.

Taryn relaxed and winked at Jocelyn. She leaned over in her direction as they took their time walking.

"I learned a long time ago that even when I'm feeling slightly out of place, if I put on the right suit, magnificent heels and a complimentary purse, it strengthens my confidence," she admitted.

"I'll have to remember that. I love a nice suit. I tend to wear darker colors like black, blue or dark gray. That's what most people tend to wear around the office."

"Don't let that be you. If you want to stand out, wear what makes you feel good, look good and shine good, not for others, but for you."

Jocelyn smiled over at her as they walked up to the conference room door.

"I appreciate that. I think tomorrow will be a dark pink kind of suit day," Jocelyn beamed.

Taryn waited for her to open the conference room door and then paused when she didn't move forward.

"Is everything, okay?"

Jocelyn turned in her direction and made sure they couldn't be seen through the long glass wall of windows on either side of the large redwood door.

"Adrian said when you arrived that I was to warn you about something."

Taryn, still confident, felt a tinge of hesitation.

"Okay."

And she waited.

"Your family is here and a little uptight. They were here extremely early and requested a sit-down with Adrian before you arrived, which, of course, he didn't grant. He did greet them nicely even though they seemed to be angry and on edge. When they arrived, they came with additional people who were not included on the invitation to be here for the reading."

"So, how many people are in there?" Taryn asked without looking into the room. She remained behind the door.

"Now, only your two uncles, your aunt and two cousins. Per your aunt wishes in the instructions to the firm, no spouses were allowed to be here. She also made it clear that there was to be no one at the reading who wasn't going to be beneficiaries of anything. There will be another lawyer from the firm in there. He's actually already seated in the room, hopefully, keeping your family calm. His name is Cyphus Tyree. He represents the interests of the charities and other non-profit organizations that your aunt left donations to. The other family members were not happy when they were escorted out. Even angrier about that are your aunt and uncles who are in the room. Adrian wanted me to warn you of how unhappy and quite unpleasant they are."

Taryn exhaled and smiled.

Hearing all of this wasn't new to her.

"Luckily, what you're saying isn't news to me. They've been angry, unhappy and unpleasant for as far back as I can remember," she whispered. "I'm learning how to deal with them. With my aunt gone, I've developed a new level of no-tolerance of their crap. Trust me, I'm good. Adrian..."

Taryn stopped talking. She almost revealed saying that he had given her a warning the night before of what she may encounter. That would be too much information sharing. She changed her thought and smiled.

"I'm sorry?" Jocelyn asked.

When she didn't complete her thought, she'd left her words hanging in the air, confusing her.

"Adrian did warn me ahead of today, so I'm ready for them. Thanks for reminding me, but I'm all good."

"Shall we enter?" Jocelyn questioned.

Taryn ran her hand down her red suit with white trim around the collar and cuffs. With her hair up, and her stance, one of stately stature, she nodded her agreement.

"Yes, we shall."

The minute she entered the room, Taryn made sure that the first pair of eyes she connected with were Sherita's. She hadn't seen her cousin since the night before when she left to go one floor below to see Adrian. She had eventually sent Sherita a text to let her know to lock up because she wouldn't be back until the morning. She remembered smiling brightly when Sherita immediately texted a ton of smiley faces, clapping hands and heart emojis.

When her cousin looked her way, the wink she received had her relaxing her shoulders. That was the smiling face she needed to see. She winked back, relaying that they would connect later on regarding how her night with Adrian went.

By the time she got back to the apartment after leaving Adrian's place, Sherita was already up and out for an early morning meeting she had. She knew that her cousin was making a few connections while she was home in New York for a short period of time.

"Hey cousin," Sherita said, speaking up first before anyone else in the room did. Taryn wasn't expecting much of a greeting from them.

"Hey, yourself."

"You look absolutely stunning in red this morning. In fact, you look totally refreshed."

Taryn laughed with Sherita knowing that the reference was made to what happened between her and Adrian the night before.

"That, I am," Taryn jokingly replied.

She then turned to the rest of the family.

"Good for you, girl. We'll talk later," Sherita said.

"Good morning," Taryn said with her blanket morning greeting to anyone in her presence who was interested. What she wasn't going to do was be rude. She wouldn't feed into the narrative that her family wanted to set when it came to her. They were the ones with the issues, not her. She never saw herself as uppity or better than them. They assumed that how she was without really getting to know her. Too much time was spent being bitter for no reason.

Taryn didn't direct her greeting to any one of them, but to all of them. To her surprise, the response was unexpected.

"Sherita is right; you look beautiful, as you always do," Valencia said.

Taryn cleared her throat and then responded.

"Thank you."

Her uncles both looked her up and down before her aunt nudged them, as they sat on either side of her. That's when they finally spoke.

"I see a lot of Misha rubbed off on you. She always was a snazzy dresser. Do young people still talk like that?" her aunt asked.

"I think they still do, yes, and thank you. A lot of who I am I got from her."

"So, where is this lawyer guy? Is he coming back? I take it we're all here?" her uncle Antony asked.

Taryn chuckled to herself. Every time she saw her uncle, all she could think about was how Julianna always said her uncle was still, to this day, chasing that 'H' in his name. She held her composure though. She was about to answer him when Jocelyn pointed to a seat for her to sit in closer toward the head of the table where she assumed Adrian would be sitting.

"Mr. Jarreau just texted me that he's on his way," Jocelyn replied to the room.

Taryn turned her head when one of her uncles breathed out a heavy, impatient sigh.

"It's a good thing. We've been waiting long enough. I'm a busy man too, just as I'm sure he is," James added to the conversation.

"Uncle, I'm sure you are. Keep in mind, you arrived two hours before the scheduled time; you all did. I told my mom we have to be patient *and* kind until the actual start time. Now that we're all here, minus those who were here uninvited, this meeting will start soon enough. Can we tone down the aggressive attitude this early in the morning?" Sherita asked.

Taryn eyed the room.

"Yeah, well, it's easy for you to be so happy and cheery just like Taryn here. I'm sure Misha provided well for you in her will. You had a relationship with her. She treated us like unknowns. She probably left us a dollar each just to show us that she could," Antony unhappily declared.

"Not now, uncle; not now," Sherita pleaded sternly.

Before anyone else could say a word, the conference room door opened and Adrian walked in, closing the door behind him.

Taryn didn't know where to look after her eyes quickly strolled over his form and the sexy strides he made to the head of the conference table. Adrian smile at everyone as he walked. She was happy when their eyes met and he didn't make an effort to spend more time gazing at her than he looked at others. He was being professional even while she was remembering the way his body moved on top of her, under her, on the side of her – just all around her. She loved him in a suit, but damn he was fine naked and all rugged. She took in the obviously expense brown suit, with a crisp tan shirt and matching striped tie. Her mind screamed at her over how this man could definitely wear a suit.

When Adrian took his seat, his eyes landed on her for a few seconds. Something told her that he was letting her know that he was remembering their night. Though he was being about business, his look told her that he didn't want her to think that what they shared was over. She responded with a slight smile.

"Now that we have everyone here who is supposed to be here, we can go on and get started. Let me first introduce everyone before we get started. I will start with myself. I am Adrian Jarreau, managing partner of this law firm, Jarreau,

Gerard and Associates. My firm has represented Alexander Rivera and Misha Maxwell-Rivera for over thirty-five years. In the beginning of the relationship with them, my father, William Jarreau, was the managing partner along with his best friend, Armand Gerard. My father has since retired and along with me, the firm is owned and managed by Armand's son, Zacarious Gerard, who happens to also be my best friend. After her husband passed away, Ms. Misha made it clear that all of her personal and business matters would remain with this firm until her passing. In this room with me is one of my assistants, Jocelyn, and a junior partner, Cyphus, who is here representing the organizations that Mrs. Rivera has stipulated a charitable amount will be distributed to."

Adrian then turned his attention to Jocelyn.

"It's nice to meet everyone once again. I want to let you know that this meeting is being audio and video recorded, so please be mindful that everything you say will be a part of the permanent record associated with the reading of this will," Jocelyn explained.

Jocelyn tapped on a keyboard in the middle of the table and a large screen came down from the ceiling.

"Thank you, Jocelyn," Adrian said.

Adrian noted the date and the exact time, Taryn assumed, so that it was a part of the permanent record.

"It's nice to meet you all," Cyphus weighed in. "Please let us know if you have any questions once Adrian begins."

"For the record, in this room we have the family of Mrs. Misha Maxwell-Rivera, who are here for the presentation of her last will and testament. In front of me and to my right we have her brothers, James Maxwell and Antony Maxell. Seated between the two of them is Valencia Clayton, sister of the decedent. On the other side of the table and to my left we have her nieces Taryn Novack and Sherita Clayton. At the end of the table we have her nephew Leonard Maxwell, son of James Maxwell. Can you all please give a verbal affirmative that I've noted your names correctly," Adrian explained.

Everyone did so. Taryn was last.

"I agree as well," she said, giving a hearty smile to Adrian.

"Thanks everyone. All of you are present here today because Mrs. Rivera requested your presence. Each of you are mentioned in her last will and testament. Please note that the recording of the last will and testament was done in front of five witnesses of this law firm and notarized over five years ago. That date is recorded on the official documents that were signed and filed with the Surrogate's Court of New York. Today's recording will be added to that file. I will also note that in the recording, Mrs. Rivera made it clear that no part of her last will and testament can be disputed. She has spent years making sure her will was and is ironclad. What you will hear today are her final wishes. Any attempt at a dispute by any family member or organization mentioned in the will today will forfeit any monetary, property or material asset stipulated to them. I need everyone around the room to state that they acknowledge, understand and are aware of what I just stated even if you don't agree with the outcome of the reading. Your acknowledgement has to be verbally recorded. If you do not agree, you can state that as well, though it will have no bearing on what is included in the will," Adrian explained.

"Um, should we have attorneys with us?" Antony asked.

Taryn looked at her uncle and tried with all of her might to not roll her eyes at him. He was her least favorite of them all, but she respected him because he was family. She turned her eyes back to Adrian and decided that it was his handsome face that she would focus on.

"Mr. Maxwell, you may secure an attorney after today's meeting if you choose, but no other attorneys were needed for the reading and hearing of the will. You will be given a written copy of the portions of the will that you will need. The permanent record can be found with the courts and here at my law firm."

"Okay," Antony said.

"Antony, be quiet and just do what is asked. There is no need to try and get all legal at this point. It is what it is. Let him speak so that he can play the recording," Valencia said.

"Thank you. Before I play the recording, please go around the room as Jocelyn is pointing to you, and state your name and that you acknowledge what I just explained to you. Jocelyn?" Adrian said and pointed to her.

Taryn waited until it was her turn again and she boldly declared her name and her acknowledgement.

"Thank you, everyone. Are there any other questions before Mr. Jarreau begins?" Jocelyn questioned.

Everyone said no. Without any further delay, all eyes turned to the large screen as first Adrian appeared on screen explaining what they were about to view followed by her aunt. As her smiling face graced the screen, Taryn broke down crying before being comforted by Sherita. She hadn't planned on a video of her aunt talking to be how they would hear the will. She was unprepared for how her heart broke knowing that her aunt was gone. No one in the world could ever replace the love, support and devotion she'd experienced her entire life from a woman who didn't have to take her in and raise her. Where she thought the memorial service would be the hardest day of her life, this reading was the hardest day so far. There was no telling how much harder her grief would be to get through.

She composed herself as the recording briefly stopped.

"Taryn, are you okay? Do you need a minute?" Adrian asked.

"No, no, I'm good. The immediate shock of seeing her hit me kind of hard. I'm okay now. Please continue."

With that, she settled into her chair and listened like everyone else. Her aunt spoke so eloquently in a manner that only she could do and was known for. Taryn could see where she got her own confidence from. Hearing her go through what her final wishes were with grace and solid determination left no doubt that she was clear about what she wanted. While focusing on her words, Taryn also thought back over memories of a wonderful life that the woman on the screen made sure she had. Her thoughts also turned to the letter her aunt had left for her. Briefly, her eyes turned to Adrian who faced the large television screen at the end of the room, right in front of him. Before she looked away and with everyone else turned and facing the screen, he winked and smiled at her before turning his eyes back to the screen. She did the same before anyone caught them gazing at each other.

The reading and hearing of the will was a necessity; she knew. More than that, she wanted it to be over so that she could have a moment with Adrian. She appreciated anything her aunt left her, but unlike her family, that wasn't a priority for her. She would give it all up just to have more years with her aunt. As her aunt read through everything she was leaving to her loved ones, Taryn knew that the family drama was only beginning. She heard just as they had what her aunt's final decisions regarding her estate were. The others around the table would not be happy. No one could have imagined, first her aunt's total wealth and second, the way she distributed her wealth was a complete shock to them all, especially to her. That was clear from the way all eyes turned to her once the recording stopped.

At the end, Adrian noted the date and time. Though everyone received something, the largest part of her estate would be hers. What was to happen next, she was prepared for. She knew, based on the outcome, that if it was as it turned out to be, she would end up being even more hated by her family than she already was. That was disappointing, but not unexpected. She turned and faced her family and waited.

11

Adrian waited through the silence in the room after all eyes first went to Taryn and then to him. He didn't care much about what anyone in the family had to say about the reading of the will. He was concerned about how Taryn was doing knowing what her aunt's wishes were. He had known all along. He knew it would be overwhelming in the beginning. He and his firm were here to help her deal with it all. He let the silence live in the room. It was clear that they all needed a few minutes to take in what they'd just heard.

When he first entered the room, he wanted to pull Taryn into his arms and kiss her as if it would be his last time. She couldn't have known, but he saw her when she walked off of the elevator. He was making his way to the conference room when one of the junior associates stopped him to get some advice on a case that had been assigned to him. He and Zac made a practice of always taking the time to lend an ear and advice to the other lawyers in the firm without feeling the need to take over and do their job for them.

While the associate talked, his eyes took in all of Taryn in the most perfect red suit he'd ever seen on a woman. He was remembering the same color red of the sexy thong and bra of the same color the night before. He has now discovered a newfound love for the color red.

Taryn's curves were clearly defined in the two-piece suit. For a second, he was concerned when she stood staring into space as if she didn't know what to do. He wondered if she was rethinking even being at the firm. They didn't have a chance to talk before he got up and left her in his bed in the early morning hours of the day. He knew she needed the rest; as did he. He had kept them up pretty much all night. Once they kissed, he was a goner.

Every part of him wanted every part of her. It was clear that she felt the same way. Either he reached for her or she reached for him. The loving would commence once more for what they thought would be the last time of the night. He'd lost count of the number of times they loved on each other. When he woke once daylight shown bright through the wall of windows in his bedroom, reminding him that he hadn't closed the blinds as he usually would, Taryn was still deep in sleep resting on her stomach with her head resting on one of her arms. He was glad her face was turned away from the bright morning sunlight. If she needed extra sleep, he didn't want her disturbed.

Getting out of the bed, he closed the blinds, tossing the room into darkness. There was just enough light for him to see her form under the think blanket that he'd finally covered them with after she fell asleep as they spooned with her cradled in his arms. When he looked over at her with her one leg and cheek peaking at him from under the cover, his body was screaming for him to forget leaving and get back in bed with her. To say the struggle was real with the decision to go or stay was fact.

As tired as he was, he couldn't immediately find sleep when she'd finally fallen asleep in his arms. He didn't want to lose the extra time to caress her body while pulling her as close to him as he could get. Their night had not been planned. He didn't know if she would wake with thoughts of regret. He wanted to enjoy the quietness of the room while his head was still filled with the number of times she welcomed him into her body and hopefully, into her heart. She was already deeply engrained in his.

Knowing he had to get up and out early, he left her a note explaining where he disappeared to and set the coffee maker to provide her with a cup. He referenced that for her as well. Most of all, he let her know that the reality of being with her was just as potent as his dreams of her were. He left it open for her to decide if they could spend time together. He was ready if she was. He let the ball remain in her court knowing all that she had to deal with in the coming weeks. When his eyes landed on her when she arrived, he also thought about the day that she would go back to her life in Paris. He was already fraught with how to say goodbye to her when that day came. He'd never fallen for a woman this hard and fast.

"That's it? That's all she gave us? Nothing else?"

"Antony?" Valencia questioned, raising her hand up to stop him.

Adrian's eyes once again landed on Taryn before turning to her aunt and uncle, wondering if he would need to step in to keep the conversation civil.

"What? Don't tell me you're not thinking the same thing. I see she left you a little more than me and James even though you treated her worse than we did."

"How dare you?" Valencia shouted.

"Mom," Sherita interrupted.

Adrian watched it all unfold. His only concern was if any of them turned their anger toward Taryn. That's when he would step in.

"He's wrong, honey. None of us, other than you, Taryn and Leonard, treated her in the best of ways," Valenica noted.

"LJ," Leonard corrected. "I don't like being called Leonard."

"Okay, then, LJ," Valencia said.

"Why are you so quiet?" Antony asked James.

Adrian turned his attention to James to see what his reaction would be. He wanted them all to get out any frustrations they had before he stepped in to see if anyone had questions that didn't have to deal with any contesting of what they had all just heard. That, he would not be entertaining.

James looked around the room. Adrian locked eyes with the man when his eyes landed and didn't move from him.

"I'm quiet because we just heard what our sister said. There is no need in getting angry. Listen, she left me three million dollars. Let me say that again. She left me three *million* dollars! Her will cannot be contested or anyone who tries will get nothing. Besides the money, her will pays off my house and any outstanding bills I have acquired up to today. That means I am officially debt free. I will not complain. Like the two of you, I wasn't nice to her. I'm thankful for what she did leave me. If you want to squawk about what wasn't yours to begin with, you do that. I'm not messing that up just to have an argument about someone else's money."

"Are you serious? She left Taryn sixty-million dollars. *Sixty-million-dollars*? Did anyone know that she had this kind of wealth? I sure as hell didn't. Taryn gets the apartment here in New York and the houses, even the one at the lake. She gave more to charity than to us. Why did she leave Valencia five-million and only three million to the two of us? LJ got the same three million and we are her brothers."

"We don't know anything about his relationship with Misha. What my son was left is of no concern of yours. Misha didn't have to leave us anything. Are we done here?" James asked.

Adrian sat up and paid attention when James addressed him.

"Yes, we're done. Jocelyn will provide you with next steps unless you have additional questions for me."

"We don't," Sherita chimed in just when Antony was about to jump back in with more gripe.

"Don't speak for me," Antony chided her.

"Don't talk to my daughter like that," Valencia yelled.

"Why not? She just tried to speak up for all of us. I guess she would be okay since she got five million like you along with all of her debt wiped out. Did you hear me say that Taryn got everything? She's just a niece," Antony said boldly.

Adrian saw Taryn shift in her seat. He was about to jump in to stop the bickering. Before he could, Taryn spoke up. He waited through the few seconds of her gathering her composure before answering. When she straightened the lapel of her suit and leaned forward, he got the feeling that she wouldn't need anyone to speak up for her.

"I was much more than her niece. If you had been around all of the years that I was growing up with her and Uncle raising me, you would know that she stepped in as the mother that I no longer had. None of you looked at me with a kind face, smile or anything for my entire life. You didn't like my father, so you didn't care for my mother after she married him. Auntie told me all about that. She didn't want me to ever forget it. I loved her. She loved me. There wasn't a day of my life that I didn't feel loved and wanted. Until her last breath, she never left a conversation with me without letting me know that I was loved. I don't care if she had left me nothing at all, I have the memories of the love she and Uncle gave me that has helped me become the woman I am today. If you're worried about money, you need new priorities in life. Auntie is who I miss more than I desired what she left me. If you want to be angry, you do that but don't you *dare* come for me as if I won't come back for you," she yelled.

"Now, wait a minute," Antony interrupted.

"No! I am speaking now. I have put up with sneers and evil glares for a long time. I, like Auntie, don't owe you *anything*. I respect you as my uncle but if you continue to come at me with disrespect as if I didn't matter to her or this family, I will quickly forget the respect I should have. You will not like that side of me. Auntie has spoken. Be thankful that you were at this table. She spoke and it's done. Don't come for me with that, I was only a niece thing. You were her brother, and you didn't care a thing about her. You didn't look after her or check on her after uncle Alex died. There were no holiday invites or acceptance of any of her invites. You were angry and jealous of the life they made for themselves and me. I will forever be grateful to be a part of this family even if some in this family had no love for me. Are we done?"

Taryn turned to him. Adrian couldn't stop the smile that graced his face. He wanted to jump up and cheer as she stood her ground and took control of the narrative. Taryn didn't need any help. He waited to see if Antony would come back at her for more. When he slouched back in his seat, Adrian knew the conversation was over.

"Again, any questions?" he asked everyone around the table.

He turned to Jocelyn to be sure everything was still being recorded. She nodded knowing why he looked her way.

"Can you let us know what's next?" Valencia asked.

"I sure will. You can all come with me," Jocelyn said.

No one moved because Valencia reached across the table and took Taryn by the hand.

"Taryn, I'm sorry for how we have always treated you. I know that you and Sherita have always been close, pretty much like sisters. I now don't have a chance to make things up with my sister. We always think we have more time, when in fact, time winds down fast for us all. It's good to see you. You are as beautiful as your mother always was."

Adrian watched Taryn smile over at her aunt and whispered words of thanks.

"Well, as I stated, Jocelyn will see each of you separately if you have the time to do that today. She'll explain what needs to happen next, especially in obtaining what was given to you. She'll also tell you how to submit the bills that your sister has covered full payment of in her will. If you are short on time today, please make an appointment with Jocelyn over the next few days. She'll provide you with the information to reach her directly. If you have time today, please follow her out and she'll take you to the waiting room. There are refreshments, including a continental breakfast prepared. You will each need to meet with her separately. If there are no other questions for me, I appreciate your time today. Jocelyn, please note the date and time for the end of this discussion. You can then stop the recording."

"Thank you for handling this, Adrian. I appreciate how you and your firm have taken care of my aunt and uncle over the years. She has had the greatest respect and highest accolades for the entire firm. I know how you directly helped her with any and everything she has needed over the years. I appreciate it," Taryn said.

Adrian nodded.

"Thank you," he acknowledged.

"We are all thankful. Sherita, are you hanging around? I was wondering if we could have lunch today once we're done here. Your father is planning on coming into the city in a few hours. We could join him," Valencia said.

"That would be perfect. I was planning on going out to the house later today. Lunch in the city would be wonderful," Sherita noted.

"Taryn, would you like to join us? I know there is a lot of planning that has to be done for the service. I can help with anything, if you like," Valencia added.

"Um, I can't join you for lunch but I will reach out about her service. As you heard in her stating her final wishes, she has it all planned and laid out. I mostly need to get the word out."

"I'm going to help with that while I'm staying at the apartment with her. Mommy, I'll bring you up to date over lunch. I'm sure Taryn could use some down time to take all of this in. I'll see you later at the apartment?" Sherita asked Taryn who stood and hugged her.

"Yes. I'm hoping for a quiet day today after I meet up with a few friends this afternoon," Taryn said.

Jocelyn stood and headed toward the door to lead everyone out.

Adrian stood and shook hands that were offered to him from around the table, including Antony who tried to be trouble.

When Taryn started to head out, he spoke up.

"Taryn, can I speak to you before you head out if you have a few minutes?" he asked.

"Sure."

"I'll meet you in my office. I have a few other things to go over with you. That paperwork is on my desk. I need to make one phone call and then I'll be right there. Jocelyn can get someone to escort you to my office. I'll be there shortly."

"Taryn, when you're ready, I'll have another one of Adrian's assistants escort you to his office. I'm going to walk the others to the waiting room where they can relax while I get everything together," Jocelyn explained as she led everyone from the room.

"Thank you, Jocelyn," Taryn said.

Adrian watched her slowly gather her things. They were in sync. He already knew. She was the only one who remained. When the conference room door closed, leaving them alone, Adrian kept his distance. What he wanted to do was get a morning taste of her gorgeous lips. He held back by putting his hands in his pants pockets.

"I lied," he uttered so that only she could hear him. No one was around, he knew. Still, what he wanted to say was between them only.

"Did you?" she asked, smiling over at him.

"I did. I don't have anything business related to talk to you about. Jocelyn is point on what's next. I wanted a quiet moment to check in on you. I left you asleep in my bed this morning. I wanted to rejoin you but the day was calling for me," he admitted quietly.

"You had a lot to prepare for."

"I had a great time with you last night. I know I put that in my note to you, which I'm hoping you found."

"I did and I feel the same way."

There was a knock on the conference room door before he could continue. There was more he wanted to say.

"Come in," he said louder than they were speaking to each other.

Isaiah, another of his assistants opened the door.

"Jocelyn told me to come and escort Ms. Novack to your office?"

"Yes, please do that. I'll be there in a few minutes."

Without any further words, Taryn gathered her purse and left the room with Isaiah. He looked forward to continuing their conversation in a few minutes.

**

Adrian was frustrated that the call he thought would be a quick one had taken almost ten minutes. As he approached his closed office door, he hoped that Taryn had still been there. When he opened it and found her sitting on the sofa across from his desk, he closed his door behind him and moved to lean back against the edge of his desk. For a few moments, neither of them said a word. They let their eyes do all of the talking. When his body couldn't take the distance between them even a second longer, he leaned over and reached his hand out to her. When she stood and reached for it without any hesitation, he pulled her close and did what he'd been thinking about doing since he had left her alone in his bed.

When her body lined up snug against his, moving between his long, opened legs, his arms went around her waist and his lips covered hers. He didn't care that the luscious kiss would leave his lips covered in her red lipstick. He couldn't stand another second of not tasting her in the light of day. He pulled her as close as he could with her breasts intimately resting against his chest.

Taryn's lips were soft and warm. She returned his soft and slow kiss with a hunger of her own that had his mind wondering how he had been able to survive all this time without kissing her until he needed to catch his own breath. He moaned his delight against her lips when he darted his tongue out to caress across hers. When her lips parted, he searched her mouth for the pleasure he knew he would find deep within the recesses of her welcoming mouth. He knew he'd made the right decision when Taryn's arms went up and around his neck. Tipping her head back, their tongues entwined in a familiar way that they only shared for the first time hours ago in the middle of the night. Their lips, bodies and minds didn't forget the connection that they had made that was still in play. He loved her mouth as he stroked it with his, groaning out his pleasure. He could feel Taryn's shivers of euphoric satisfaction in the way her hands played at the back of his neck.

After a few more minutes of the intimate connection, Adrian broke the kiss when he remembered he may have shut his office door, but he hadn't locked it. Anyone could walk in, though that wasn't the norm around the office. Knocking was always required when a door was closed.

Pulling back, he placed one last soft kiss against her lips.

"You have me on your lips," Taryn whispered close to his.

He smiled when she reached around him to the box of tissues on his desk. She wiped her lipstick from his lips.

"Hello," he said.

"Hello," she said sweetly in return.

"I've been waiting to do that."

"I've been waiting to receive it."

"You being on my lips brings up memories of last night when you were literally..."

Adrian held back. If he didn't change the trajectory of the conversation, he may end up leaving with her and going back to his place in order to remind them both of what it was like to have her on his lips."

"Don't make me blush. I know what you were about say. We are both thinking about it. In your office with a bunch of people on the other side of the door is not the best place to revisit last night, though I'm tempted."

He kissed her again. This time, he allowed his mouth to linger a little longer on hers.

"I wanted to kiss you awake this morning before I left."

"I wish you had."

"Something told me you needed your rest."

Taryn giggled.

He chuckled himself.

"And you didn't? The night was an extremely busy one. I woke up thinking about it."

"I promise you – if I had kissed you awake, we would have both been late getting here this morning. Did you enjoy yourself?" he asked.

"You couldn't tell? I more than enjoyed myself."

"Any regrets?" he asked.

"Not a single one. Are you serious? Again, you waking me up this morning would have been welcomed. I understand that you needed to get to the office. Dealing with my family needed preparation."

"I was expecting a lot worse especially when your uncles showed up with extra people. They were pissed when I had to turn them away. You handled your uncle. Now, that was unexpected. I'm glad you spoke up. Your aunt once said to me that one day when she was no longer here, that I should make sure you stood up for yourself against them. Looks like only Antony may try and give you some trouble about what was left to him. If so, point him in my direction."

Taryn wiped across his lip again with the tissue.

"No need in giving your staff a reason to gossip. You would not be able to explain away this red lipstick, unless they are used to seeing it," she quipped.

"Oh, you got jokes," he said, leaning down to kiss her again. He frowned when after the kiss, she moved out of his arms.

"Someone could come in. You still have to work here," she said before making her way back to the sofa.

"I could send everyone home and we'd be alone to do whatever we want around here. I'm more concerned about another way they would be able to tell that I'm aroused if they look at me. My intentions for today really were professional until I laid eyes on you looking amazing in this suit. You are so beautiful. Did I tell you how happy I was that you came to see me last night?"

"You did. You also showed me again." She kissed him. "And again." She kissed him again. "And then yet, again."

"I aim to please you with another again and again anytime you want."

"I like the sound of that."

"Look, I know we didn't plan for last night. Still, it was one of the best nights of my life. I've desired you for a long time.

I'm hoping I can entice you to have dinner with me, perhaps tonight? I wasn't sure if you were busy or not. I know you have a lot to do. Then I heard you say you were meeting up with friends today."

"I am. That's for lunch. I would love dinner with you tonight. I'd like to unwind with some great company after the stress I went through not knowing how today would go. It wasn't too bad. I knew my uncle Antony would be a problem. My aunt said he has always been the troubled child."

"The others surprised me."

Taryn nodded in agreement.

"Actually, I thought all three of them would be a problem. My aunt surprised me, especially when she took my hand and gently squeezed it."

"Sometimes, it's good to put family drama behind you. I hope you all can do that. If not, I want you to be happy. When it comes to that, I hope I can be a part of what makes you happy, starting with dinner tonight. One of my favorite restaurants is in the city. My firm represents the owner. They make some of the best soul food around New York. You game?" he asked.

"That I am."

He held onto her, laughing when she moved her lips out of his way. She was serious about making sure his lips aren't covered in the color of her lips. For seconds on seconds, neither of them said a word. His hands caressed her back. When they reached her behind, she winked her pleasure at how his roaming delighted her.

"Taryn, is there anything I can do for you?"

When she looked up at him with a sexy smile, he had been thinking exactly what she was relaying to him.

"I can see that you're thinking the same thing. Keeping things tame since we are at your place of business, I will say that I'm looking forward to tonight. Unwinding with you over some good food is a perfect evening."

The office phone behind him buzzed. Without taking his eyes off of the most beautiful sight in front of him, he pressed the speaker button after quickly looking at the incoming number.

"Yes, Isaiah?"

"Mr. Zac is trying to reach you. He's in court and asked if you could join him there. They're on a break but he needs you to come to assist once court is back in session. It appears that they've run into a snag that's leaning against the firm losing. He said he really needs you front and center. I believe you know the case but let me know if you need me to pull the history."

"Yes. It's Stoney Snyder's case. Either call or text him and let him know I'm on my way."

Taryn moving away brought on a level of disappointment at the loss of her closeness.

"You need to go and so do I. I'm going to make an appointment with Jocelyn for tomorrow."

"In the afternoon?" he asked and then blew her a kiss.

"Late afternoon. Should I pack an overnight bag for tonight?" she asked, walking toward his office door.

"Only if you think you'll need clothes after dinner. I'm glad you're thinking of the night beyond dinner. I didn't want to be presumptuous. You already know I want you; that's a given."

"Yes, it is a given. If you're going to be naked, when in Rome..." she offered and laughed out loud.

"Consider my place Rome; I'm good with that."

Walking over to her, he placed a quick kiss on her lips before opening the door for her.

"Get another tissue," she said, this time placing a quick, yet lingering kiss on his lips.

"Tonight," he said softly.

"Yes."

Adrian hummed heading over to his desk. He turned around and Jocelyn was in the doorway.

"I have a document I need you to sign. I didn't want to interrupt you."

When she smiled over at him, Adrian tried to play it off. Jocelyn walked over to him, pulled a tissue from the box on his desk and pointed to his lips before handing him the tissue.

"Damn," he exclaimed.

"Don't worry. You know I am the keeper of all of your secrets. Let me just say, I love all of it! Perfect choice," she said before turning and leaving the office, closing the door behind her.

"Perfect indeed," he said while wiping lipstick from his lips after getting on last taste of the strawberry sheen she left behind on them.

Looking toward the door where Taryn had been standing, his mind drifted to reliving the night before.

"Sweet."

12

"She left you what?" Julianna yelled into the phone.

"You heard me. I get the apartment here in New York and all the other properties; not just the one in Maryland and the lake house. She left them all to me to either keep or sell. They were put in a trust for me along with the money I mentioned."

Taryn was still in disbelief. She left the law firm only a few moments ago. Before the call with Julianna, she spent the first ten minutes just wandering the street trying to figure out if what she'd heard that her aunt left her was actually what happened. She decided to put a conversation off until after lunch with a few friends she'd reached out to, now that she was back in New York. The lunch was fun and she was happy to catch up on what had been going on in everyone's lives. She didn't mention anything about the reading of the will. That wasn't the group to have that discussion with. She needed someone to vent to about it.

After leaving, she walked a little before getting a taxi and going back to the apartment. She spent the rest of the afternoon and into the evening trying to think through the fact that if she never wanted to work again, she didn't have to. On the flip side, she could make all of her own dreams come true. That was the purpose that her aunt left everything to her. She was grateful and scared at the same time. She had a lot of planning to do.

"Girl! That is something. You are officially a multi-millionaire. I knew about your trust fund, that you have yet to touch had a few million in it but this is major!"

"She also had another account that was deposit only. She's been putting money into that since I was young. I stopped to see Adrian's assistant before I left out. I wanted the information on this other account that had been set up. The origin wasn't clear. Seems like when my parents died, my aunt opened an account using the money left to me by my parents. Their life insurance policies totaled over a million dollars. That along with money they had in their accounts is what she used. She never touched that. Nor did she tell me about it. There is over ten million in that account," Taryn whispered as if she was trying to keep someone else from hearing her business. No one else was around. Sherita was still out with her parents.

"I can say I have a friend who is worth millions; not that I would tell anyone. That's amazing! I guess being your aunt's only child, in a way, would mean she would trust you with her estate. Did she leave your aunt and uncles anything?"

Taryn was in the middle of the walk-in closet in the apartment going through one dress after the other in order to find the perfect one for her night out with Adrian. She held up one dress after another in front of her in order to find the right one.

"The uncles each got three million and all of their outstanding debt paid. Trust me, they will run it up again. My aunt got five million and so did Sherita. My cousin, LJ, who was also close to my aunt got three million. We were her only nieces and nephew and she looked out for us."

"The three of you took care of her. I know LJ lives in Las Vegas but I remember you telling me that he would fly back to New York to check on your aunt. He also called her a few times a week to check-in."

"Yeah, like me and Sherita, he's been doing that since he was young. Her siblings were terrible, but they didn't deny their kids having a great relationship with my aunt. We had a lot of good times as kids hanging at the apartment. She left a lot to charity as well. That was expected. I plan to donate to several charities that I'm passionate about as well."

"Have you heard from the publishing company? I know they want to know about her unpublished manuscripts."

Taryn remembered that part of her aunt's will. She knew of two manuscripts, not including the one she was currently editing for the publishing house. To her amazement, her aunt had left an entire new mystery series of ten novels that were complete but not edited or published. She also left three other novels with instructions that she was to either have them published under the current publishing house or if she was making plans to start her own publishing house now that she could afford to, she could publish them all herself. Her aunt's obligation to the current company ended upon her death. The only novel obligated to them was the one she brought to New York with her on the plane.

"They have. I spoke to Eloise while I was on my way to lunch with some friends. They know about the one novel that I'm currently working on. Eloise said she received some legal documents from Adrian's firm letting her know that their contract, after this last book, with my aunt was terminated per the contract she signed. Eloise knew about that. I did tell her about the other books. She wants to talk to me about a new contract to publish those."

"What did you say?"

"That I haven't decided what to do with those. She left those for me. I know they want them but you know what, I'm still thinking of starting my own publishing firm in a year or so. Eloise told me that she would be willing to negotiate with me for any unpublished manuscripts that my aunt left me. She also wanted to talk about a possible promotion for me. I know it's her way to keep me and the manuscripts in-house. I have enough to think about right now. That's last on my list."

"That's perfect. You now have the funds to do that however you choose. I'm happy for you. You know I would love to jump ship and work for you if you start your own firm. I enjoy working or Eloise, but I there is an option to work for my best friend, I'd love that."

Taryn was exited. On her cab ride home, she thought about who she could hire to help her get her own business off the ground. She hadn't decided on anything. Having Julianna as a part of that would be amazing!

"You will be my first all. You know that. I want to have people around that I trust when it comes to planning out my future."

"Are you going to keep all of the properties?"

"Of course not. I do not need all of that. I want the lake house. I definitely want the Ocean City property. That's right on the water. It's so beautiful. I have a million great memories of going there every summer."

"And New York?"

Taryn paused.

She stopped going through dresses and went back into her bedroom and sat on the edge of the bed. She moved the many bags that she'd left on the bed from the shopping she did after lunch. She wanted something special for her date with Adrian. The night before wasn't planned. She wanted to entice him with a sexy nightie for later. When she thought of New York, her focus turned to Adrian the minute Julianna mentioned the apartment.

"I don't know. Though the apartment is paid for and would only require the upkeep, insurance and taxes each year, it's a lot to maintain. It's a lot of space for just me. I don't require a lot. You know that. Unlike the other properties that were kept as vacation homes, this wasn't that. It's more than that. It's a home that was lived in all year round. I live in Paris. On the other hand, this is home. It's where I have always belonged. I don't know what this place is going to be like without my aunt in it. I don't know what the future will look like without coming here to see her. Do I want to keep it? Right now, I'm thinking no. Then there is Adrian."

Taryn stopped with that thought. The start of her conversation when Julianna called her before she had the chance to make the call was to tell her about her night with Adrian. After several moments of cheers, catcalls and loud words of celebration from her best friend, she was able to go into details without sharing all of the intimate parts of the night. Besties are great, but there are some things about relationships that women shouldn't share with each other when it comes to that intimate time with men. Jules understood that. They were always on the same page that way.

"Do you see more with him than the time you'll spend together while you're in New York? It seems like you're both open to taking advantage of the time before you go back to Paris. Uh, friend, you do know that people have long-distance relationships that actually work."

"I know. This thing with him is brand new. We only had last night, so far. I mean, day one kind of new. We had great sex last night and even better talks before and after. He kissed me today in his office and I lost a few brain cells. He had me thinking of what life could look like if we remained in each other's lives. I wondered if maybe keeping the apartment was a good idea for when I visited here."

"You mean visited him."

"I don't know what I mean. I didn't know we would share like we did last night. Now that we have, I don't want to rush into what I would like to have with him. I want to go one day at a time. Then I remember that at the end of the day, I do have a life in Paris that I will have to get back to."

"You don't have to. Your aunt saw to that."

Taryn got up and walked back into the closet. She should have left the clothes laying out on the bed instead of hanging them up. She needed to make a choice. Adrian would be out front of the building waiting for her in about two hours.

"She did. Still, I love my life in Paris. I love my apartment, my job and my friends. I've built an amazing life there."

"And you're thinking you're not the type to make a big change for a man?"

"I don't know who I am when it comes to Adrian. At least not yet. All I know is that last night was out of this world. We're going on a date tonight. I love being in his company and not just because I've seen him naked."

"Oh, so it's because you've seen more than just what was under that towel," Jules kidded.

"Yeah, whatever."

"What are you wearing tonight for your date?"

"I brought a few cute things while I was out today after lunch with Carla, Maizy and Craig. I forgot how much I missed hanging out with them when we were in college. We plan to get together again before I leave."

"Doesn't Craig live in Chicago?"

"Yes. He works for an investment firm there. He flew in earlier today after hearing about my aunt. He'll be in town until after the service, which I still need to schedule. Sherita and I are going to work on that tomorrow. I'm planning on doing the service next week. I need to meet with the funeral home director and then the church. You'll get to hang out with us when you arrive. Are you still coming in early next week?"

"I am. I've already put in for the time off. The staff who worked closely with your aunt on her novels have all been granted time off to attend the service in New York."

"Yes, I saw the email about that. I plan to send them the service information within the next day or so in order for everyone to make the necessary arrangements. I'm grateful for the support."

"Your dress for tonight?" Jules asked.

"Oh, right. I'm leaning toward this navy wrap dress I bought with me from home and these matching heels. I stopped and got my nails done before I came back to the apartment. I wanted something fresh. I always stop in at my favorite salon when I'm in New York."

"You know that place will always be home even if you sell the apartment. You could always get something smaller to have when you do go back. I'm already claiming that you and Adrian will have the most amazing love affair that will be for an eternity. You'll figure it out. I'm always here if you need an ear and unbiased opinion."

"I know and I appreciate you. Being back in New York brings back memories of hanging out around Manhattan, Brooklyn and especially Harlem. I used to love sneaking off to the Bronx thinking that my aunt would never know. She had eyes everywhere. There have been so many people who have been reaching out to me since I've been here including a lot of Harlem business owners. Speaking of people I've been hearing from, guess who called me several times today."

Taryn left Jules wondering as she gathered everything she would need to get a quick shower to get ready for her night out. Sherita, who spent the afternoon with her parents decide to spend the night with them at their home.

"I can only guess. If I had to pick a name, I would say Nathaniel, the snake," Jules said, her dull tone emphasizing how much she disliked him, as her bestie should.

"Your guess would be right. He heard that my aunt passed away and asked if he could see me. I didn't take the call. I let it go to voicemail and listened to it. He's got something up his sleeve. He was too nice on his message. Apparently, he's in New York. Get this, he called me his baby on one of the messages."

"He's certifiable."

"That he is."

"He's after money. We both know him. He's smelling the money your aunt left you. Be careful, Taryn. The likes of him is never a good thing. I can already smell the toxic scheme he's planning. He has an ulterior motive and it's not leading from his heart. It's more that he's bleeding from his wallet hoping yours can line his pockets."

"I don't trust him. I definitely don't trust his motives now."

"Yes, you have to be careful. That's why Adrian would be perfect. He has his own wealth and a lot of it. He won't have a need to hustle a way into your life to get his hands on what you have. Men will be dropping from the ceiling like S.W.A.T."

"I know. It will come with the territory. Right now, I only have eyes for Adrian. Like you said, he's got his own millions; he doesn't need or want mine. Besides, he's not that kind of person. My aunt would have peeped anything negative or unkind about him. She loved everything about him. After being around him one day, and not just the sex part, I'm drawn to him. I was glad when he asked me out. We're both looking forward to learning more about each other."

Taryn took the dress and laid it across the bed. She found the perfect jewelry and perfume to accompany the look and feel of the night. She wasn't worried about an ex-boyfriend when she had a man like Adrian who was interested in her.

"There you go."

"Oh, and Sean sent a large bouquet."

"Him, too, huh? Watch these men. That's all I can say.

"He also called me yesterday to express his condolences."

"I'm glad you have Adrian, even if it's a secret for now. He's a great guy. The way he keeps you smiling, I love it. Thanks to your aunt for making both of you see the light."

Taryn heard every word. The idea of her aunt signing off on Adrian being someone that she should be open to being pursued by brought tears to her eyes. She sat on the dark purple and silver comforter next to the dress and listened to the silent whispers of her aunt's voice throughout the apartment. She could almost hear the years of words of encouragement that she'd heard all of her life. Her aunt wanted nothing but happiness for her. She knew that she'd find it even if she was alone without ever finding the perfect mate. Still, her hopes were for lots of love, a husband and tons of babies. Could that actually be in the cards for her?

"He's quite remarkable. Before last night, I only knew him in passing. I still think back to the night of that gala when I got the chance to really talk to him and learn more about him. I think that my aunt had a hand in he and I connecting that night. If so, I'll always be grateful to her. Not much came of that night other than a remembrance that we connected on a surface level. I never connected with a man so easily, not even Nathaniel throughout our relationship. Last night with him was a natural as breathing."

"That's because it was meant to be. Don't over think anything. Just enjoy it all. I know you have a lot to take care of. You will get that done. Sherita is there to help. You know I will help with any and everything when I get to New York. As your bestie, you can count on my presence at this time in your life when I know you're grieving like never before. That's what best friends do. We drop everything to be there for each other. You would do it for me. When my sister died in that accident a few years ago, your face was the first one I saw in the hospital that wasn't family. I couldn't believe you got on a red-eye flight right after I called to tell you she was in the hospital. You didn't even know that she had passed away. You are my sister. If you need me today, I'll be on my way."

"Don't you dare. Your scheduled arrival is perfect. I know you're getting over being sick and you just got back home from business travel. I promise you that I'm fine. As you can tell by my date tonight, I'm not sitting around crying around the clock. Auntie wouldn't want that for me. Me with Adrian is having her smiling from ear-to-ear in heaven. I'm fine. You would know if I wasn't. Besides, if I wasn't, you would already hear from Sherita. You know she would be calling you if she thought I needed extra support to get through. I need to get off of here. There is a man who will be waiting on me soon. I love you, Jules. I'll see you in a few days."

Checking the time on her phone, she grabbed what she needed and headed toward the shower. Before she reached it, her phone pinged. She was prepared for one last text from her bestie but instead, found a text from Adrian. He wanted her to know that he couldn't wait to see her. He was on his way home to shower, change and bring the car around to the front of the building.

She tingled internally with more excitement than she thought she could pull together for a man out in these dating streets. Adrian was different. He broke down all negative vibes she sometimes felt about dating in this day and time. Just when she thought it was hard, in walks him and all of his magnificence from his swag, looks, personality and character. He put her at ease. That was all she needed to know to let her guard down completely by living in the here and now. It was time. She replied back with kissing emojis as she danced into the bedroom's adjoining bathroom suite.

13

Adrian pulled his car up to the curb, parked it with his flashers on and raced inside of the apartment building. He didn't want to keep Taryn waiting too long. Parking in front of the building was not allowed, so he knew he needed to hurry. Time, though, stood still as he entered the lobby and Taryn turned in his direction. Though she moved at a natural level of speed, to him, it was slow motion. Her hair was down and flowing around her shoulders. She had on a body-hugging navy-blue wrap dress that accentuated every single curve he remembered getting acquainted with the night before. Vision of their bodies entwined and rhythmically moving in perfect sync together sent his body on overdrive with desire. Her perfect statuesque legs in high heels had his mouth watering. He remembered climbing between those legs quite a few times. Each time had him wanting more and more.

Letting his eyes travel up and down her entire body, stunted his ability to talk or even move. It was as if there was a beam of light shining only on her. He had no other option than to focus on her.

Any words he thought he would say as a greeting were lodged in his throat. He didn't know if there would ever be a moment when Taryn's beauty wouldn't leave him speechless. He started to walk further but his feet felt like lead, almost as heavy as his tongue felt in his mouth. What he did with his life before she came into it, he didn't know. What he did know what that he was the luckiest man on the planet. She was going out with him tonight.

"Whew! I swear I will have a heart attack if you show up on another date looking this gorgeous. Have you seen yourself?" he declared.

"I melt when you look at me this way. Thank you! You look amazing too."

"The two of you look great together. Y'all are perfection together like that Aaron Pierre guy and the actress, Teyana Taylor."

"That's Mufasa!" Taryn blurted out and doubled over in laughter along with Adrian.

They turned in the direction of Tony, the security guard on duty at their building for the night.

"Thanks, man," Adrian said, greeting him before he and Taryn turned and headed out of the door.

"Nice ride," Taryn exclaimed as he helped her into the car.

Once he joined her inside, he turned toward her. Before responding, he leaned over and kissed her quickly.

"I needed to do that. Kissing you has already become one of my favorite things to do. The feel of you gives me life. Thanks, about the car. I don't drive often, but when I want the freedom from being driven everywhere, this is my go-to car."

"What model is this?" she asked.

"It's the Maserati Grecale."

"The black exterior and interior fits you. How much do you love cars? Do you have like a fleet of cars?"

"Absolutely not. You can only drive one at a time," he chuckled.

"Is that right?" she humored him.

"I have a Navigator, also in the garage. I also have a few vintage cars that I've rebuilt and refurbished over the years. I keep those at my home in upstate New York. It's one place I go to get away from the city. It's quiet with the closest neighbor about two miles away. The two mustangs were gifts from my parents a few years ago. What about you? What do you drive when you're home in Paris?"

Adrian pulled out into traffic and headed for their first destination – dinner. Following that, he had plans to take them to see a play on Broadway that he's been dying to see. Thankfully, he was able to ask Sherita if Taryn had seen it and her cousin said it was on Taryn's bucket list. The minute he heard that, he decided to help her check that one off.

"My blue beauty is a Mercedes C300. I've had it for about two years and she drives like a dream. I don't drive a lot when I'm at home. I love walking. Most places I love going to are within walking distance from my apartment and my office."

"That's what I love about being in New York. I love being able to walk everywhere. My favorite restaurants are all close by. Friends are nearby."

"Where are we going tonight?"

"Dinner at a spot in Harlem. Then we are going to see a play on Broadway."

"Food and a play. You already know me so well," she joked.

"I'm paying attention. Would you like to listen to some music?" he asked.

"No. I enjoy the sound of your deep voice."

Adrian tried to hide his smile. Getting complimented was not new for him. He really loved it coming from her.

"I'm glad that's a thing. I'll talk more."

"Then tell me more about anything," she said.

He looked her way while they were stopped at a light.

"Can I tell you about another time when I came close to asking you out?"

"Oh? You did?"

"There was more than one occasion of me knowing I wanted you."

"Tell me."

"One day, quite a while ago, you came by the law office with your aunt. I think you were here for a visit. Your aunt mentioned you were on your way to lunch and she needed to sign some papers. You were in a mint green pant suit with a white top that had a big white bow at the neck. Your hair was pulled up. That was the first time I noticed that your ears had a lot of holes in them. I wasn't close enough to count them, though I was intrigued."

"Six in my left ear and seven in my right."

"Beautiful. I came out to say hello to you and your radiant smile had me hooked when I saw it. You made me nervous. No woman has ever had that impact on me. I was close to asking you out. That's when my dad and your aunt joined us. The two of you left right after that."

"Why didn't you ask me? I would have said yes."

"I mentioned it to your aunt a few days later to see if she had any reservations about me doing so. Before I could get a full sentence out, she told me that she wished that I had already done it. I thought about it even more. Something in me wouldn't let me do it. It wasn't you; it was more about me and where I was in my life. After that you were gone. I saw you a few times after that but you were never close enough for me to approach you. I wasn't sure what you thought about me after that night in the hallway."

"One day I'll tell you my thoughts about that night – the real ones. Let me just say that, I couldn't get you off of my mind. We talked about it, but we haven't really talked about it. I could only imagine what...well, I'll just say, there isn't a woman in this world who wouldn't want to be on the other end of your attention. I'm one of those women. I was then. I still am now."

"We have both been holding back, apparently," he replied.

"Can I ask, why now? What changed?" she questioned.

"You are a much-welcomed distraction. That's not even the right word. You're a welcomed addition to my life at the perfect time."

Before they could continue, Taryn's cell phone pinged. He noticed that when she checked it and quickly put it back in her purse, her expression changed. She was no longer smiling.

"Are you okay? If you need to get that, go ahead."

"No, no. It was nothing."

Just then it pinged again and then again. Her fake smile as she reached for her phone again told him that whoever or whatever it was, it was definitely something. He started to ask her again if everything was okay.

Taryn turned her phone off and he let it go.

"We're almost at the restaurant," he said, hoping to put a smile back on her face.

"I forgot how much I love Harlem. Just being here makes me feel good. I miss New York."

"Have you ever thought about coming back?"

"To live?"

"Yeah."

"I've thought about it often. I don't know what the future holds."

"Perhaps it will hold something that would make you want to come back this way."

When she looked over at him and smiled, he greeted her smile with a wink. He did what he'd set out to do. He wanted to take her mind off of anything that had to deal with her phone that took it away. Perhaps his way of thinking was too soon to address, but he was hoping beyond hope that she would stay around beyond being here for the time being. What he wouldn't be was pressure. They were too new with each other to talk about anything beyond what they were enjoying. She has enough to worry about.

"Perhaps. The future has a lot of unknowns."

"Well, not the immediate future. There is the restaurant – our current destination," he said and pointed before turning the corner to find a parking space.

"Adrian?"

He turned in her direction just as he was about to get out of the car to go around to her side.

"Yes?"

"Thanks for being you. Being around you is so refreshing. I can't really explain it, but you are a breath of fresh air at a time when I thought I would spend weeks here depressed. I miss Auntie. I will use your words and say, you are a welcomed distraction. One day I'll explain more about what that means. For now, tonight is extra special to me. I needed this."

"Anything for you."

He meant it. As long as she would allow him, he wanted to be not only what she needs but also, what she wants.

"I just realized I forgot something."

"What? Something you needed for dinner or the play?"

"No. I packed a small overnight bag."

He grinned from ear to ear with what he knew had to look extra cheesy to her.

"Baby, around me, you won't need any clothes later unless you feel it's necessary."

She looked at him and then looked away. When her eyes landed back on his, there was a smoky, seductive and rather enticing look to them.

"It's not clothes as much as it is lacy, stringy and not a lot of material. I bought it just for you to take off of me, but I can forgo it if you'd like," she jested.

"Oh, please. We're in the same building. Our first stop will be to get that bag. I want you to be amazed at what my tongue and teeth can do when it comes to removing lacy garments from your body. Whew, woman. You make me want to skip dinner. If I wasn't starving, I would whip this car back around and head in the direction we came from."

"Later?"

When her head moved in his direction across the car, he took the hint. While his hand caressed the side of her neck, he lightly pulled her closer for the kiss that he knew would be full of promises for later. They were just really getting into the kiss when a car horn interrupted them. He had to move the car.

"Definitely later," he replied sexily against her lips.

He couldn't wait to see them pucker after being thoroughly kissed. The night wasn't coming to an end soon enough for him. He was happy knowing they had all night. He planned on using every single second, minute and hour of diving them pleasure upon pleasure.

14

"If I never see another play, *Hell's Kitchen* was everything! I'm talking incredible from the first word to the last. I will admit that *The Lion King* is and will always be my favorite play, but this is a close second. Just wow! Perfect company, perfect dinner and now the perfect play."

"I'm glad you're enjoying yourself."

"Best date ever! You do how to treat a woman right."

"I aim to always please. You make it easy to do. I don't know if I said this earlier or not but thank you for wearing that dress. When they played music to slow dance to at the restaurant, you moving so easily into my arms helped make my night. If you haven't realized it yet, I enjoy being close to you. You feel like you were meant to be in them. We make a beautiful couple."

Adrian stole the words out of her mouth. She thought the same thing. He may not have been aware, but women in the restaurant kept giving her secret thumb and index finger snaps after pointing to him. She knew that there was no secret in the place that they were focused on each other throughout dinner and dancing.

"I think others thought so as well. You turned many heads, mister attorney," she laughed.

"No, we turned many heads. Just as women saluted you, there were men handing out thumbs up when it came to you.

They know a gorgeous woman when they see her. I'm glad that tonight, you are mine and I am yours," he replied.

"Only tonight?"

"Not if I get my way."

Taryn turned and looked out of the window. It was late but they had just drove by an area near Central Park where people were milling about. They had plans back at his place, but for now, she wanted to be out and about. She hoped what she was about to suggest didn't put off the love they wanted to get into that night.

"Can we walk around here a little? It's such a beautiful night. The bright lights of the city bring back many memories – all good. I know it's getting late."

"We can do anything you want to do at any time. You're in heels. Are you sure?" he asked.

"Oh, then how about a quick plane ride to one of those resorts that has those bungalows over the water?" she joked. "These are comfortable shoes. I wear heels more than I wear flat shoes."

Adrian was stopped at the red light and looked around for a garage or street parking. When the light changed, he headed in the direction of where he saw a car pulling out. Once he was parked, he turned to her before the exited the car.

"I have one thing I want to mention based on your comment."

"What comment?"

Taryn quickly thought back over everything she'd said. When she looked in handsome his face, she knew what it was. The determined look on his face told the story. She was joking but clearly, he was already making a plan simply because she said it.

"Do not kid about taking a quick plane ride anywhere. I know you were joking but trust me when I say, before the sun could make another appearance, I could have plans made for us to take that trip. If you say it and I can make it happen, I will do that especially if I know you need to get away."

"I should have known because I know that you are a man who follows through. Soon? For now, a walk?"

"I got you. I want you to know that your needs, I got you."

"Including later?"

"Especially later."

When Adrian got out of the car to come around to open her door, she fanned herself. She loved the idea of being with a man who doesn't just talk a good game but follows through on any and everything. She whispered a silent thanks to whatever she did that was so good that she ended up deserving of a man; not really a man, but this man. This amazing man who had her feeling like a queen just by a look or a touch.

He opened the door and took her hand to help her out. He held out his arm to her to place hers around his as they walked.

"Did you always want to be a lawyer?" she asked as they strolled.

"I did. I never wanted to be anything else. As a kid, I admired all that my dad did. Fast forward to now, I get great satisfaction out of every person I help. I want to do so much more."

"You mentioned the other day that you were expanding your mentorship program. What is that about? I have been meaning to ask about it," she inquired.

"The law firm is growing fast. We're bringing on new junior partners who will also help with our popular mentorship program. We have partnered up with several high schools and colleges to bring in students to work in the office as assistants, researchers and runners; especially those who have an interest in staying on the good side of the law. We had such an overwhelming response that we're looking to add in additional schools and more students. The ones we have now have been doing a remarkable job. We've seen them transition from wearing every day street gear or school uniforms to wearing suits, ties and for the young women, dresses and power suits. We require that kind of attire from our staff, all of them. The kids wanted to fit in. We have businesses who donate to the program which helped with the purchase of work clothes for the students. They go with us to court, we have mock trials for them to participate in and they love it all. It gives them a perspective into a life where they can make a difference. The first four college students we had are currently in law school. Besides the paid internships we offer them, we have other partnerships with those who offer etiquette classes, interview classes, tutors, college-prep classes and some money in their pockets. We are looking to expand to offer similar programs at other companies who deal with musicians, athletes, business owners, chefs and a lot more. We want to keep kids on the right path to success."

"Adrian, that is wonderful. I knew you had a big heart. You had dreams and you have followed them. I like that. I'd love to partner up with your firm where I can. When I first heard what my aunt left me, I knew I wanted to do a lot for the youth. Partnering with mentorship programs is definitely a dream for. Before you say that I don't need to do that, yes I do. More people need to as well."

"If you want to, I'll stay out of it and connect you with the mentorship program coordinator."

"Thank you. I need to find other programs to give to. No way can ever spend all of that money. I want to do something great with it that helps others."

"You wear your heart on your sleeve. I'm a lucky guy. I can tell you that."

"Not just you; so am I."

He kissed her shoulder and she shivered. What a man.

"What about you? Do you have dreams beyond where you are now besides helping others?"

"I do. Only Sherita and Julianna know this one thing about me. I want to own my own book publishing company one day."

"Oh, I see that for you. With all the unpublished books your aunt left you? That would be a great start for you."

"I've been thinking about that too. It would take a lot which I'm not sure I can pull off at this juncture in my life."

"Taryn, you can do anything you want to do. We both know that what your aunt left you is enough to make all of your dreams come true, which includes helping others. That was the whole purpose of what she did. She could have easily added those completed yet unpublished works to her contract with her publishing company, but she didn't. She wanted you to have them. I hope you never give up on any of your dreams. If there is ever a time where I can help you with any part of that, all you have to do is say the word."

Taryn snuggled in closer to him as they walked. Something in her knew that his words were not just smoke and mirrors. He meant every word. She stopped walking and turned to him as throngs of people moved about around them on both sides.

"I wonder where we would be if you had asked me out before now. When I say before now, I'm not talking about our night together. I'm talking about back when you thought I wouldn't be interested because of what your dating life was like."

"I don't know, sweetness. We may not be where we are right now, at this getting to know phase. Yes, sleeping together already has sped up this getting to know each other. I still wouldn't change that either. I like where we are. I'm happy you said yes to me now."

"Let me apologize for something," she said.

This walk wasn't a good idea. It's not what she really wanted. She needed his touch. She needed his feel. She needed his kisses. She needed all of him.

"What's that?" he asked.

"I don't want to be out here walking. I mean, I love walking around New York. It's always one of my favorite things to do in the city. Not tonight though. Can we go back and say yes a few times tonight? What I really want right now after dinner and the play, is you; only you."

She tried winking at him the way he did at her which was always enticing. His reaction shocked her. Adrian doubled over in laughter so fast that he caught her off-guard.

"Blunt is exactly how I like you. I'm not sure I'll ever be able to say no to you."

When he turned them around to head back to the car, she giggled as he quickened his strides.

"Adrian, if you don't slow down, I'm going to fall flat on my face. You're walking really fast!" she kidded.

"You have no idea how much I want to pick you up and run to my car. Don't be surprised with the speed at which I plan to get us to the building. Oh, and I haven't forgotten about the sexiness you have in that overnight bag that we are definitely going to stop and pick up. I promise not to keep you up late. I know you have early morning meetings. I won't promise that you won't yawn throughout the day, just as I'm sure I will. I have a crazy busy day tomorrow which will probably turn into a late night. I'm glad we have tonight. I'm on client overdrive. I'm also out of town for a few days."

"Someplace interesting or is it a work trip?"

"A little of both. I have some clients who opened a casino not long ago in Chicago. I'm heading there with friends to hang out with the fellas. I also have to talk business while I'm there. They'll soon work on plans for revamping a casino they own in Las Vegas. I'm going to go over changes to those contracts with the owners. I figured I'd get some R&R in while I'm there."

"I'll be busy these next few days working on the funeral arrangements. I'm hoping to have the services next week. I don't want to drag this out. If not next week, then early the following week."

"You should probably think about the following week. There will be people coming from all over the world; don't forget that. Sherita is helping you, right?"

"She is. My best friend, Julianna, is coming in to help also along with some friends I have in town who plan to stay close to be the rock I can lean on."

When they reached the car, Adrian leaned back against it and pulled her flush to his body. She couldn't get close enough.

"I am here. Even while I'm out of town for the next few days, if you need me for anything at all, you call me. I will answer on the first ring. I don't care the time of day or night. Of course, you know I'll be at the service. Just tell me what you need and you have it."

Taryn nodded as thoughts of her aunt filled her head. At the same time, tears filled her eyes. Adrian saw them and quickly wiped them away. He then placed a soft kiss on each eyelid.

"I really miss her. The world is already different without her in it. I know I will move beyond this grief of once again saying goodbye to a piece of my heart. I'm glad I have so many people in my corner. Friends and fans have really stepped up to let me know how much they care, not about my aunt, but about me too."

"That's because like your aunt, people know you are a person of high caliber, standards and character."

After one quick last kiss, Adrian helped her get into the car. As she sat down, her phone buzzed. She forgot that she had turned it back on after the play. She hadn't meant to. It was a reflex. Now she wished that she hadn't. She quickly looked at the screen and saw that there were two missed calls and texts from the same number; it was Nathaniel. What she thought would be an old flame sending condolences has turned into something more sinister. His calls and texts were a shock to her system. She quickly read a text and thought about what Adrian had just said about her having good standards and character. Nathaniel's text was a reminder that not everything about her was of good caliber.

When Adrian opened his car door and got in, she quickly slid her phone into her bag to forget about it for now. Nothing was going to distract her from the rest of her night. Nathaniel and his threats about their past together would have to wait.

"You look troubled. What's up?" he asked while starting up the car.

"Nothing at all. I'm just preparing myself for the rest of the night. Then I realized, even though we've only been together once, I believe that there is no way to prepare for you."

"None at all, baby. You bring out devil in me. I can promise you that it will be unforgettable, that's for damn sure. It has to be."

When the corner of her mouth turned up into a sexy grin, she remembered that he said he liked boldness. She was feeling that way when she reached over and allowed her palm to caress that area on his lap that she was feigning for.

"Bold me?" she said.

When she attempted to move her hand, Adrian held onto it.

"All the way home! If I didn't have to drive and if we were not in the day of cameras everywhere..." he declared.

Adrian's deep, melodic voice was all it took to get her body throbbing in all of the right places. His words prepared her mind for the pleasure she would soon be experiencing.

15

Taryn could not have imagined the crowd that turned out for her aunt's funeral, especially the fans who stood outside in the rain to bid farewell to the woman that came into their lives with her bewildering crime story novels. What she penned allowed her fans to forget about all of the cares of the world while taking time to step away and live in the fantasy of her characters and stories.

She was overwhelmed time after time as one speaker after the next took to the podium at the church where her aunt made sure that she rarely missed a Sunday. They each recalled their most memorable moments with the world-wide known author, Misha Rivera. Most recalled stories of her life with her husband, the love of her life. Taryn could barely contain the love that poured from them to her with their kind words.

When she woke earlier this morning all prepared to take in this moment, she wasn't ready for the flood of emotions that she sat still on the first pew in the church holding in. Every part of her wanted to burst into tears each time her eyes laid on the closed white and soft pink casket in the front of the church. There were so many flowers that most couldn't even fit across the front of the church. Many were still being delivered to the apartment as well. Thankfully, since Julianna arrived in New York a few days ago, she and Sherita had spent a lot of time making sure the extra floral arrangements were delivered to local nursing homes and hospitals as she herself had been attempting to do since she first arrived in New York. They were all beautiful with most in her aunt's favorite color, pink. As her eyes scanned around the church, there was a sea of pink everywhere with people doing justice to her aunt's memory by dressing in her favorite color in various shades.

Next to her on the front pew was Sherita. On the other side of her was Julianna. At the end sat her aunt, uncles and cousins. Other family members, most she'd never met before had also filled the two pews behind her. She knew that quite a few of her friends from college were there as well. Seeing the come through to show support, she cried like a baby when they each walked up to give her a hug.

Included right behind the family, was the extended family she and her aunt had acquired from the publishing house. There was staff from the Paris office, along with the two offices in the United States, including the one where Julianna worked in California. There wasn't an empty seat in the massive church. What gave her comfort was any time she needed to find that perfect set of eyes that relayed to her that everything would be okay, she found when she turned her head to the left. That's where Adrian sat with his father and the entire staff from the law firm on the opposite of the church. Whenever she looked at him, his presence, his gaze, his wink was what she needed on the hardest day of her life. He told her he was closing the law firm for a few hours so that everyone who wanted to attend could. Her aunt and uncle had been one of the most well-known clients they'd ever had.

There was so much love everywhere.

No one knew about them being together yet. Except, perhaps Jocelyn. Adrian told her that she caught him with lipstick on his lips that day the will was read. She'd been at the office a few times since then and tried her best to avoid Jocelyn. She was embarrassed. She didn't want to put Adrian in a bad spot. Luckily, Jocelyn whispered to her that her and Adrian's secret was safe with her until they were ready to tell people. That was over two weeks ago. By now, a few more people knew. They had run into someone on his staff while they were out having dinner recently. She was terrified. Adrian took it in stride and invited the lawyer to sit and chat with them for a few moments. Before he left ten minutes later, they were all laughing and joking.

Like Jocelyn, he congratulated them on being a couple. He noted how much happier Adrian seemed. He told her he would explain that comment at a later date.

More than anything, she wanted to have him closer to her, especially after that. Adrian had no problem with people knowing about them. She decided not to have reservations about it anymore either. Over the past few weeks, they had fallen into a routine like two people who had fallen in love. She had. She wasn't sure about him. Though she hadn't spoken the words, something she had never said to a guy before, the love word certainly lived in her heart.

Time with Adrian had breathed new life into her. For now, until they were more public, it would not have been appropriate to have him sit with her at the service. What she appreciated was on the ride over to the church in the limousine, he'd sent her a text telling her that all she had to do was look slightly behind her and to her left and there she would find him if she needed a comforting glance; a safe space. He had come to mean so much to her. Having him in her line of sight helped her make it through the service. He knew exactly what she needed.

She was glad that she was able to say her final goodbyes at the start of the service. Making it through her memories would have been hard after hearing everyone else speak so eloquently. With the service over, she stood as the casket rolled past her. For her final farewell, she let her hand rub across the casket as the funeral staff slowly walked it down the aisle. It was at that moment that the tears she'd been holding in for most of the service began to fall down her cheeks. She didn't want to fall apart in front of all these people. She stepped out of her pew with Sherita on one side of her and Julianna on the other. They walked slowly with her to the entrance of the church. Standing at the top of the stairs and seeing the casket disappear inside of the hearse was more than Taryn could handle.

She wondered what would happen if she collapsed right here on the front steps of the church. Her legs felt heavy. Her heart was in so much pain that she felt like any minute, it would burst out through her chest cavity because of the grief she was going through. Her head turned slightly from side to side, wondering if anyone could see her struggling. She worked to keep her composure in front of the hundreds and hundreds of people surrounding the church. She held a smile on her face as others walked up to her to express their condolences for her loss. Her aunt wasn't just a loss. She was her connection to life. She had been her everything. This life without her was going to be hard. She couldn't fathom how much harder it will be as the days, months and years continued.

With her friends staying close, she felt crowded even though she knew they were her rocks at a time like this. Throughout the service one or both of them would hold her hand or rub her arm to comfort her when cries wracked her body.

Her thoughts turned to Adrian. She didn't want to be obvious by looking around for him. She needed his touch. She felt safe in his arms. She loved her cousin and her friends, but for the first time in her life, she wanted the soothing touch, his hug and reassurance from the man who made her feel loved and protected. He'd been that and more for her during their time together.

When she started to move down the steps, her legs wouldn't cooperate. She was having a hard time catching her breath. She was scared. Hiding the impending anxiety attack from those around her was going to be hard. She didn't want to be the focus of everyone's attention as she lost all control on the steps. Just when she was about to just let it all go and let her steps fall where they may, there was the most soothing sound in her ear.

"Come with me, baby. I'm right here. Hold on for just a few more seconds and I got you. All you have to do is turn around and step this way. Just turn around, baby," Adrian said softly in her ear from his position behind her.

Taryn took in a large breath and turned to Julianna and then Sherita who were holding her arms tightly.

"You heard your man, go girl," Sherita whispered. "He's got you. We're not going anywhere."

"Go, Taryn. He's right behind you. Hold it in for one more second," Julianna encouraged.

Taryn couldn't speak. If she opened her mouth, nothing would come out other than the crying and wailing that was caught in her throat.

She turned her head in Adrian's direction just as cries were about to tear her to shreds. She saw the soft, inviting smile on his face. Her eyes landed on the hand he stretched out to her while his other went around her waist. It was clear, he didn't care who saw how he was stepping up to care for her. Right now, she didn't either. All she knew was that she needed to get out of the crowd. She needed a moment to herself. Adrian was rescuing her even from herself.

Shouting in her head for her body to cooperate and turn to head back up the steps, she felt Adrian's slight tug on her arm. Turning her body just as tears began to fall, she pushed her legs to cooperate. Adrian led her back inside of the church. She tried to focus but found it hard as every step she took, she wanted to collapse to the floor.

"Son?"

Taryn heard the voice of Adrian's father behind them as he tried to hustle her away from prying eyes.

"Pop, I got her. I promise you, I got her," he said before moving her down a side hall with a quick pace.

Taryn was about to collapse when she saw a blurry figure of a man pointing in a direction down another hall. Her legs gave out just as Adrian reached down and picked her up in his arms. He quickly rushed her away from where anyone could see her. She reached her one arm around his neck and held on as her willpower disappeared. She let out a wail from the depths of her soul that she never knew existed. She screamed her aunt's name again and again, in the midst of soothing words from Adrian that filled her ears. She didn't know where they were going but she felt comfortable enough to let everything out. She had to. There was no space in her heart, mind or body to hold anything else inside. She cried harder than she ever had, right into the lapel of Adrian's suit.

"I got you, baby. I'm right here."

His voice was the level of serene that she needed. Within seconds, they were inside of a room with the door closed behind them. When she thought he would place her on her feet, he didn't. Adrian sat down on a long sofa with her in his lap. He held her close. He kissed her cheeks. He rubbed her back until her wails subsided.

"Thank you," she said softly.

"You looked like you were about to fall down the stairs," he said.

"I didn't realize you were that close to me to notice. I was so overwhelmed. I think I've been trying too hard to hold it all in for too long. I couldn't anymore. From the celebrities speaking, to the choir singing all of my aunt's favorite gospel songs to finally realizing that she was gone. Just too much. I would have collapsed if you hadn't shown up. You swooped down from out of nowhere."

"Your own personal superman," he joked.

She needed his laughter right now.

"Yes, you are. Did I hear your dad's voice just now?"

"You did. I'm assuming he's full of questions. At this point, I don't care. All I care about is that you're okay."

"I am now. I needed to get that out. I'm good now. Can we sit here like this for a little longer?" she asked.

"We can sit here as long as you need to. The burial isn't until tomorrow afternoon, so you don't have to rush out."

"Don't you need to get back to work?"

"Today? Absolutely not. Today is about you and what you need. If that's me, you have my attention. What do you need?"

"You. Just you, right now. I don't want to deal with all the people. I know they're expecting me at the repast, but I can't do it. There are too many cameras flashing; too many questions. It's a lot. I know how popular and loved she was, but this being in the spotlight thing is not for me. All of this has made me realize how much I love my solitude."

"You don't have to go. People may look around for you, but I believe they'll be too busy diving into that large spread of food the caterer is preparing. Are you sure you don't want to go?"

Taryn nodded her head so fast and hard that her chin almost touched her chest.

"I'm positive. Is that improper etiquette?"

"People will understand. I think my father is planning to go. I'll ask him to speak on your behalf. I'm sure Sherita and Julianna will help with that too. It'll be fine. Do you want to go back to your apartment?"

"No. I want to go to yours. Do you feel like my company? I know it's a heavy day. I can't promise I'll be the best company."

"There will never be a time that I don't want your company. Sit tight for a minute while I speak to my father and your cousin."

Adrian stood and placed her on the chair.

"He's going to have a lot of questions," she uttered.

"He will. I'll answer them another day. Today, my only priority is taking care of you. I'll bring my car around to the back of the church so that you can avoid more cameras in your face. There are a lot of them set up across the street from the church. I'll have Sherita bring you out the back in a few minutes. The order for the remainder of this day is rest; and lots of it. I'll order some food. We can stop at your apartment and pick out some comfy clothes. Then, I'll put some movies on and let them watch you as you sleep," Adrian joked.

"I don't need clothes. Aren't you the one always telling me that? I just need one of your t-shirts. I love wearing them. You'll hold me close?" she asked just before he kissed her deeply.

"All day and all night long."

**

The minute Adrian stepped out of the room and into the long hallway, he saw his father talking to Zac near the front door of the church.

"How is she?" his father asked when he walked up to them.

"She's better. I don't think she's going to make it to the repast. Taryn needs a break from all the paparazzi. It's a bit more than she's used to."

"And you know this because?" his father asked.

He looked to Zac, who looked the other way. The cat was out of the bag.

"We've been spending a lot of time together. It's not something we've been broadcasting."

"Beyond business, son?"

"Yes. Way beyond business. If you're about to give me the third degree about getting involved with her due to the closeness of the business relationship, you should save that. I'm not explaining myself when it comes to her. I'm in love with her. Too late for any talks about boundaries or crossing the line with a client."

Adrian wanted to say more but his father put his hand up to stop any more words.

"Son, that is the furthest thought from what I was going to say."

To say he was shocked would be an assured affirmative.

"It is?"

"You and Taryn were always meant to be. It was only a matter of time. I knew it. Her aunt knew it. We spoke about it a few times. We knew you were a perfect pair long ago. We needed you and Taryn to figure that out. Took you long enough!"

"So, you don't think it's wrong?"

"Have you forgotten how I met your mother? I worked for her father when I was in college. That was touchy but I didn't care. I saw her and knew I wanted to spend the rest of my life with her. You being in love with Taryn isn't a surprise. Your mother called it. If she wasn't out of town looking after your aunt, she would have been here today. I'm only hanging around to make sure she's okay and to see if there was anything I could do to help."

Adrian exhaled his happiness. He wasn't in the mood to hear anyone question what was happening between him and Taryn.

"Can you go to the repast and speak on her behalf, apologizing for her absence? She wants to get out of the spotlight. Crowds like this bother her. I'm going to take her home so that she can relax. I'm going to quickly talk to her cousin to let her know and then we're out. Zac, will you get the staff back on track in the office? Let them have the time at the repast. They can trickle in at their leisure, or, I'll leave it up to you if you want to give them the rest of the day off."

"Good plan. I'm on it. Let Taryn know I'm thinking about her. You know if you need me, call me," Zac said before he stepped away.

"I'm going to make my way to the repast. I'll check in with the two of you later. Take care of her, son. She's going to need you. That connection with her aunt was a strong one. I don't want her to think that she doesn't have anyone. I'm glad she has you, but she has me and your mother too. Your sisters have been texting me all morning worried about Taryn. They know what her aunt meant to her. Let her know that she has an entire village that I'm happy to now say, starts with you."

"Thanks, dad and you're right, it starts with me and always will."

Seeing Sherita and Julianna still standing at the top of the stairs in a group he assumed was more of Taryn's friends, he walked out and asked Sherita to step to the side.

"How is she?"

"She's fine. She needed to cry it out in private. The public stance of the past few weeks that she's been in the midst of scared her. She needed a moment."

"Is she coming out? The limousine is waiting for us."

"You all go ahead to the repast. Taryn wants to go home. I'm going to drive her. She needs to relax."

"You're sure, she's okay?" Julianna asked walking up to them.

"I'm sure. She just needs a little space."

Adrian noticed something weird happening between Sherita and Julianna. Sherita kept looking at a man who stood alone on the opposite side of the steps. The guy was trying to act like he wasn't checking for them, but he was. If he was trying to be inconspicuous, he was failing.

"Um, okay," Sherita said, her eyes cutting back and forth to the guy.

When Julianna kept doing the same, Adrian grew concerned.

"Is there a problem with that guy? You're both sort of off kilter."

"Well, he's someone we know. No biggie. You take care of our girl. We'll hold things down at the repast. Tell her I'll see her when I get home later."

"She'll be at my apartment. Stop down if you want. She would love to have both of you check in on her."

"No need as long as she's with you and not alone. If she needs us, tell her we will be one floor up. Do I need to bring her anything?" Sherita inquired.

"She said she doesn't need anything, but can you bring her some clothes? Maybe some of those leggings and a shirt along with some socks?" Adrian asked.

"I got it."

"Good. You know I have her. Can one of you come with me? I'm going to get my car and pull around to the back of the church. If one of you can walk Taryn out, that would help."

"I got her," Sherita added.

Adrian gave the guy one last look before heading back into the church. He was most certainly acting strange and stood out. He'd place that thought in the back of his mind for another time. Something was telling him that this wouldn't be their last encounter. For now, his complete focus was on getting Taryn home and out of the mayhem.

16

Adrian exited his car and gave his driver the evening off, knowing that unless there was a serious emergency, he wasn't planning to come back out. It wasn't often that he left the office before ten or eleven at night. He was learning to prioritize something other than work.

"Good evening, Mister Jarreau. This is an early evening for you, sir."

Adrian smiled and greeted Harold as he opened and held the door open for him.

"You are correct, my good sir. Sometimes, I forget what it's like being home at this hour."

"I'm glad you came in through the front entrance instead of the garage. You have extra mail that couldn't fit into your mailbox. I have them locked up in the office if you have a minute or I can bring them up later if you choose," Harold said.

Adrian, like the other residents in the building, loved the white glove service Harold and his team provided.

"I can take it all with me now."

Harold nodded and Adrian followed him into the concierge's office off of the lobby. Thankfully, the office contained a one-way mirror that allowed Harold and the other staff to see if anyone walked up to the building and needed assistance. He stood right outside of the door and waited."

"How are your wife and daughters doing?" Adrian asked.

Taking the mail and gathering it all in his arms, he looked down at the large stack and wondered why there was so much of it.

"They're all doing great. My youngest is graduating high school this year. The oldest if graduating from Morgan State University this year."

"You're having a busy year ahead of you. I hope you're taking time off to enjoy the festivities with them and not feel like you need to rush back to work."

"I'm working extra days now to give the other guys some time off because I'm taking about a month off to enjoy this celebratory time with both girls. Looks like you're taking a bit of your own advice these days. I've seen more of you than I usually do," Harold said, locking the door and walking behind Adrian toward the bank of elevators.

"Oh?" Adrian questioned. He waited before punching his code into the keypad to call the elevator down. He had to use the first elevator to the left of the four in the large hall. That one would only travel to the top four floors in the building.

"I've seen you with Miss Misha's niece. She sure is beautiful. She's special, huh?"

Adrian started not to answer. He didn't talk about his personal life when it came to women. That was usually off-limits. There was no doubt that his casual dating life wasn't a secret. He had a healthy dating life. Taryn was different. It was clear Harold saw that too. For once, he was excited to talk about a woman with him. He turned from the elevator and faced Harold. They looked up when Marty, another member of the building staff took the post on the outside of the apartment. Adrian knew that would give him a little more time to talk about Taryn.

"She is. She's very special to me. I've been caught off-guard. She's always been beautiful. I've had the chance to really get to know her and she's so much more than that."

"I saw the way you looked at her the other night. The two of you were having a late dinner in the café here in the building. The best thing the owners have ever done was to add the café. The fact that it's open twenty-four hours a day has been the biggest plus to the residents, especially those who work crazy schedules like you."

"I do love that I can get a meal, a sandwich or just a snack in the middle of the night. It's not the healthiest time to be eating, but it's handy when I'm up late."

"I've never seen you smile as much as you were when you were with her that night. It was good to see."

"I'm beyond smitten. Let's keep that to ourselves for now, if that's okay with you."

"I'm happy for you. I'm extremely happy for her. I don't know her too well. She was already living outside of the country when I took this job. Ms. Misha talked about her all the time. She was so proud. I will miss the building's most popular resident."

"It was good to see you at the memorial service the other day."

"There were a lot of residents from the building. Too much media was there, but I guess that goes with her level of celebrity."

Adrian shook the hand that was extended to him.

The elevator door opened and he hopped in.

"Good chatting with you, Harold. Congratulations on the achievements of your daughters."

When the doors closed, Adrian took out his phone and recorded a note to himself to make sure he handed Harold a financial gift for both girls.

Putting his phone away, his thoughts turned back to Taryn. He was hoping beyond all hope that she had followed his suggestion to put her feet up and relax without the need to worry about things that she couldn't control. After the funeral, she'd been on roller skates trying to handle her aunt's affairs. Not everything was going smoothly. Deciding that after a week of working from early morning to almost midnight each night, he decided to call it an early evening. Of course, as soon as Zac heard that he was freeing up his evening, his friend had called some of their other friends and planned a guy's night out. He was all for that until he got to his car and got a text from Taryn that her plans to go out with friends fell through. They hadn't seen each other all week. They were both free. He had a remedy.

After a quick call to Melvin and Zac, whom he was supposed to meet for a game of golf and networking at the golf course, apologizing for not being able to connect with them, he focused on getting home. Tonight, he wanted some quiet time with Taryn. He now needed to make time for Taryn since they were dating. He was learning to balance life better so that it included her.

Since they connected on an intimate level, not just sexually, but a tenderness of their hearts, he understood what it meant to live life to the fullest with those who mean the most. Taryn had broken through every barrier he'd had in place that helped him stay focused on work and not a personal life. He thought he knew what was important. He was learning.

The elevator opened on his floor. As he walked toward his door, he wondered if he would open it to find his love there. The possibility that she wanted some alone time was on his mind. When they spoke, they hadn't made any plans to be together tonight. The idea lived in the air. He would respect her wish if she decided not to spend the night with him. With the week she's had, she may want her own quiet time.

As soon as he reached his door, he smiled. There was music coming from the other side. Taryn was here. Couldn't be either of his sisters, who also had keys to his place. Neither of them was in New York this week.

There was nothing but delight when he opened the door to a candle-lit lined foyer. Dropping the mail in the basket on the table at the door, he closed and locked it and then headed in the direction of the beautiful sounds of a woman singing off-key, his woman.

Walking through the living room and beyond the dining room, he reached the kitchen. His heart skipped several beats at the scene before him. Taryn was in the kitchen cooking something. What, he didn't care, though the aroma was delectable to his nose. He was mesmerized by the sight of her in his place, singing and dancing around in a hot pink satin, short two-piece pajama set. She did exactly what he'd hoped she would do. He wanted her to be here.

Leaning against the kitchen wall frame, he waited and took all of her in.

"I could get used to this," he finally said.

Without thinking, he licked his lips.

When she turned and smiled, he was not only happy that he hadn't startled her. He was excited when she put down the baster and raced to him. He had only a second to brace for her leap into his arms.

"You are the best sight ever!" Taryn yelled.

Adrian wanted to confirm that they were on the same page, but she made sure that his lips and tongue were too busy being devoured by hers with the kind of heated, fiery kiss that he had come to enjoy and love.

Holding her body in his arms with her legs wrapped around his waist, he let all thought leave his mind except for how good she felt in his arms. He took over loving her mouth in a way that made him want to forget doing anything other than walking with her in his arms into the bedroom. Sinking into her silky, smooth body was on his mind.

Taryn moaned into his mouth. He took great pleasure in deepening the intoxicating kiss, dueling with her tongue in a desire that could only be tamed temporarily. The kiss sealed the deal for him. He would always want her. When they finally parted, it was so that they could breathe. That was clear from the extra effort they needed to calm their raging hormones and hearts.

"Damn! Can I go out and come back in again so that we can put this kiss on repeat?" he asked before kissing her sweetly one last time as she slid down his body. When she moved to walk away, he pulled her back to him, this time with her back to his front. He held her close, placing soft kisses from her chin to her neck.

"I need to check dinner. There's no need to go back out. You can have as many kisses as you want at any time. I'm just happy to see you. I wasn't sure how late you'd be," she said.

"I was going to be late. Then you told me you would be back earlier than you had planned since you weren't going out."

Taryn walked back over to the stove and checked the pots.

"You changed your mind about going out with your friends? I was going to leave this warming for you."

"It smells amazing in here. What are you cooking and why are you cooking? We could have ordered."

"I know. I wanted to surprise you with this meal. Besides, I needed something to do while I waited for you. I didn't want to work on anything, read anything or do anything else that dealt with the estate. I wanted to do something that had me thinking of only you. I know you had plans to go out with Zac and some of your other friends. I'm sorry if my call had you changing your plans in any way. That was not my intent."

Adrian removed his suit jacket and placed it on the back of one of the eight stools at the black and gold kitchen island. He moved around the counter toward the stove to look in as many pots as he could.

"Don't apologize for that. I can hang out with those fools anytime. They understood. Neither of them even questioned or tried to counter. They get it. What in the world are you cooking? This kitchen smells amazing."

"Well, I know about some of your favorite foods from our talks. I wasn't sure where to get everything. I haven't lived in New York in a few years. Things and stores have changed. When I would come home to visit my aunt, she always cooked. She loved cooking for me."

"I see she taught you well."

"She did. We are having seared lamb chops and broiled jumbo shrimp. I know we both love salad, but I wasn't in a salad kind of mood. Plus, I wanted to start with the main course and not mess it up with a salad appetizer. There are sauteed veggies over yellow rice. I'm simmering a light creamy sauce to put over the top of that. Your timing is great because everything is almost ready."

He was speechless. There was a woman that he was surely falling in love with, in his kitchen cooking for him. He wanted to alleviate her stressful day by doing something for her like cooking for her. Taryn never ceased to amaze him.

"I was going to prepare something for you when I got here; that is, if you were here. I'm glad you are here."

"You have to be tired."

"I am, but seeing you here has given me new life. I know you did not find any of these fixings for this meal in my kitchen. Where did you get them?"

"Oh, right. I started to explain that. I called Zac. He didn't tell you?" she asked.

Adrian shook his head from side to side.

"I called the office and asked to be patched into him. I explained why and your assistant helped me. I asked him where around here you shopped for fresh food to cook. He told me about the Whole Foods store not too far from here. He mentioned that I should pick up some fresh strawberries from there because they are the best. I knew they were your favorite. Now I know where you like to get them from. They're in the refrigerator in a sauce from a recipe I found on the internet. I'm in the middle of setting the table. I hope I didn't go too far going through your cabinets. You have a lot of them. I wanted to find something nice for us to eat from," she explained.

Adrian looked to the end of the island to where she had placed a table setting for two with his black China.

"Look anywhere you want. You chose well. I love the black set. I don't get to use it often. I'll finish setting the table since you're cooking."

When he walked toward the dishes, Taryn hopped in front of him. She stopped him with both hands up on his chest, pushing him back a few steps.

"Don't you dare touch a thing. I have this covered. As you can see, I'm already dressed for relaxation and rest; that is, if you want an overnight guest," she asked, beaming at him with her big bright eyes.

"You're joking, right? I try not to be too demanding of your time in my bed. If it were up to me, you'd be here every night."

"Good. That means, you need to get out of those work clothes. Then and only then can you join me."

He turned to head toward the bedroom when he stopped.

"Do you want to talk about anything about your day? You sounded frustrated when we talked when I got in the car."

Taryn shook her head hard and fast from side-to-side.

"No, Adrian. Not tonight. It's a lot. I don't want to talk or think about any of that tonight. No work talk. No doing any work either. I don't want to talk about anything that isn't about me wrapped around you, snuggling under a blanket and watching a good movie. You know how much we both love movies. All I want tonight is you. If we're talking, we're talking about happy things. As soon as you shower and change into something sexy for me, we can eat and get our night started. How does that sound?"

Kissing her one last time, he stepped away so that he could get back to her and to the quiet night he couldn't wait to spend with her.

**

Taryn turned back to what she was doing. She cringed when her phone rang knowing who it was. The incessant phone calls and texts with demands for her time were at a point of plaguing her at this point. She grabbed it to stop the ringing and saw the label for the caller that she'd added to the number; do not answer. When her phone pinged, she looked toward the bedroom where she could hear the shower going. Adrian would be busy for a few minutes. She didn't want to but then decided to listen to the message that was left. Her body went rigid hearing his voice.

"You can't keep ignoring me, Taryn. We not only have history but we have business to discuss. It's too bad we didn't get a chance to talk at the funeral. Why you have ignored me since then, I don't know. I'm not going away. I'm going to keep calling until you respond. Perhaps if I sent you a few seconds of our video, you'll know it's a good reason to return my call. I'm tired of leaving voice messages. I would hate for you to see yourself all over the internet. Imagine that. The niece of the world-famous writer found to have not such a squeaky-clean background. Get your checkbook together and call me or it's on."

The message ended as abrasive as it had started. She wanted to scream. She hated being taken down memory lane to a time in her life that she wanted to forget about. Before she could turn the phone off and put it in her bag to hopefully forget about it until another day, it rang again while it was still in her hands. She was about to force it to voicemail when she saw Julianna's name on the screen.

"Hey Diva!" Julianna yelled with extra enthusiasm.

Taryn couldn't smile or come back with a quirky retort. The voicemail message consumed her mood.

"Hey," she finally said, somberly.

No way could her best friend miss her tone.

"Okay, what gives? I thought you were waiting for that hunk of a man of yours to get there. I'm sensing something that's not so happy. What's going on? I was calling to check on you. We haven't spoken much since the funeral. I'm sorry I've been so busy once I got back to L.A."

Taryn paused, exhaled and then said the name. Julianna would understand.

"Nathaniel."

"He's causing trouble? More threats?"

"Him being at the funeral was trashy considering I know his motive for being there; *money*."

"Oh, my goodness. He's still pestering you? I thought it stopped. This is harassment."

"He won't stop calling and texting me. He wants money. You know what he's threatening to do."

"Girl, you need to tell Adrian. He's a lawyer. I'm sure he can find something to get Nathaniel out of your life."

"I can't. I don't want him to know. I don't know if I can handle seeing disappointment in his eyes."

"You're talking about something you did in your early twenties. Were you even twenty then? I don't know. You can't let Nathaniel do this to you. He's basically trying to blackmail you. That's illegal."

"I know but if I don't do what he's asking, can you imagine what could happen if he follows through? Also, I need to think about Adrian. People know we're seeing each other. Even if they don't, they will if my secret is revealed. I can't hurt him. What if this ends up ruining his name just by being connected to me, especially in a romantic way? I would die if I hurt him in any way. He's been amazing to me. He's the kind of man any and every woman would love to have. This could turn into a smear campaign that would draw Adrian into it. I can't."

"Okay, then what are you going to do? I know you're not thinking of paying him?"

"Maybe I should."

"That won't make him go away. It will only have him come back for more at a later time."

Taryn paced across the kitchen floor. She looked up when she heard the shower turn off. Her nerves kicked into overdrive.

"I have to think about what I'm going to do. Just not tonight. I need to clear my head. I want to focus on Adrian tonight; nothing negative."

"I get it. Look, call me tomorrow. Have you picked when you're going back to Paris? Perhaps, you're planning to stay in New York?"

Taryn smiled at the idea of not leaving. Now that she was wrapping up the issues with her aunt's life and last wishes, all she wanted to do was relax.

"I'll be going back. Not right now though."

"Where is Nathaniel calling you from?"

"In his messages, he says he's still in New York. You know he doesn't like Paris. Considering his mother lives and works there and he's caused enough issues there to never want to return, I know he's hoping to catch up with me while I'm here. He wouldn't dare come to Paris. Too many burned bridges for him there."

"I guess that's a safe place for you to not run into him."

Taryn's eyes widened when Adrian walked in her direction with a large gold towel around his waist. Her eyes went from his feet to his smiling face and then to the towel that was hiding what she was in need of tonight.

"Jules, I will call you in a few days. I love you, sis."

"Oh, I guess your man is in the room."

Taryn licked her lips and smiled when Adrian winked at her.

"Bye, Jules."

Without waiting for a response from her, Taryn ended the call, turned her phone off and placed it in her bag that she'd left sitting on the kitchen counter.

"You didn't have to end your call," Adrian said walking up to her.

When his body pressed seductively hard against hers until he had her pressed against the wall, her arms went around his neck when he lifted her body from the floor and placed her legs around his towel covered hips.

"You, in a towel still glistening from your shower, is all the reason I need to not be on the phone. I'm also wondering if dinner can be postponed for a bit," she said kissing his lips.

She got her answer when Adrian released the towel from around his waist, leaving him standing and holding her while completely naked. She could feel him. Her response was to grind her hips in response to how he was holding her.

Clearly, she didn't have to ask again or wait. Adrian turned with her in his arms and walked them into the bedroom after giving her seconds to reach behind him to turn off the last pot that was still boiling. She was ready for what was for her and her only before dinner could be consumed.

She always loved having dessert before dinner anyway. With a hot, sexy man like Adrian who desired her every time they were together, there was no way food was the priority. They could do that much later. She needed what she could feel until her brain turned to mush. She had already forgotten about anything else that had almost ruined her sexy mood for the night.

The minute Adrian pressed her body into the soft mattress, her mind cleared of everything but the feel of him.

17

Adrian had hoped to leave the apartment early in the morning without waking Taryn. They'd had a late night. The sun wasn't even up yet. Though he could have used a few extra hours in bed, he had a meeting with two of the firm's junior associates who were making their debut in court later in the day. He was planning to run a mock trial to be sure they were heading in the right direction with the case. Doing this would give them the confidence to take the lead. He had agreed to meet them in the wee hours before most of the staff arrived for the day.

"You're already up and dressed? Why didn't you wake me so that I could go upstairs?" Taryn said while his back was turned to her.

Straightening his tie, he turned around, walked over to the bed and kissed her even further awake.

"Upstairs? You have a big day ahead of you?"

"Well, no. Sherita and I may have lunch later. She's coming back to town today."

"I forgot she went home after the funeral two weeks ago. She's back already?"

"She has a meeting at your firm today to go over some legal documents. She'll be here for a few days. I forgot to ask her about the hospital benefit gala you mentioned. I hate for her to come to town and I'm there and she's not."

"I somehow forgot about that event in a few days."

"The gala?" Taryn asked him as she got out of bed. His eyes focused on her nakedness until she wrapped herself up in a white satin robe.

"You are so gorgeous, baby."

When he moved in her direction, she wiggled her finger back and forth before he reached her.

"Don't think about it. You're already dressed. You don't want to be late for your mock-trial. Don't forget you told me all about that."

"You don't have to get up and leave because I'm leaving. You know the code to the apartment. You already come and go here as much as you want. Stay and get some sleep. I know you need it."

"Yes, I do. It's all your fault."

They laughed together.

"My fault? You mean before or after you kept rolling over on top of me just before sleep would kick in for either of us?"

"I swear, I have never been this wild sexual demon before you. About the gala. You said you forgot. Are we still going?"

Adrian paused. That's not what he wanted to do. His plan was to get them away from the city for a few days. Now that she could take the time and focus less on business or anything about her aunt, he wanted them to take a road trip to one of his favorite places."

"I honestly forgot about it. I have something else in mind for us. I bought a table for the firm, as I do for most fundraisers like this gala. I don't always go."

"Oh? Like what?"

"How busy are you for the next three to four days? I don't want to keep you from something important."

"Now that the hardest part is behind me? Not much. Last week when you came home and I was in the kitchen cooking, that had been a stressful day. I'm in a better place now. The realtor handling the sale of the apartment has been trying to reach me to talk about showings before I go back to Paris."

"Don't remind me about that. I know it's on the horizon. I want to take advantage of the time we have while you're here. No focusing on packing the apartment or handling any more details, at least for a few days. I have an idea. Are you open to hearing it?"

"Yes, I am."

"If I can move a few things around on my schedule — actually, I will move a few things around on my schedule, would you like to take a road trip with me to a quiet getaway spot?"

"A getaway spot? Where?"

"Upstate New York. My family owns a secluded log cabin that overlooks Keuka Lake. The most gorgeous view during the day and at night. It's quiet with no one else around but me, you and the animals living around in their habitat, not bothering us. I go there when I want to disconnect from the matrix, my form of shutting everything down and out and finding time to restore myself when life gets the best of me. I would love to take you there. I feel like you could use some time away from all that you've been going through. You've been on a rollercoaster ride for weeks. I could use the time away also. I don't do that enough. It's an updated log cabin with four bedrooms and two large family rooms. You can have a room for yourself if I'm in your way of getting your quiet time. There are two kitchens that can be fully stocked with one call from me. They have everything needed for me to make you some of the best food you'll ever have. There's a hot tub, a fishing dock, swimming pool, huge library, large wraparound deck and most of all, quietness like you wouldn't believe. We also have a small yacht that we can take out on the lake. I can call our management company to have the cabin aired out. We can stop on our way up there to get supplies. I want to cater to you. What do you say?"

What a man, she thought. Nothing about all that they were sharing and what he was becoming to mean to her could have prepared her for the onslaught of feelings of not having to be strong all the time. Adrian was continually doing his best to allow her to just be. This soft era of the past few weeks that he's helped provide for her was heavenly.

"You're stepping away from work? Don't you have a big case that you're sitting second chair on with one of the junior associates on Friday? I know that's big for you."

Taryn immediately kicked herself for disturbing the narrative of him making her a priority.

"I can get Zac or one of the other senior associates to do it. Today's court case is the most important one because they've never been first and second chair. The case on Friday is nothing I can't bring Zac up to date on to then dish out to another attorney. I don't step away often. If I am, they know I need it; so do you. Let me do this for you. Unless you really don't want..."

"I do," Taryn interrupted and then chuckled when she realized she had screamed out her excitement.

"Haha," he quipped.

"I'm sorry. I didn't mean to say that so loud. What about the gala tickets?"

Adrian thought about it.

"You said Sherita will be here? Maybe she'd like to go in your place. I hate that she's coming and now I want to take you away. She's coming to see you. I can give another attorney my ticket. Zac is going. He can give the ticket to someone."

"She would love an opportunity to get all dolled up for a fancy event. With her newfound wealth, she'll probably want to make a donation. I plan to make one. She's enjoying making the road trip. She only works three days a week, twelve hours a day, so she has plenty of days off to do what she wants. Right now, that's coming here."

"Is that a yes then?"

"I need to learn to just say yes when I know that's what I want to do. You are so wonderful to me. I've never dated anyone as caring as you before. Oh wait, did I assume that we're dating. I'm nervous. What is wrong with me?" she sighed at hearing her own words.

"Baby, we are absolutely dating. There was never a question on my end. Don't worry about me or my schedule. I want to be all about you and have you be all about me even if it's only for a few days. Until I have to say goodbye to you when you go back to Paris and we figure out what long-distance will look like, I want this time with you; time I didn't know I needed and wanted. Whatever time we still have before you leave, I want to live it up. There is also a nice pub there. They have pool tables, darts and a large room in the back with vintage arcade machines. You'll love it. Most of all, I like how you feed me," he said in a voice that he knew, from their love of movies, she would recognize what he was imitating.

"No. Not the *Little Shop of Horrors*, Audrey II voice?" she joked.

"I love that movie! Yes, that was the Audrey II voice you just heart."

"Adrian that is one of my favorite movies!"

"I'm already adding it to our viewing list while we're at the cabin. We have so much in common. You get that right?" he asked.

Taryn danced around in a place. She was feeling it too.

"I'm excited. I'll be here for a while. I think I'm going to get back in your bed and sleep a little longer, as long as you're okay with me staying here."

"Baby, I'm already out the door. Get as much sleep as you want. I'll call you later. I'm sure I'll need to hear your voice."

"Any time you need to, I'm a phone call away. I'll check with Sherita to see if she wants the ticket. She may not know anyone there, but trust me, she'll make a few best friends easily."

"Who is she meeting with at the firm?"

"Zac. He's taking the lead on educating her on what to do with her new wealth like you're doing with me."

"Okay, then she'll know Zac. I know that he's going. She may meet a few others while at the firm today. She'll be fine. Let me know before I ask if Zac wants it for someone else. It'll give Sherita something to do while you and I are tucked away from the world."

Waiting until his lady love was snuggled up in his bed on top of his pillow, Adrian turned the overhead light out, throwing the space into pure darkness. Before leaving, he went over to her for the kiss he needed to send him on his way before leaving the bedroom and the apartment. He took the elevator down to the main lobby where he exited to his car, driven by his usual driver to keep him from having to be in traffic. Before he could get in, he turned at the sound of his name being called. To his surprise, his sister Amira was racing in his direction.

"Hey big brother!" she yelled before hugging him tight.

"Sis! What are you doing here at this hour?"

"I figured I would either catch you leaving or still in your apartment. Why are you heading out this early?"

"Work calls at many different hours of the day. Again, what are you doing here? You didn't call to tell me you would be in town. Is Adore with you?"

"No. I flew in and landed less than an hour ago. I came right here hoping I could stay with you for a few days while I'm here."

"No mom and dad's house?" he asked.

"Ugh, not this time. I'm here for a party this weekend and then I'm heading back out. I'm going to stop by the house a little later. Mom's going to ask me if I'm staying with them. I'm hoping to tell her that I had already planned to stay with you."

Adrian looked back at the building and then at her.

"I would usually say yes, but, uh..."

"What? A woman? Wait – Taryn? Is it Taryn?"

"You know about her?"

"Yeah. I had to find out from Adore. You tell her everything," Amira huffed.

"I'm sorry about that. I was going to tell you too. She found out because one of her friends saw me out with Taryn."

"She's up in your place?" Amira asked pointing to the glass lobby door.

"She is and she's sleeping. Do you want to stay at my house? You can use the car. It's in the garage."

He started to apologize for not letting her stay at the apartment as he usually would. Before he could get a word out, Amira shoved her hand out at him.

"Keys? Car and house, please! Can I have Cara and Monet over? I promise, no parties or anything. They're in town too."

"Amira, if I hear of anybody else up in my house, this will be your last time staying there when I'm not there. I mean that," he said handing her the keys to one of his two cars in the garage. "You know how I am about my cars."

"I can't use the truck?"

"No. I'm using it for a road trip."

"You and Taryn? I want to meet her."

"And I want her to meet you and Amora. I talk about my two bratty, spoiled rotten, yet highly intelligent and beautiful sisters. Maybe later today?"

"Okay, I'll take that. I want to tell her how sorry I am about her aunt. I loved me some Ms. Misha."

"I know. We all did. Reason a million of why I don't want you to disturb Taryn while she's sleeping."

"Your house is a nice consolation prize. I promise, no one other than Cara and Monet. We will keep it clean."

"No drinking and no guys."

"I wouldn't do that and you know it. I get why you're reminding me. I promise to handle your house with care. I love you. Can we still tell mom and dad that I'm staying with you here? She'll blow a gasket if she finds out I'm at your house and you're not there."

"I got you. Don't let me down. Not even a single scratch on my car. Love you sis," he said getting into the car.

He wasn't even sure she heard him. Amira had already disappeared into the lobby of the building to take the elevator down the garage level.

He shook his head at her fast exit and then told his driver to get him to the office quickly. He was already running late. He took out his cell phone and sent Taryn a quick text.

"Sweet dreams," he typed.

He chuckled to himself. He was a goner for sure. Truth is, he wanted to send a text more from his heart. One like he loved her. Now wasn't the time. He was patient.

18

Traffic to the cabin was lighter than Adrian had expected. Leaving early in the day, he was sure that they would have run into major rush hour traffic. He smiled over at his good luck charm. Taryn was fast asleep. He chuckled remembering her promise that she was the perfect companion on a long car ride. Twenty minutes after packing the truck with everything they would need for four days away, they hit the road, and Taryn had fallen asleep.

When they had stopped at a railroad crossing, he reached into the bag behind her seat and pulled out a fleece blanket she had packed and covered her with it. He reached around her body and lowered her seat. Now she could really get some rest while he drove them to their destination. Denying himself the chance to caress her cheek and think back to the night before where they relaxed in his media room watching an old favorite, *Love Jones* while eating popcorn smothered in butter and hot sauce. He was quickly becoming a fan of her favorite snack – a definite acquired taste. Taryn was his favorite acquired taste. Thoughts of her often took him away from being all about work and instead, being about living a happy life with her. They each had their own money. He was learning that there is more to life than money. Right now, his happiness came with the woman next to him feeling safe, comfortable and happy in his arms. With the train now moving on, he was able to get them back on the road.

After taking the many winding roads and taking in the mountainous views, Adrian took the final long, hidden road that would take them to the cabin that was also hidden amongst a massive number of trees. When the lake came into view, he knew he was close. He looked over at Taryn as he took the last turn to the long road that would take them to the cabin.

This place was his family's home away from the fast life of working and living in the city. Just being there could be exhausting.

Taryn slept the entire ride up. He hated having to wake her soon. She'd been asleep in the passenger seat of his Black Chevy Suburban for well over an hour. Turning onto the private road for the last mile, he smiled when Tony and Shira Bryson waved wildly as he drove up and parked in front of the cabin. The two of them have been managing the property for over five years, back when his parents first bought the house.

"Hello, Adrian," Tony said first while rolling the window down and turning the truck off.

He placed his finger over his lips and pointed to a sleeping Taryn.

"It's good to see you both," he said, quietly slipping out of the truck. He made sure there was barely a sound when he closed the door to the truck.

"The cabin is all ready for you. Shira got everything on your list for the pantry and refrigerator. She even got a few steaks which are in the freezer. Are you sure you won't need anything else? I thought you would have asked us to pick up more than you did.

"No worries. I got everything else we'll need. If not, I can make a run to the store. Thanks for airing the place out."

"That's never a problem. Your father called and asked us to have the boat brought out of dry-dock for you too. It was delivered about an hour ago. It's clean, tied up and docked safely at the end of the pier. There are all new linens as well. If you want Lenny to drive it if you want to go out on the open water, he's on standby. Do you need anything else?"

"You guys are the best. I think I have it from here. I have to wake up my girlfriend and then get everything out of the truck."

"Need help with that?" Tony asked.

"I think I'm good. I know you've been working on this place for two days. I'll let you get back to your life. As always, I am most appreciative."

Shira walked off and Tony stayed and moved closer to him.

"Have you ever brought a woman here before?" he asked.

Adrian smiled. He considered Tony more than just the man who maintained their property. He considered him a friend.

"In the five years since we've had this place? She is the first one."

"Aw, you must be serious about her," Tony said looking to the truck and then back at him.

"Yes, I am."

"I'm happy for you. If you feel anything like what I feel for Shira, you and she are both lucky. Enjoy your time here. If you need anything at all, I'm a call or a text away. The pool has been uncovered, cleaned and ready also."

"You've thought of everything."

"Are you sure I can't take your things inside?" Tony asked.

"I'm good."

"Okay, then I'll let you to your lady. If you go to the pub while here, let me know. Shira and I can join you. Good to see you."

"Likewise, Tony."

Once they got into their truck and turned toward the road, Adrian went around to the passenger side door and opened it slowly. Taryn stirred a little just as he was about to lift her up to take her inside in hopes that he wouldn't break her sleep. When her eyes opened, he winked and placed a quick kiss on her lips.

"Hey," she said softly. "We're here?"

"That we are."

She stretched and he smiled brighter.

"How long have I been asleep?"

"Actually, close to two hours."

"I'm sorry. That makes me a terrible driving partner."

"Baby, we were up late and then up early to get on the road. Besides, you haven't been sleeping your best lately. When you fell asleep and you were peaceful, I wished we could have had a few more hours of drive time. I was fine. I was about to carry you inside so that you could sleep some more."

"No, no, I'm awake. I didn't realize I had fallen asleep. Last thing I remember, we were talking about our favorite comedic movies while listening to music," she joked.

"Yes, we were. The minute I talked about how much I loved Eddie Murphy's *Beverly Hills Cop* movies, one, two and four, but not three, I looked over and you were out cold. I pulled over and relaxed your seat back further, turned the music down and tried not to hit any potholes in the road, though that was a test of my patience," he kidded as he held Taryn's hand so that she could step down out of the truck.

He couldn't help letting his eyes roam over all of her from her blue capris to her white top, tied at her waist. Her Pandora charm bracelets glittered brightly in the high sun and as usual, her natural beauty had his heart thumping a few extra beats. Everything about her was perfect, inside and out. As she took in the beauty that was the cabin and the property around it, he moved to the back of the truck to grab their luggage. He would come back out to grab all the food after giving her a quick tour of the inside.

"Your description and the pictures didn't do this place justice. You already know how much I love cabin life."

"Yes, you told me about the one your aunt owned and left you in her will. I hope I get to see it one day."

Taryn turned slightly and smiled at him over her shoulder, moving her long hair out of the way so that he could see her face.

"I'm already thinking about spending time with you there. You will love it as much as I know I will love being here. In fact, I'm already in love with it. You were right about how peaceful it is here. Is that your boat?" she asked, pointing to the end of the dock.

"It's my dad's. He and my mom love being out on the water. My sisters and I got our love for the water from them. We'll be here for four days. I would love to take you out on it. Are you good with boats?" he asked, grabbing their luggage.

When Taryn tried to reach for something to help, he waved his finger letting her know that he had it all covered.

"I love them. When I'm home in Paris, one of my favorite things to do is a boat ride. I live walking distance from one that also boasts some of the best food around. I love being out on the water."

"That's good to know. As far as the best food, I can guarantee you that you're going to love my grilled lamb chops in my dill, onion and garlic sauce along with my grilled veggies. I love city living but there is nothing like having cooked food from the grill. Then there is my grilled fish. I have some chef level meals planned for us."

"Baby, you've brought enough food for us to feed an army while we're here."

He leaned over and kissed her lips again. When she touched his face, holding him on her lips a little longer, he was reminded that kissing each other was something they loved to randomly do, just because. He wasn't sure when he'd turned into a big fan of public displays of affection. Before her, he never did so with other women. This wasn't just a, just because, kiss for him. He was in love. Kissing felt different than with anyone else. The idea both pleased and frightened him.

"Go on inside and look around. I'll start bringing stuff in. I plan to cook us dinner, but for lunch, I want to take you to this new restaurant called Bederman's Inn. My sister wanted to come here a few months ago, but my parents wouldn't let her unless I accompanied her and her friends. Bederman's Inn catered for the big party here at the house and the food was amazing. I figured we could relax after I give you the grand tour and then change for a late lunch. That will give me some time to marinate the chops and jumbo lobster tails for the skewers."

"*Mmm*, that sounds delicious. If I am about anything, it's definitely seafood."

Before she got too far, Adrian was about to pick up their bags to put them under his arms when Taryn turned back in his direction and walked back up to him.

"Are you okay?" he asked.

"I am so much better than okay; all because of you. Like what you did for me at the church when you knew I needed to step away from everyone, you knew that I could really use this time away. I've been so busy wrapped up in wills, trusts, the apartment, family, funeral planning and a million other things. I can't believe I didn't even bring my laptop with me. That is usually an extension of who I am."

"Not when you're with me. We are both busy work creatures. Out of habit, we tend to think of work and all that it involves as soon as we wake up. We are taking a break from that for the next four days. You didn't need to review or edit any novels or deal with the publishing company. The reason I have such a large team at work and amazing partners is so that I could get away from the ideal that I always had to be present and in control at the firm."

"How often do you come here?" she asked.

"When my mother demands family time away, I'm always here. We also have two other places, but this one is closest without having to take a flight. Maybe twice a year I come here by myself to decompress. I need to do that more. I've never brought a woman here before."

Taryn leaned back and turned her head to the side. He could see the wheels turning in her head about what his revelation meant.

"Really?" she questioned.

"Really. You're special to me. I wanted to show you a place that was special to me."

"I'm honored. You always make me feel special."

"If there is ever a time where I am lacking in my job of making you feel that way, I hope you'll tell me."

"Adrian, you are one person who I know that with you, I am guaranteed to always feel special. Does your family know that I'm here?"

Lowering his hands from her waist, he gathered her hands in his. He had a revelation he wanted to share with her.

"Yes, they know. I haven't mentioned it, but I told my parents that you and I are seeing each other. They are happy for us. My dad expected it would happen. My sisters also know. They can't wait to meet you. Amira was in town this week, but she never did make it back to the city before we left today. You'll meet both of my sisters soon. Everyone seems to have known that you and I should be together except us."

"I'm glad we know now."

"My father did everything but push me out of the door this morning when I stopped by early this morning before you woke up and we got on the road. I wanted to check in on a few things. The minute he saw me he pointed to the elevator. I got the message. I went back to the apartment, finished getting my stuff together and waited on you. He threatened to throttle me if I even sent a text to check on a client."

Taryn laughed at him as he maneuvered the bags through the door that she held open.

"Oh, your dad knows what's important."

"He and my mom have been together since she was a teenager. My dad had a job working for her father when he was in college. She was a senior in high school. They have the best love story. At least for now."

Adrian purposely allowed his eyes to focus and stay on Taryn's. He wanted her to imagine what those words could mean; especially for them. He wanted her to think about them beyond now. He wanted their love story to one day be the best one every told. In due time.

"There is always room for improvement on any story," she finally said.

That gave him hope.

"What do you think of the place?" he asked when they entered into the massive open family room.

"I'm thinking that you may have a hard time convincing me to go back to civilization after being here for four days. I love this large open space. I already see that my favorite place to relax will be on this gigantic sectional. I've never seen one this big. Looks like it can seat up to twelve or fourteen people."

"It may. For the next few days, it will be just enough space for me and you to roll around on. Go look around and I'll get the food. Before you offer, don't even think about helping. I want you to relax and let me take care of you for four days. I'm new at doing it. Am I wrong for saying that I believe you are new to being taken care of to the point that you will leave here in the most relaxed state that you've ever been in?"

"Other than my aunt and uncle? No. If you're talking about a man? Never. You are a rare breed, sir. I think I like you," she said and winked at him.

"You already know! I'll be right back."

Adrian sprinted to the truck and looked at the number of boxes and bags of food in the back of the truck. To the left of the food was his briefcase with his laptop. He had no plans of taking it out of the truck unless there was something they needed to search the internet for. He smiled to himself knowing that this side of him that he had never been introduced to was the part of him that he never wanted to let go of again.

19

Taryn woke slowly after the best afternoon nap that she could remember ever having. Perhaps, the reason was that she and Adrian were out on their family's boat, more like a yacht because of the size. She was relaxing on the covered deck in her bright yellow bikini swimsuit. During her nap, he must have covered her with a thin blanket because she didn't remember covering herself.

Sitting up, she looked around to find Adrian relaxed on a chair with his gaze on her. The lake was quiet. The only sound she heard was the soft music playing through the speakers on the yacht. She leaned up further, yawned, though she was well rested and turned her head where her eyes landed on an Adonis-like vision in front of her. Her head was screaming, *"my man, my man, my man."* Adrian was that and then some. It took her some time to come to the realization that she was madly in love with him. The thought had her smiling from ear to ear.

"Have you been sitting their staring at me the whole time I was asleep?" she asked turning around to ace him.

"I would say yes, but that would make me sound like a creep. You in a bikini just made every part of my life worth living."

Taryn sat up and turned her whole body around. She leaned back on her elbows and eyed Adrian from head to toe.

His hairy chest screamed sexy. His physique covered only in black boxer brief swim trunks tantalized her. Her desire for him grew with each passing day. Her love for him surpassed any feeling she thought she would ever have for a man.

"Adrian?"

He raised his sunglasses and locked eyes with her.

"Yes, baby?"

She paused. Finally allowing her mouth to say what her heart has been feeling, she let go of any hesitation or reservation. She was ready.

"I love you, too."

She waited. His response didn't make her wait.

"And I love you."

"I know. I heard you the other night," she admitted.

"What?"

Adrian removed his glasses and placed them on the small table next to him. With mythical Zeus of Mount Olympus, god-like precision, he moved from his chair and moved across the open deck on his hands and knees toward her until his body covered hers. She laid flat on her back and moved her arms to circle his neck as

he aligned his body with hers.

"We were in bed asleep. At first, I thought that I was dreaming. Then I realized what I heard you say. It wasn't a dream, was it? You pulled me close to you, spooning me from behind. I felt you nuzzling my neck. I heard you whisper that you loved me; twice. I wanted to say it. I felt it. Saying the words were hard for me. I lose everyone I love. I knew you meant it. I mean it too. Not just because you said it, but because I know it and I feel it. I love you. I love your love for me."

Adrian lowered his head. When their lips met, this time it was more alluring than ever before. No doubt it was because she finally put her love for him into the atmosphere.

The kiss sent Taryn's body spiraling into a heated haze that showered her entire being. His lips were soft. They loved her lips and then each cheek before he moved down to her neck. She extended her head up to give him the greatest access to her. When his mouth extended down her body toward her breasts, she was ready for anything; including making love with the man she loved right on the deck. When his mouth traveled back up to her lips, she didn't feel disappointed. She felt loved.

"I didn't know you heard me."

"I've heard you whisper it every time since then when you think I'm in a deep sleep, but I wasn't. I loved hearing it."

"We've talked several times about how lonely you've felt in the world. I've wanted to tell you ahead of that night, but I didn't want to scare you with my feelings for you that grew deep very fast. I didn't want to put you off. I wanted you to be ready to hear it knowing that every word that I spoke was true. I remember that first night when I said it. You're right, I thought you were asleep. You had drifted away from me to the other side of the bed. I know how you love being in my arms. It's where I love having you. When I pulled you back to me and held you close, a love so strong and powerful overtook me. I could no longer hold the words in that encompass my feelings for you."

"Do you believe me when I say I love you? I'm not saying it because I know you love me. I truly love you, Adrian. You have filled a part of my life and my heart that I'm not sure I ever saw for myself. Not at this heart-to-heart kind of level of love that I've never experienced. I was scared. Being this vulnerable is new for me. I don't ever want to lose this love I have for you."

"I'm not going anywhere. It's me and you."

"What about when I go back to Paris? I know you've said we can have and survive a long-distance relationship. Do you believe that?"

"Yes, I do. I don't want either of us to question if our love is strong enough. We each have a life and yes, it takes us to two different parts of the world. We will figure it out. Let's not start questioning if what we feel is real enough to get us through what I see as an easy plane ride away. When I told you that I would be anywhere you want or need me to be, it's true. I will miss the hell out of you for sure. Whatever choices you make, you have to make them for you and not for me. I'm promising you that I will be your man here, there and everywhere. I believe that one day, we will be in the same place, loving each other and as far as I'm concerned, married with kids of our own to love. I'm in no rush. If I get to love you, I'm good. If we get to spend quality time together, I'm good. My love is your love. That can be here on this boat, back in the city, in Paris or even on an island in Fiji. Hearing you say you love me is music to my ears."

Taryn nodded. She was unable to speak. A lump had formed in her throat. Unshed tears welled up in her eyes. Even with a threat looming that could ruin it all, she held on to the belief that right now may be all that she was going to get. The words were on her tongue to tell him about Nathaniel and his threats or what she knew was him blackmailing her. She wasn't ready. They were on a lover's getaway. She didn't want to damage their few romantic days away with anything that would change the mood.

"I dread leaving you. I know I have to get back to my life. My aunt's affairs are getting wrapped up faster than I thought. It seems, most of what I thought I would have to do she had already put in place upon her passing. Maybe she knew that her time was coming to an end on this earth."

Adrian stood and pulled her up to her feet.

"I think she didn't want you so worried about details that it would consume you. She wanted you to get back to living as soon as possible while not dwelling on the fact that she would be gone. You'll forever mourn the loss, which I think is healthy; others don't think so. Missing a loved one is not always hard. When you have happy, glowing memories, that's where your focus should be. She wanted that for you. She wanted me for you and you for me. Nothing can come between us."

Taryn's heart hurt at hearing his words. They should make her feel better, but they didn't. She wasn't so sure that nothing could or would come between them. She had a secret.

"Do you ever feel like your life is too perfect? I mean like, we see how people struggle with life, love and relationships every day. Look at where our country is with so much division, yet here we are in this bubble of love, laughter and good living. Some days, I'm afraid to be this happy and content."

"Be as happy as you want to. As for our happiness at a time when others are struggling, we do our part. We give unselfishly in all kinds of ways. You and I have a chance at something remarkable; the kind of love that not everyone experiences. I love you with everything in me. If you ever feel different, let me know. That means I'm not as focused on my woman as I am on everything else in life. Deal?" Adrian asked.

"I still can't believe any of the women you've been involved with haven't gotten you to this point. Have you ever been in love before?"

"Never. That's because none of them were you. Now, how about we go for a swim."

Taryn turned to face him.

"Do you ever spend the night on the boat? I know there's a bedroom below and a full bathroom."

"I have before, yes. Do you want to tonight?"

"I do."

"Consider it done. We can go back to get what we'll need. Then I can lock up the house and notify the local law enforcement that we'll be on the boat all night. We do that so that our location while here is always logged. It's important for safety reasons."

"I can't wait to show you the homes my aunt left me that I'm going to keep. I'm finding that I love what I do when it comes to my career. What matters more to me now is living and loving life."

Adrian hugged her around the waist. She rested her hands on his chest.

"Tonight, when I'm making love to you, don't be shocked by the number of times I say I love you. I don't want to say it only when you're asleep. I want you to hear it, feel it and delight in it when you are wide awake. I'm just saying, I may set some kind of record!" he jested.

"You? Only you? Trust me – now that I am no longer holding back on saying how much I love you, you may find me yelping it into the night air!"

Adrian pulled her by the hand back to the edge of the boat. "More music to my ears, baby!"

In the next second, they took the leap together and splashed into the water. They dunked and splashed each other with pure love. Taryn realized this was her today. She couldn't focus on what may come tomorrow. Her plan was to let the coming days take care of themselves. Especially when it came to Nathaniel. She was afraid, yes. Today, she was in love. That's all she wanted to focus on.

20

"The baby isn't mine."

Adrian barely got out a hello once Melvin walked into this office. He'd just ended a call with his friend and client, Tellum Blackstone. As the lawyer for him and his brothers, Byrum and Callum, he promised them that anytime any of them needed him to work on a legal deal for them, he'd make himself available.

Tellum had just brought him up to date on a new location of an old resort site in Tulum, Mexico that they were looking to buy and refurbish. They were being offered a deal that Tellum believed they couldn't pass up. The previous owner was about to lose the old property in a tax seizure. They needed him to look over some legal documents to be sure the sale could happen and wouldn't come back to haunt the brothers later if things were not as clean and clear as they thought. He'd barely had a chance to breathe in a new breath when Melvin walked in. He'd called from the lobby for a quick meeting. He couldn't turn Melvin away. If he dropped by without an appointment, it had to be important. Now he knew what the impromptu visit was about.

"The baby?" he asked.

"Yes."

"You mean the one you told your wife about that you could have possibly made with another woman? The stripper, correct? The case I've been working on?"

"Yeah, that one. The timing is off by a month by how far along she is. I paid a guy to keep an eye on her. She was tearing into my pockets like you wouldn't believe. Her latest request was for a new apartment right here in the city. Sabrina is reconsidering leaving me. I'm still in the doghouse with her."

"She still has you sleeping in the guestroom?" Adrian chuckled.

When Melvin first told him about the part of their house that he was moved to, he had to scold him again for being so reckless. He had spent more than a few evenings bringing Melvin back from the virtual cliff he found himself on when he came clean with Sabrina.

"When I told her a few days after I talked with you about it, you were right. I didn't want the baby coming out looking like me, especially since all of the kids I have now look just like me."

"Dude, did Sabrina even try? Or your older kids' mother? You are right. I've never seen a bunch of kids who look exactly like their father only. You have strong genes. Close the office door, sit down and tell me what's going on. I'll have Jocelyn pull your file and send it to me. I'm assuming we can pull the supporting documentation and the papers for child support and cancel it all? It's a good thing you haven't signed the papers for that apartment that she wanted you to buy her. You were planning to pay for the first year upfront."

"Can I sue her for the payments I already paid her for the past few months? I mean, it wasn't a lot considering how much I have. But still, I want it back."

Adrian took a pause to ask Jocelyn to bring in the papers he needed and to email him all the electronic files for Melvin's latest extramarital entanglement.

"I'll bring the paper copies in a few minutes. Check your email for the link to his file on the secure network."

"Thanks, Jocelyn."

"I bet you a dime to a dozen that when she saw me she started pulling everything. She's the perfect assistant. One day when she moves beyond you, I'm going to hire her."

Adrian shooed him off.

"You can't afford her. More than an assistant, you need a babysitter; and I'm not talking about for the kids."

"Haha, for me, right? Funny."

"It's clear you need someone around to protect you from yourself."

"Hey, bro. That's what I pay you for."

"No, you pay me to help you clean up after the fact. Tell me what happened so that I can figure out the next step. First, are you sure Sabrina isn't going to divorce you?"

"I'm sure. She came into the guest room last night and told me that she texted me a picture of a new G-Wagon she wants. She'd like it by the weekend. That Benz wagon is hitting my pockets real deep. If she doesn't leave me, I would buy her an island."

"After you buy her the wagon I know you're going to get her, you should think about taking her on a getaway. You need a break from all the temptations here in New York. A client I was just talking with when you came in owns several luxury resorts. I'm talking about top of the line while also being fun. They're all adult only resorts so you'll have to leave the kiddos at home with the nanny. Or you can take them but you'll have to put them up at a hotel off the resort. Take her on a nice getaway vacation and it may get you back into your bedroom. Now, this stripper. Let me hear it."

"I think I'm going to look into that. Sabrina could use a break from the kids. We need to get that spark back."

"You can do that as soon as you learn to keep it in your pants. Spill."

"I paid a guy to keep tabs on her. If she was going to cost me a bucket load of money, I wanted to make sure she wasn't lying about the baby. No doubt she is pregnant. Me being the father is something I needed to know for sure. He found out that she was mixed up with this guy. They thought they were discreet. I told her that I wanted her to show me this apartment she wanted in the city. We agreed to meet there to sign the lease. When she arrived, I brought along a doctor to explain that taking a non-invasive prenatal paternity test would not hurt her or the baby. She has been stringing me along saying she was having a risky pregnancy. I wanted proof. The minute the doctor looked at her, she told me that the pregnancy was probably further along. I offered a lot of money if she went with us to the doctor's office for an exam and a test. She finally came clean and said that the baby probably wasn't mine. It was a scheme cooked up by this guy she was seeing to get money out of me. They scammed me. Perhaps you're right that I need a babysitter. I was with her a few times, I went with the story she told. You know me, like you said, I have a problem keeping it in my pants."

"What do you need from me?"

"I want to sue her for the money I gave her thinking I got her pregnant. I've been paying her on the side for months, from the day she first told me."

Adrian leaned back and shook his head from side to side. It was time to drop some wisdom on his friend who thinks with the wrong part of his body.

"At this point, I think you need to walk away and focus on your family. Do you really want me to take all your dirty laundry to court? What do you think Sabrina will do if everything is aired out publicly? Walk away. Count it as payment toward getting a scammer out of your life. Love on your wife, man. It's going to take a lot for her to trust you again and you know it. Shake it off and move on."

"Well now. Listen to you all full of wisdom and advice about love. I guess your lady love has done a number on you."

"She has and you know what? I wouldn't have it any other way."

"Taryn, right? Man, talk about acquired wealth. Estimates of what her aunt was worth are all over the social media sites."

"Yes. We are in love and that matters more to me than anything. I have money, she has money. That's not an equation we focus on."

"In other words, she can buy you dinner and take you on nice trips," Melvin joked.

"She could, but I would never let her. I'm old school, my brother. I am my father's son. He raised me to take care of my lady. I will support any and everything she wants to pursue. I will protect her. I will love her. Too many people make things about money. I just want to love her. She knows that. What we have works."

"Sounds like it works well. I'm learning a lot from you. I hope to meet this wonderful woman of yours one day. Do you mind giving me information about the resort you spoke about?"

"I'll do you one better. I'm going to put you in direct contact with Tellum Blackstone. He's a big-time sports guy. He knows who you are. I'll text you his private contact information. Don't give it to anyone. I'll let him know you'll reach out. Take care of your wife. Stop all this playing around. If she gives you another chance, take it. I have discovered how good life can be with the love from one good woman."

"This coming from a man who didn't pass up a sexy woman, ever. I can remember you having a new beauty on your arm with each new week."

"Taryn is the beginning and the ending for me. She's the full package. There is no reason for me to ever turn my head in the direction of another woman. When I say she checks all the boxes, I mean that."

Melvin stood and walked toward his office door.

"I hear you and I understand. I like this new, in love Adrian Jarreau. I appreciate you always having my back. You work hard to keep me on my toes. I'm listening. This latest indiscretion has me listening. I hear you loud and very clear."

"That's what I like to hear. I'll go over the paperwork to prepare a document for this woman to sign, absolving you from all responsibility for her and her baby. This will be the last one?"

"Scouts honor!" Melvin cheered before leaving the office.

"You weren't even a boy scout," Adrian hollered to his back as he hustled down the hallway.

Jocelyn came into his office as soon as he was alone.

"What do you need from me?" she asked as she typed away on her iPad.

"We need to close out his file; at least for now. Something tells me he'll be back here before too long with another issue. Let me take a quick look at everything and I'll send you what I need you to do."

"Sounds good. You're heading out soon?"

"Maybe not."

"Maybe so. You were going to see your mother before heading home early. You mentioned doing some work from home, possibly with Taryn close by? You purposely had me move some things around so that you had a free evening. I love that I've been doing that a lot lately. Should I call your mother or Taryn to let them know you may be tied up?"

That was the last thing he wanted.

"No need. Since you've already cleared my calendar, I'll keep my original plans."

"Good. Do you want me to order something for you and Taryn to have for dinner?"

Adrian rounded his desk and sat down, taking out his phone to send Melvin the information he promised. He'd reach out to Tellum and his final call would be to get what he needed for his dinner plans at his place for later in the evening. He was moving away from any help in planning a night for his woman.

"No, I have it all taken care of."

"You sure?"

He smiled over at her seeing the shock on her face.

"Surprised?" he asked.

"Of course. I know you've been doing everything yourself lately when it comes to her. I'm happy about it. This new you has grown on me. I love seeing you in love."

"I love being in love. Feel free to take the rest of the afternoon off. I know you could use some downtime."

"You sure?"

"My one and only offer! I'm in a great mood today," he declared.

"I'm already gone. Have a good night!"

Adrian leaned back and crossed his legs up on his desk. "I plan to."

**

"When are you coming back? This hotel in Las Vegas isn't going to pay for itself. You should have let me go to New York with you. She hasn't given you the money yet? I thought you said it would be easy money in the bag. You've been gone a month."

Nathaniel wore a path on the hardwood floors of his New York apartment. By now, he had hoped he'd have money wired to his account from Taryn. Even though she was doing a good job of ignoring his calls, he knew she listened to his messages. His threats were clear. The only reason he was still in New York was because of the big pay day he was hoping for. There was no way Taryn's aunt had died and not left all her wealth to her niece. He only needed to wear her down until she gave in. With his mother no longer a source for his expensive lifestyle, the timing was perfect to have his next big pay day, thanks to Taryn and their time together back in college.

"I told you I'm working on it. I'm close to getting it. You calling five times every day isn't going to make it happen any faster. The suite is paid for. I may be running out of money but it's not all gone yet. Besides, they know I'm good for it. My name alone carries weight."

"Oh? I tried to get an advance at the casino to play and they denied me. I gave them your name. I was still told that I needed to front the money to play. I'm getting tired of being here by myself. I'm lonely. I miss you."

Taylor was working his last nerve. Did she really think that they were more than just two people bumping uglies? It was all about the physical for him. At this point, he was tired of her augmented body parts. Anyone could buy them. Being back in New York and seeing Taryn and her natural body parts accentuated in all its perfection had him still desiring her. He always had since back in their college days when they were a couple. He'd tried several times over the years to win back her affection, yet, to no avail. If she didn't want him, that was fine with him. He had leverage that would at least have her paying to get rid of his presence in her life.

"Be patient. I'll be back in a few days."

Nathaniel smiled to himself. He loved playing women for what he needed from them. Little did Taylor know that he wouldn't be returning to Vegas. In a few days when he had his money from Taryn, that he was sure she was going to give him, he would change his cell phone number yet again only to disappear so that Taylor would not be able to find him. He was glad he never told her where his apartment was in Manhattan. He may not be the son of the year, but his parents made sure he always had a place to live. That's why they always kept the bills paid on his apartment.

What he needed to do was to confront Taryn face-to-face since his calls went unanswered. It wasn't as if he wasn't aware of where she was staying. What angered him was that it appears that she's in a relationship.

He was planning on seeing her over a week ago and ended up on the street of her apartment building. As he was making his way toward the entrance, he saw her get out of a large sleek black SUV. She was smiling and giggling when the driver came around, lifted her up and kissed her like they were long time lovers. She was smiling like he's never seen from her before. He stood still and watched like he was an obsessed stalker. Maybe he was. Out of nowhere, jealousy hit him on a level he'd never experienced before. He knew Taryn had dated and been intimately involved since they broke up years ago. Still, he'd never had a front seat to her locking lips with anyone.

Moving close to the wall of the building next to the apartment, he lightly smashed his fist against the black and gray marbled building. He saw fire. He didn't want to see Taryn happy and possibly in love. He wanted her afraid and solemn that he may be able to ruin her life. Knowing that perhaps now wasn't the time to confront her, he decided to wait.

Before he turned and walked away, there was something familiar about the man. It took him a few minutes of watching them for him to remember where he knew him from. It was the funeral. He was the man that from his place in the back of the church, he saw Taryn turn her head to look at that same man quite a few times during the cemetery. He hadn't thought much about it until seeing them together now. Before turning, he thought of a new plan to get the money from Taryn or at least get her to return his call and then give him the money he wanted. He still had an ace in the hole to have her bowing to his will. Perhaps, he could even get one more roll in the hay from her. She was young when they hooked up. The way she was kissing on the street, he could imagine her behind closed doors these days. He'd love to find out.

"I'll see you soon, Taryn. Real soon," he said to himself before turning and going back the way he'd come. He would return soon. First, he needed to find out more about the man she was now involved with. One he knew was he'd also seen his face before. There was a billboard in Times Square that he remembered seeing before. Her latest boyfriend was a major presence in the legal world. It seems, not only was she hitting it big from her aunt, which was always the case but more so now that she has more money, but she was also connected to a powerhouse. The idea of bringing down her house and maybe his too could possibly get him the money he was demanding from her. Perhaps, even more than his original request.

Nathaniel's sinister laugh echoed behind him as he turned the corner. He'd be back real soon.

21

"How is getting the apartment on the market going?"

Taryn exhaled loudly so that Julianna could hear how tired she was just from walking the New York street and worry about the apartment. She was less than a block from it. She was more than ready to go inside to out of her heels. She was making great time after getting off of the train – something she hadn't done since being back in New York. There was a time that her aunt had to bribe her to stop taking the subway everywhere and instead take a car service. Now and even then, she found it hard to explain her love for the subway. She loved being able to get everywhere just by taking a trip down the subway stairs. There were times, unlike today, when she didn't even have a destination in mind. She just sat back and watched the sights.

Today, she spent time at the bank going through the contents of her aunt's safety deposit box. She was surprised she still had the box. She found keepsakes that her aunt had collected over the years. She decided to leave everything inside. She would revisit what to do with everything later. After a few more stops of her busy day, she was finally heading back. Julianna called just as she had exited the subway platform.

"Let's just say that I accomplished all that was on my to-do list for today."

"Are you making it to the end of your list? I know most of the apartment is empty. Have you decided if you're going to get a smaller place for when you visit New York or is your plan to stay with Adrian when you come to town? I take it things are still going great?"

Taryn felt a shrill of excitement sear through her body at the mention of his name. The struggle to one day leave and go back to her life in Paris was real. She had a reason to second-guess leaving and his name was Adrian Jarreau.

"I don't know what I'm doing yet."

"Have you thought about a timeframe for leaving? I keep asking and you haven't said anything yet."

Taryn nibbled on her bottom lip as she hustled through the busy foot traffic on the sidewalk.

"I don't know yet. Most of what I needed to take care of while here has been done. I can certainly take care of other things from Paris. I must eventually get back to my life there. My only issue is this time with Adrian. It's been everything."

"I'm happy for you. I love seeing and hearing you smile. Don't even think of asking how I can hear you smile; I just can. Anything else going on? You know what I'm talking about?"

Just like that, in an instant, Taryn lost her smile.

"The calls are getting more persistent and demanding. I don't know what to do at this point. I don't want to see him."

"See who?"

Taryn jumped when a familiar voice spoke from behind her. She knew who it was. When reality set in, she almost tripped over her own feet, but he caught her before that happened. She turned her head as she pushed away from the way he was embracing her knowing he would say he was rescuing her. The idea sickened her. So did him touching her in any way.

"Nathaniel, what are you doing here?" she questioned.

"Nathaniel? He's there? Where? At your building?" Julianna pressed from the other end of the phone.

Taryn didn't say anything else.

"I've been waiting to talk to you. Do you know how crazy people think you are just standing on a New York street? You would think they would mind their business. You look beautiful. I've been trying to reach you. I see your phone does work," he said.

"Don't you dare hang up. Keep walking and go into your building. You don't need to talk to him."

"I'm okay, Jules."

"Oh, that's Jules? Tell her I said what's up. I saw her at the funeral and she acted like I had the plague or something."

"Tell him that's exactly what I think when I think about him. No, don't say that. Just walk away. Or, keep the phone on so that I can hear the conversation. If he bothers you, scream!" Julianna yelled.

Taryn did just that. She didn't disconnect the call. Instead, she lowered the phone and held her own against Nathaniel.

"I've ignored your calls for a reason; it's clear I don't want to speak to you."

"Why? You don't care about your image? What about that of your lawyer boyfriend? I expected more from you. We have history. Didn't I warrant even one phone call? What about one thanking me for being supportive by coming to the funeral? Nothing? Nothing at all? Okay, bet. We're here now, so we may as well talk. All you have to do is go along with my proposal and you'll never hear from me again. Well, unless you want to. We used to have a pretty tight connection. I have a video to prove it."

Taryn felt sick to her stomach.

"What do you want? I don't have time to stand here and go back and forth with you."

"You got my messages. You already know what I want. You can leave and go inside your building if you want to. I get it. You don't want to be reminded of your past but that's exactly what happens any time you hear from me or see me. I'm right, huh?"

"No, you're not. It's hard to not when you're standing here outside of my building. This is stalk-ish behavior."

"What? We're just two old friends having a friendly conversation. I would hate to have to keep coming here. Maybe next time I'll see you with your boyfriend like I did a week ago. The two of you were all over each other right here on the street. Looked like you were coming back from a trip or something because he took luggage inside of the building for you. The two of you looked quite intimate. Can I meet him?"

When he leaned over and asked that question right into her ear, Taryn moved further away. She looked around nervously to see if anyone was watching them. The last thing she wanted was to be any closer to him than she was. She could smell alcohol. His eyes showed something else; that he was most likely high as well. She didn't want to talk to him in this condition. One of the reasons they split so many years ago was because of his proclivity for drugs and alcohol at an extremely large amount of usage.

"How dare you show up here? I'm not giving you any money. Stop calling me. Do not come by here anymore."

With smugness that she wished she could forget she ever knew about, he smiled in a way that frightened her. Standing up to him wasn't working; that was clear.

"What would you high profile boyfriend think of your past?"

"You're drunk or possibly high. Go get yourself cleaned up," she admonished.

"Does he know that back in the day you used to indulge with me in a few things like drinking and smoking weed? Oh, and of course, there is all the things we did on the video that I still have. We were something back then. You were such a stuck-up princess back then. You still are extraordinarily beautiful; that's for damn sure."

"Leave Adrian out of this!"

"Oh, sweetness, I can't do that. You have been ignoring me and casting me to the side like I'm a piece of gum on the bottom of your shoe. I'm tired of it. What I'm asking you for is nothing compared to what I know you have. I'm only asking for a little bit of it."

"I'm not giving you anything! Not one red penny."

"Keep trying that and see where it gets you. I think I'll make an appointment with your boyfriend tomorrow at his law firm. We have some things to talk about; maybe even compare a few notes," Nathaniel chuckled.

Taryn didn't like the sound of that. If she knew anything about Nathaniel, he would absolutely do just that.

"Stay away from him."

"Then do what I asked and we're done. I'll give you two days. That's it. If you don't come around to your senses, I'll give him an ear and eyeful of who he's involved with."

"He won't care."

"Well, keep ignoring me and we'll find out. Two days, Taryn. I'll be back in two days."

Before she could come back with a retort, Nathaniel jogged across the street and headed away from her and her building. She was glad that Adrian was still at his office and didn't come upon them talking outside the building. Nathaniel would be hard to explain to him.

Just then she remembered Julianna was still on the phone. She could hear her screaming her name. Putting the phone back up to her ear, she hustled inside of the building, ignoring the concierge at the desk. She needed a space where no one could see or hear her.

"Are you alright?" Julianna asked.

As soon as the elevator door opened, Taryn hopped in and breathed a long breath while she paced around the small space.

"Did you hear all of that?"

"I did. Don't tell me you're considering giving him money?"

"What am I going to do? What if after two days, he goes to see Adrian? Oh, my goodness, I wouldn't be able to look at Adrian again after Nathaniel confronts him. What am I going to do?"

"Well, not give him the money, for starters. Second, talk to Adrian. I know he'll understand. Who didn't do stupid things back in our college days? You were young, rebellious and trying all kinds of things. You didn't do anything we all didn't do."

"Oh? Did you record a sex tape with your boyfriend and then let him keep it?"

"Well, no. I didn't do that, but you were young. Adrian went to college at an HBCU, pledged a fraternity and played sports. I'm sure he has done a video or two himself. We don't know. He may understand."

"He won't understand. I need to leave New York. I have to go. I can't think here. I have Nathaniel breathing down my neck. I want to love all over Adrian but then with this hanging over my head I feel like I'm keeping something from him. When I look into those brown eyes, I'm being dishonest by not sharing this with him. Nathaniel is just vile for what he's trying to do. Who keeps a video all these years? Why would he do that?"

"You didn't know he had it?"

"I remember making it. We were both drunk that night in his apartment. We just did it. He wanted to watch it later. By morning, after the alcohol and the high from the night before, I forgot all about it. I really assumed he would delete it after he watched it. I had no idea he would keep it and try to use it to blackmail me. He must be in a bad place."

Taryn entered the apartment and went straight to her old room, one of the few places that still had furniture. She and the realtor still needed to meet to talk about staging the apartment. For now, she needed to get out of town.

"I wish you wouldn't make a rash decision like just up and running back to Paris. You have a good man that you're in love with. Give him the benefit of the doubt that he will help you and not hold it against you. I don't want to see you do this to yourself. What will you tell Adrian? Surely, he's not expecting you to just up and leave. When are you thinking of going? I wish you wouldn't. Please don't do this."

"I need to think, Jules. I can't do that here. As soon as we are off the phone, I'm going to make arrangements to fly out tomorrow."

"You're not even going to see or talk to Adrian?"

Taryn was so confused. More than that, she was afraid of what Adrian would think and see in her if he found out. She didn't know what would happen if she didn't give Nathaniel the money. If he released the video on the internet, her connection to Adrian could hurt him and his business. She would never be able to live with herself. She needed time away to think. She needed to get back to Paris.

"I'm seeing him tonight. I'll tell him that I'm done with things here and that I'm needed back at the office. He knows I have to get back to my life. We have already talked about having a long-distance relationship. He's onboard for that. I'll tell Nathaniel that I need a little more time. It's a lot of money that would have to be moved. That should bide me some time to think of how to approach this with Adrian or even if I'm going to do that. He doesn't deserve to have his life turned upside down because I was once stupid enough to be involved with someone like Nathaniel."

"Please reconsider. Didn't you say Sherita was coming into town tomorrow evening? This departure looks and is abrupt. It's drastic and over the top. You're a critical thinker. Let's talk and figure this out. I can fly to New York and be with you when you tell Adrian. All you have to do is say the word and I'm on the next flight from Los Angeles to New York."

"No, Jules. I don't want you involved in this. Just let me get home and back to work. I'll think through this. I don't want to chance Nathaniel showing up at the apartment again. He may not know that Adrian lives here too. I don't want him running into him. He knows what Adrian looks like. That would devastate me. If I'm not here, he won't pop up. Just let me do this."

"You're going to leave Adrian just like that. There is no planning, no warning, no discussion, no nothing. You just turn into a puff of smoke."

"I know it sounds crazy. I need to buy some time. Going home is the only way to do that. Trust me, okay? I'll spend my night with Adrian and let him know that I'll be leaving tomorrow. He'll be shocked but I'll come up with something. This is best for me and for him. I don't give two shakes about Nathaniel. I wish he would crawl back into the hole he crawled out of. I promise it will be okay. I'll call you tomorrow? Please support me with this. Please?" Taryn begged.

After a round of loud huffs and puffs, Julianna finally agreed.

With the call ended, she raced around the room and started packing what she would take with her. With Sherita coming to town, another person she needed to tell a lie to in order to explain her sudden departure, she could have her pack up the rest of her things and send them to her. Her biggest concern was how she would handle Adrian. She didn't want to leave him yet. She wasn't ready. Still, she knew it had to be done. They would have this night together. She wanted to love all over him like never before. It may be some time before they saw each other again. If he meant what he said, they would survive long distance. She needed to know and hoped beyond hope that there could be a resolution that got Nathaniel off of her back while keeping the man she loved in her life. She had some planning to do. First up were flight arrangements. Then she would prepare for her romantic dinner and night with Adrian. This wouldn't be an end. It would be a pause until she got her life together. She needed some time to do that.

**

"You're what?" Adrian pressed for the second time in the past five minutes.

His eyes followed Taryn as she got out of bed to grab a bottle of water from the beverage fridge built into the entertainment center in his bedroom.

Hearing her say that she was leaving to go back to Paris took him by surprise. The idea of it came up in several conversations but this is the first time he noticed that she was uncomfortable telling him.

"Do you want a bottle?" she asked him.

"Really? You dropped this bomb and your first question is if I want a bottle of water? Taryn, what's going on?"

He sat up and swung his legs over the side of the bed, turning toward her where she moved to kneel on the long bench at the foot of the California King bed after grabbing one of his t-shirts to cover her body. They had just spent the last hour making love after an evening of quiet after a long week of them both being busy a little over a week after returning from their time at the lake. This was not the conversation he expected they would have. She looked up at him with a sad face. This wasn't a simple chat about her going home. Something was going on. He needed to know what.

"Don't be mad, please," she pleaded.

"Baby, I'm not mad. What I am is confused. I knew the day would be coming, but how you just dropped this is wild. Talk to me."

"We knew that I would have to go back to my life."

"I know. Long distance and all. I know."

"Do you still believe that?"

"Of course I do. I love you."

"I know this seems sudden."

"Taryn, we spent this entire evening cooking, talking, relaxing, making plans for a trip to the Hollywood Bowl in Los Angeles. Let's not forget about the house your aunt left you that's in Ocean City that you wanted to go check out. Amongst a few other things we talked about, you seemed ready to do some of those things. Not once did you say that any of that had to change. When are you leaving?"

When Taryn hesitated, Adrian braced himself for her response. He was trying not to be upset that they are having this conversation pretty much in the middle of the night after passion that was off the charts had just happened.

"Tomorrow."

That one word. He wanted to pinch himself to see if he was dreaming. He wasn't.

"Tomorrow? And you're just telling me? Did you not know this when you arrived? A few days ago? When we were away?"

"There are some things that have come up at work that I need to get back to. I didn't find out about it until earlier today. I've been trying to come up with how and when to tell you. Since I'm leaving in the morning, that time is now. I didn't want to ruin the romantic atmosphere of the night."

"What was that? Was that you saying goodbye to me? I thought you never wanted to say goodbye. We have had several talks about our relationship. Even when you wanted to walk away because you thought things may not work because of the fear you have around losing everyone you care about and love. You once told me that you weren't sure you could promise me that you would give our love a try. You were afraid. I promised you that I would be here no matter what. You said no when I asked you to promise me that you would try. Still, you did. We collectively fell in love and dared anything to come between us. You gave me your heart; I gave you mine. The way you made love to me just now was out of this world. Not that our sex life has been less than stellar before tonight, but there was something different about it. Was this your way of sharing our last night and making sure it was memorable?"

Taryn crawled across the bed and wrapped her arms around his neck. She maneuvered her body behind his with her legs on either side of his. With her head laid on his back, her arms around his chest, he held on to her hands and leaned his head back until it rested on the top of hers.

"This is not goodbye, by no means at all. The way I love you could never have me walking away from you."

"I feel like you're running."

"From you? Never."

"From something else?"

"Babe, no. I just need to go back."

"Taryn, I am aware of that. I assumed we would have talked through what this would look like with more time before you actually left. But hours?"

"I don't want to be away from you."

"Okay. All of your business here is taken care of? Is there anything you need me to do after you leave?"

"No. Just keep loving me. I'll be back soon."

"Or I'll be in Paris soon. I don't want you spending a lot of time flying back and forth. Leave that to me. I'm sad you're going."

"You're sure nothing is wrong? We're good."

"We're perfect. The sooner I go, the sooner I can get back here to you to do the things we are planning. I still want to go to the show at the Hollywood Bowl. If I'm in Paris, I can fly and meet you in Los Angeles. I just need some time to handle some business. I've been away a little longer than I had planned. Who knew I would fall in love and find my greatest joy in life in your arms? I certainly didn't but I did. That means you are stuck with me. Can you not be upset with me for springing this on you like this?"

Knowing that this day would come, he relaxed his body and trusted her words. Reaching around, he pulled Taryn around until she straddled his lap. If he was only going to get a few more hours with her until he'd have to miss her presence like crazy, he was going to make sure he loved her enough tonight to last them until they saw each other again. Something unsettling was still in the space between them. He would allow her to do what she needed to do. Hopefully, whatever the real situation was, she would feel comfortable enough to share that with him.

He pulled the t-shirt up and off of her body, tossing it to the bedroom floor. The way his lips were feigning for hers, he didn't want any tension between them with her leaving. He only wanted to love on her. He didn't answer her with words. He let his body, especially his lips speak for him.

Raising her chin so that their lips were aligned, he took her lips in a fiery kiss that melded not just their lips and tongue, but their hearts and minds. Taryn's arms circled his neck as she moaned her please into his mouth the minute he used his tongue to part her lips for his salacious entry.

"I love you," he muttered against her lips, adding his over sizzling groan of pleasure. "I'm going to miss you like crazy," he added. "Just remember, if you need me, a call is all I need and I'm there."

Adrian turned their bodies so that Taryn was flat on the bed, his body covering hers. The only thing on his mind was loving her and giving them their fill until only sleep could keep them away from each other.

With the room in total darkness and him preparing for another hour of titillating loving, Adrian was consumed with becoming one with her. What he didn't see were the tears that flowed from her eyes.

22

Three weeks after Taryn abruptly left New York and him, Adrian was in a horrible mood. Walking with heavy, determined footsteps toward his office, there was no doubt that his mood was evident to everyone he passed by. The quiet atmosphere was evident when the usual lively banter would cover the air around the open office area wasn't in full effect. Today was not the day for him to stop and talk to anyone.

The plan for the day was to spend it in his office going over the new cases he needed to assign along with reviewing applications. To say he wasn't faring well with Taryn gone would be an understatement. His call with her last night didn't help any. It wasn't that he didn't enjoy each and every phone conversation. The evening before was off. Taryn wasn't herself. He'd picked on that right away.

Entering his office, he went straight to his desk, tossing his brown leather backpack on top of it.

"I hope there wasn't anything valuable or sensitive inside of that bag. You crashed that thing down like you're mad at the world."

Startled by Zac's voice, he tossed up his middle finger behind his back.

"Zac, why are you stalking me this early in the morning?"

"I had to come check out the office gossip about your moodiness lately. What the hell has you in a stink?"

"What?"

"I mean, is there something other than Taryn leaving a few weeks ago?"

"Ugh, man – I cannot believe the level to which Taryn has gotten under my skin. You know I have never had a woman with this kind of impact on me."

"It's called, being in love, my brother. You've never been in love before; at least not like this. You are known for being in lust," Zac declared humorously.

"Don't act like that title isn't bestowed on you as well. We both had a lust for beautiful women."

Zac pointed at him.

"See? That's what I'm talking about."

"What?" Adrian questioned.

"You said, had. You didn't say have. Not that you don't lust for Taryn because, goodness, a man from mars could see that. Anyone around the two of you for more than a few seconds can feel the heat. Lust and love? You are done, Adrian. There is nothing wrong with that."

"Is that so? What about you and Sherita? I walked in on the two of you in your office the other night. If I hadn't, you would have been deep. First of all, does Taryn know?"

"Absolutely not. You better not clue her in either. We swore to secrecy that you wouldn't say anything. Sherita was already embarrassed enough."

Adrian chortled loudly.

"Embarrassed is not the word to describe the vibe I got from what I was seeing in her."

"True, true," Zac said, swiping down his long, full growing beard.

"See? Don't talk about me.

"Whew! I'm really feeling Sherita. It's a good thing you locked my office door on your way out that night. At first, Sherita thought you would go right home and call her cousin. I assured her that you wouldn't do that. We have a code between each other. She said she and Taryn had sort of the same kind of code."

"She still hasn't told Taryn about the two of you? About how you hooked up after that gala I gave her Taryn's ticket to?"

"No. The same way that you are shocked at how fast Taryn left New York? It's been bothering Sherita too."

"What did she say?"

"She was surprised to get a call from Taryn saying she was leaving that day."

"Hold on a second. Taryn didn't tell Sherita until the day she left?"

"That's what she told me. She'd gone back home but had plans to return the weekend to have another meeting with the realtor about the apartment. When they talked, Taryn asked Sherita to do her a favor and meet with the realtor alone because she had to get back home to Paris. She asked Taryn if there was an emergency or something. All she said was there was something that couldn't wait. Her leaving came out of left field. She was planning on telling her about us when she came back to town. The next week is when you walked in on us in my office. Sherita is certain that something is troubling Taryn but she can't get it out of her. What is she saying to you?"

Adrian stood and paced around his office. He walked over to the large window overlooking New York City. He was now aware that the feelings he'd been experiencing that Taryn was keeping something from him were not just about him missing her.

"Nothing that would allude to what's really going on. I wanted to take her to the airport. She wouldn't let me. She said she hates goodbyes at the airport. Man, she was already packed and ready to go. I was shocked as hell. I don't even know when she booked the flight. I've been in a bad mood ever since. I'll apologize to the staff. I've been a grumpy ass bear for no reason."

"No, there's a good reason. There is something going on with your woman and you haven't unlocked the key to the situation. Maybe it's time you took a trip to Paris."

His grin told Zac that they were already on the same page.

"You're preaching to the choir. I've got a few things to do but then I'm on a flight out of here. Can you hold down the fort until I get back? I should only be gone a few days. She didn't leave here because she had planned to. Something sent or pulled her away from me and sent her rushing back to Paris."

"You're about to do exactly what I expect that you would do. I'm not sure what's taken you so long to take that flight. I'm glad you are."

"Last night."

"What about last night?" Zac asked.

"We talked for over an hour. There was a sadness to her voice that broke me. She tried to hide it but I felt it through the phone. I don't know what happened on that last day here in New York, but it was something. The trip to the Hollywood Bowl that we were planning to take?"

"Yeah?"

"I bought a ring."

"What?" Zac pretty much shouted.

"I showed it to my parents. I was planning on a lavish proposal. I was going to rent us a beach house in Malibu and have it decorated while we were at the show. I want to marry her. I'm hoping she feels the same way. Things pivoted for us that last day. I need to know why. I need to know if she sees a future with me like I see one with her. First, I need her to trust me with any and everything. That's why I'm flying to Paris. She has to trust me."

"Good for you, brother!"

"Thanks, man. I appreciate it. I'll keep you posted on that front. For now, I need to see what's bothering my lady. You sure you're good around here?"

"Please. Stop playing with me with that. Can you take a look at the stack of new potential hires while on your flight? I can handle everything else. My choices are first on the list in your email. Let me know if you agree and if you see a few other potentials. Also, the partnership and mentorship list of companies, celebrities, athletes, etc., are also in your email. We talked about rolling that out with a big kickoff at the Marriott Marquis. I need to get the team on putting those plans in place. Pairing up high school and college students with mentors is a way of guaranteeing that we're doing our part to bring up the next generation of power men and women in business."

"Consider it done. The flight is long enough that I'll email you my recommendations before I land. You know, you and Sherita need to tell Taryn you're seeing each other, unless it's not serious."

Zac held up a hand to stop him from saying anything else.

"Oh, it's pretty serious. We're going to Atlantic City to see Gary Owen live at Harrah's for an overnight trip. You know I don't do trips with women. I'm not in love, but I definitely looking forward to heading down that path like you have. Sherita is an amazing woman. At the gala that night, I thought I was being creepy spending the entire night getting to know her and monopolizing her time. She was refreshing. When I kissed her at the end of the night, I saw stars. Can you believe after years of playing the field that you and I not only have connected with incredible women, but they are also related? Look, I will talk with Sherita about that. If it comes up between you and Taryn, you can tell her. It's not a secret. She'll find out regardless. I'm sure Sherita will be fine with it. For now, handle whatever you need to handle for and with your woman. I'm holding down the fort. Besides, our dads are both here this week for two high-profile clients they clinched from another law firm who only want to work with them."

"I'm glad they agreed to stay connected to the firm after they retired. We get a lot of business because of their track record; especially older, established clients."

"You got that right," Zac declared. "Now, get out there and apologize to your team, Scrooge," Zac laughed.

"Yeah, yeah. I got you."

23

Adrian walked into the lobby of the publishing house where Taryn worked. Unfortunately, they had never talked about exactly where she lived. It was just after noon, so he assumed he would find her at work. Finding her here would have to suffice if he wanted to surprise her.

Standing in the center of the large three-level lobby, he looked around for the direction he should go in. Before he took a step, a large, voluminous yawn overtook him. What he should have done was catch up on some sleep on the flight to Paris. Instead, he focused on reviewing some of the cases of the law firm's junior associates. He had started with the ones that were coming up within the next few months. He and Zac agreed that he would focus on them while Zac held things down at the firm until he returned from checking on Taryn.

Gathering himself, he walked up to the security desk and waited behind two others. Once it was his turn, he watched one female security officer adjust her position while licking her lips at the same time. In the not-so-distant past, he would have found that move interesting. Being in love with Taryn, no woman could ever distract him from her. Before she could greet him, the male guard stepped up to him ahead of her and garnered his attention.

"How can I help you, sir?" he asked.

"I'm hoping you can help me. I'm here to see Taryn Novak."

"Do you have an appointment?"

"No, I don't. I can see from the level of security here that I should have an appointment and not an impromptu visit. If she's here, I'm sure she'll see me."

The guard looked down at the large overnight bag he sat next to his feet. His eyes then landed on the large backpack over his shoulder.

"You're a guest. From the United States?"

"Yes, I am. I just landed. I'm hoping she's here. Could you perhaps give her a call? My name is Adrian Jarreau."

"Adrian?"

Hearing his name, he turned and his eyes landed on the woman of the hour. Taryn was standing near the elevator with her arm full of papers and the iPad that she rarely let out of her sight. She looked like she was on her way to a meeting. He was in the presence of his love again.

His heart melted as the surprise look on her face turned first to recognition that he was actually here and to sheer delight as a smile, brighter than any he'd ever seen before, graced her face.

"Hi, baby!" he declared loudly.

Before he could move in her direction, she shocked him by dropping all the papers in the floor before racing toward him at full speed in high-heels. With her in his arms, he inhaled her sweet peach and vanilla scent. She always smelled good.

After a quick kiss, because they were in the middle of the lobby, he placed her back on her feet. He laughed when Taryn touched his chest, his arms, his hands and then caressed his face

"You're really here. I thought you were a dream when I first walked out of the stairwell. Took me a few seconds to realize you were standing here in the lobby of my building."

"I'm glad I could shock and surprise you at the same time."

"Ms. Novack, your papers?" the female guard said, handing over the items Taryn had dropped in the floor and cared nothing about.

"Oh, thank you. I am so sorry. I completely dismissed these, didn't I?" she noted, taking everything in her arms.

The woman leaned over close to Taryn's ear, but he still heard her.

"No apology necessary. I completely understand," she said.

"Um, this is my boyfriend, Adrian Jarreau. Can you get him a visitor's badge please? We're going to go up to my office. Let me call Cordell to tell him to stall the meeting I was heading to after grabbing a snack. For some reason, I now do not need a snack. I have you here!"

"One boyfriend snack, present and accounted for," he said and saluted her like a soldier.

"You are so silly. You're here. In Paris."

"I am. Happy to see me?"

Smiling at her with all of his teeth, he held back from kissing her bright, beautiful smile.

"You are the breath of fresh air I needed this morning.

"Nice office. I see as a senior editor, you are living good up in here – up in here!" Adrian quipped.

Together they laughed heartily once Taryn understood the meaning behind what he said and how he said it.

"Good one. I got that. They treat me well here."

Taryn looked away, her eyes darting away from his. Before she did, he was able to capture a sadness in them.

He moved and took a seat at the round conference table in the center of the room.

"Something's wrong," he whispered.

Her office door was still open. He didn't want to draw anyone's attention to their conversation. That short statement got her attention. She moved to the edge of her desk and faced him.

"I love you and I love that you're here. Are you okay or were you just missing me like I've missed you."

"Of course I missed you. That's not the only reason that I'm here."

"Okay, then what's wrong," she asked.

He was making her nervous.

"Baby, close the door and come here."

As soon as she shut the door, she walked with ease over to him where he made room for her on his lap. Sitting sideways, she leaned into his neck and relaxed.

"What's wrong?" she asked again.

"You tell me."

"I don't understand."

"Taryn, something is wrong. Whatever it is, you're keeping it from me. Whatever it is, it shows on your face. It's been in your voice with every call we've had since you left."

She sat up and caught his eyes.

"What are you talking about?"

"You're going to make me lay it all out for you?"

"Adrian."

"Don't Adrian me. A few days ago, during our video chat, you were happy to be talking to me but you were distracted.

Whatever was taking your thoughts away from me wasn't a good thing. I'm here because during our last chat, you seemed unhappy. Something is weighing on you. I want to talk about it. I share everything with you. Is there something that I'm not doing right that makes you hesitant in talking to me?"

"Okay, something is going on that I've been keeping from you. It's not that I am hiding something from you as if you wouldn't listen to what it was without judgement. I fear that once you hear it, you may look at me different."

"Never, baby. Never, ever. When you look into my eyes, you will always find the deepest, most passionate form of love that a man could have for a woman. That will never change. I've wanted you for too long to lose any part of what we've come to be. Talk to me."

Taryn exhaled loudly, turned her body to face him.

"I'll tell you what – how long are you staying here?"

"Today and through tomorrow night. After that, I have an early flight out. I have an important client flying in to meet with me in person. In fact, I brought that case and a stack of others that I was focused on while I was in the air. I don't want to take you away from work. I figured that I could work from my hotel while you're at work during the day and the evenings and nights would be all about us."

He was about to continue until Taryn quickly stood.

"Hotel? You booked a hotel room?"

"Well, clearly that wasn't the right thing to do. I didn't want to just invade your space since my visit wasn't planned."

"You are certifiable," she laughed.

"What?" he laughed.

"Okay, well, if you have a hotel room – a suite, I assume?"

"Yes."

"Then I'll need to go home and pack an overnight bag to stay with you while you're here."

"Wait, what? But you have..."

"What? My own place? *Exactly.* See where your mind went? What makes you think I want to sleep away from you considering you're only here a few days? Nonsense, Adrian. Don't play with me. Now, you could cancel your suite and just stay with me; the way it's *supposed* to be. Feel free to use the phone on my desk to cancel your reservation."

He pulled out his phone and sent a text to Jocelyn to cancel the reservation she made for him. That only took a few seconds.

"Done."

Taryn walked over to closet in her office and pulled out her purse. She walked back over to him with a set of keys in her hand.

"You are never to come to Paris and think you're not going to bring all of you to me day and night. No hotels unless I'm staying there with you!"

He pulled her body between his legs and held her there.

"I hear you, my lady."

"Good. Here is the key to my place. It's not too, too far, but you should still take a car service. I'll have one of the cars from my company take you there. I'll text you the code for the door. You'll need that along with the key. You can get all of your work done. I have three more meetings today and then I'm all yours. There is a lasagna I made last night in the fridge along with a freshly made salad and some garlic knot rolls. There is also a very nice bistro a block from my building that has some amazing dishes that I think you'll love. I promise not to be here too long. Every second that you're here cannot be wasted. How does all of that sound?" she asked.

The kiss he wanted and needed to give her was the only response she needed. His eyes lowered to her lips. He couldn't resist smiling when she licked them salaciously. They were covered in a rich red color, in anticipation of what was next. Neither of them disappointed the other.

He'd come this far for this and much more. Moving his hand to caress the back of her head, he joined their lips and delighted in the soft, sweet way she mewed her pleasure against his mouth. He didn't hold back forgetting to care that they were in her office. The door was shut, but probably wasn't locked. He didn't care. He had his lady love in his arms and it was important that she feel and taste how much he'd missed her.

The kiss started out slow with kisses along her lips from one corner to the other. He knew she wanted and needed more. Her hands gripped the back of his neck, holding him in place.

Taryn's mouth opened to give him more and deeper access to her mouth. He accepted the challenge as warmth flowed from his body, through his mouth and into hers were the sensation of his tongue against hers turned hot as fire. This is the kind of feeling he wanted and needed to last forever. He could feel the pulse of their heartbeats with each pass of his tongue over hers.

The heat in the room and in his body rose to an insatiable level when he had to remember where they were. What he wanted to do with her had to wait. Pulling back, he gazed into her eyes and the hooded, smokey haze he found there was its own explanation of what was on her mind.

"Later, baby. You need to get back to work and I need a shower after a long seven-hour flight. Besides, it's a little after six in the morning in New York. I have a conference call at nine this morning, their time."

"Okay. If you must leave," she smirked. "Don't forget to eat something. I know you don't like to eat much on flights."

"I won't."

He stood and shifted the hardness behind his zipper.

"You'll need a few minutes," Taryn joked when her eyes went to his pants and then back up to his face.

"All your fault. Remember, we're talking tonight. No holding back. Whatever the issue, we're tackling it together."

"I promise. We will talk when I get home. Let me get a car for you."

Taryn stopped right before picking up the phone on her desk. She turned back to him again and smiled.

"What?" he questioned.

"I'm so happy you're here. Be prepared to hear me say that the whole time. I'm going to take tomorrow off. I want all day and night with you before you leave."

"You'll have to show me your town. I've been to Paris several times, but now, I get to experience it through you. Let me get out of here."

Adrian picked up his things and headed toward the office door while Taryn spoke to Cordell about a car.

"Cordell says to tell you hello. He was on the only person not in his office when we walked through. He's on another floor preparing for my next meeting. He'll have the car brought around. I'm going to walk you down."

Before they left her office, he pulled her close for one quick kiss before Taryn grabbed a tissue from the box on her desk.

He was familiar with her doing that. She did it often when they kissed in his office.

"No need in giving my co-workers an insight to what we've been doing in here. You did not arrive with red lipstick on your lips," she laughed, wiping his lips clean of any trace.

"Trust me, they already know. I flew to Paris to see you. They know."

24

Taryn hopped out of bed, grabbed her white, shorty silk robe that she never wore at any other time.

After covering her nakedness, she tied the sash tight around her waist but didn't get back in bed. She paced nervously while waiting for Adrian to return from the bathroom. They'd just had an hour-long of loving on each other in ways she didn't know existed. He showed her what she'd been missing being so far away from him. Her body missed him just as much as her heart did. She was hesitant about the talk they were finally going to have. She was able to put it off until now. Was she ready? She wasn't sure. Perhaps, he forgot. With him in the shower, she could go and get them both a snack; maybe even a distracting topic to talk about.

Taryn made a move in the direction of the bedroom door just as Adrian walked out of the bathroom.

"Don't even think about it," he said, stopping her dead in her tracks.

Taryn turned around slowly and smiled.

"What?" she replied, trying to play like she was oblivious to what he was thinking. She knew.

"Taryn – I haven't forgotten that we need to talk. I couldn't help my animalistic need for you when you came home"

"Yes! I know. I loved it all!"

"But now, come back from wherever it was you were about to sneak off to.

"Ugh, you know me too well. How is that possible after just a few months of being together?"

"I take the time to know what I need to know about the woman I love. That didn't take long either. Are you ready to talk to me? I came a long way to see about my baby. Talk to me."

She was afraid. Still, there were things that needed to be said. This was a man who loved her. He promised her that his love would always be without attached conditions. She silently prayed that was true.

"I...I... think I'm being blackmailed."

She kept her eyes locked on his.

"What? By whom and for what?"

"Okay, let me start over. You already know the story of how I ended up with my aunt and uncle after my parents died. I was happy to have them. They provided a good life for me in New York. My last year of high school, I don't know what happened but I started to rebel. I would get in trouble by sneaking out at night to hang around the city with my friends. We would, just for the fun of it, steal things out of stores just to say we did it. Getting caught was the least of our problems because that's just how we thought as teenage girls. Caught stealing is exactly what happened. Luckily, everyone in New York knew my aunt and uncle. That infraction was swept under the rug."

"I think most of us went through a phase like that."

"I agree. Things quieted down after that. I focused on graduating, going to prom and spending my summer here in Paris with my aunt. She decided to do some writing here and thought it would be a great vacation for me. My uncle was doing a few business trips so the time was perfect. That's when I met Nathaniel. You know that his mother, Eloise, owns the publishing house where I work. She was also one of my aunt's best friends. My summer in Paris was a lot of fun. Once I was back home in New York, we stayed in touch. He even transferred to NYU to be closer to me during my sophomore year. With him, I ended up getting into all kinds of trouble. He was a rich kid, two years older than me, yet still a sophomore. That should have been my first clue that he was trouble. I got into drinking, which led to some wild and crazy times."

"Unconditional, remember?" he reminded her.

She nodded her head and continued.

"We were off and on, here and there for a long time. In my junior year, we made a video."

"Video? Of the two of you?"

"Yes. I won't play innocent here, but I thought I was in love. I went through several phases of feeling sorry for myself not having parents and being raised by my elder aunt and uncle."

"Were you drunk?"

"No. We got drunk afterward. It was the dumbest thing I have ever done. I know that no woman should ever let a man record her having sex with him. That day, my aunt was angry at me because of how I was letting my grades slip. She said she didn't care for Nathaniel but she tolerated him because I liked him. She didn't like the things she felt he was coaxing me into doing, like skipping class and spending weeks at his apartment instead of the apartment she and my uncle were paying for me to stay in with two roommates who were my best friends. I got my first tattoo back then and she was livid.

Thankfully, I got it in a place where no one could see it. She was concerned I would mess up my chances for a successful career if I started tattooing my body like Nathaniel had done."

"The heart on your hip with the bow and arrow?"

"Yes. I got it for my parents, not for my then boyfriend."

"No need to explain. I've kissed and done a few other things to your hip enough that I saw the initials around the heart. I knew it was their initials."

"I love how you notice the smallest details."

"Baby, I have to as a lawyer. I have to spot everything."

"Anyway, fast forward to now. Nathaniel and I haven't been together in a very long time. I've been in a few short-term relationships since him, but he always seems to be lingering around. I do work for his mother, so he sees me when he pops in and out of the firm. He seems to think that no matter who I'm with that he will always be the man I end up with simply because..."

"Because you lost your virginity to him. A lot of men think women are theirs for life when that happens. It's a stupid idea."

"I know. Anyway, over the years, he still has not found his footing in life. He once wanted to be a producer of rap artists. Then he wanted to be a sports agent. Then he wanted to open his own book publishing firm. He never graduated so most of his ideas have been funded by his mother. I think even she has tired of him after all these years of still having his hand out. After my aunt's funeral, he wanted to talk to me. He kept calling and texting, but I wouldn't make the time for him. While you and I were away at your family's vacation home, he left me a voicemail that only said for me to remember the video we made and how he looks at it all the time. That was followed by a stern warning that I had better call him. When we returned to New York, I did."

"You didn't meet with him, did you?"

"No. I did call him. Without all the details, he told me that he knew I was worth more millions now. He knew how wealthy my aunt and uncle were. When I laughed at him and told him how foolish he still was, he threatened to post that old video of us on the internet. Basically, he wants me to do what he wants or he will ruin my life."

"Why didn't you tell me?"

"I was ashamed, Adrian. That video is not something I ever wanted anyone to see. In fact, he told me back then that he had deleted it. Now, I know that he never did. That's creepy to hold onto something like that after all this time. He wants me and he wants money. He offered to forgo having me if I would give him a few million dollars to start his own company. His bank of mommy dried up years ago. Now he's telling me to give him money or else."

"Why did you rush to get out of New York and back here to Paris? I am all for supporting whatever you wanted to do, but I sensed a different agenda when you announced you were coming back here. We didn't have a real chance to talk about that."

"I was afraid that when I put my foot down that I wouldn't give him any money that he would release the video on social media. I wasn't just concerned about me. I was concerned about what that could do to you."

"Me?

"People know we are involved with each other," she blurted out.

"Correction. People know that we're in love. I don't see a problem there, sweetheart. Enlighten me."

"You and Zac are building an amazing law business on top of what your fathers started. You are well-known around the world. If people see that video and know that we're together, it could tarnish who you are and what you have. I could never, ever do that to you. I love you too much to see something from my past haunt not just me, but especially you in the business world. I would die if I hurt you in that way because I was stupid in undergrad."

"I wish you had told me when that clown first reached out to you. You do realize I am a lawyer, right? I mean, I am a damn good lawyer. One thing I know about is what he is trying to do is against the law, especially in New York. What happened took place in New York. Was he in New York with all of this communication and blackmail attempts?"

"Yes. That's one of the reasons I needed to get out of there. He has an apartment in New York where he's been staying. I got a call from him earlier today. I didn't answer but his message said he was at his apartment in New York and wanted to know when I was coming back so that we could talk. He knows my aunt's accounts are there. That's probably why he's hanging out there."

"Listen, so that we are clear on a few things. You are not in this world alone. I know you have family and close friends. That's all good. You also have me. I am a man who is completely, totally, unequivocally in love with you. This thing we have is forever. I will never, ever, ever let anyone hurt you in any kind of way. Especially not some fool from your past over something that could never destroy anything about who

I am, what I've built or businesses I have. He cannot touch you once I get my legal brain on this."

"What are you going to do? I'm sorry I didn't tell you. Julianna said I was being a fool for not telling my boyfriend, the lawyer that someone was trying to blackmail me."

"She was right about that. I bet Sherita told you the same thing. I saw her before I left to come here and she didn't say anything to me either."

Taryn leaned back and hit him with a questionable look.

"Sherita was in New York? In the city? She wouldn't be if she was visiting her mother. She didn't tell me she was going to New York. I talked to her a few days ago."

When Adrian's eyes cut away from her and he attempted to lower her to the floor, she stopped him by locking her legs tight around his waist.

"Yes, she's in New York."

"And you know why?" she asked.

After a few deep breaths in and out, she knew he was going to tell her something she didn't know. She couldn't wait to find out what it is.

"No secrets, right? Even if they are other people's secrets?" he questioned.

"Spill it, lover boy. What's going on? You do not have a poker face. I can read you quite easily," she laughed.

"She's in New York to see Zac."

"What! Who is? For what? Is she having a legal issue or something?"

"No. I stopped by Zac's office to tell him I was heading out to the airport the next day to see you and, something I need to remember myself when I'm kissing all on your in my office, he hadn't locked his office door. It was late in the evening and he assumed no one was around. I walked in on him and Sherita lip-locked. I mean, that was not their first time. Apparently, they have been seeing either other for about three weeks. I take it you didn't know?"

"Hell no! Yes! I love it, but wait until I talk to her."

"No, baby. You can't tell her that I told you. Wait until she tells you about it. She knows I know. She begged me to not tell you. Since we don't keep secrets anymore from each other, right?"

Taryn nodded.

"I promise," she said softly.

"Then after today, no more secrets about anything. After I interrupted them, he raced after me to the elevator to tell me that they fell for each other hard. Do you remember the night we were supposed to go to that Broadway play and instead, we stayed in bed watching movies and eating pizza?"

"I do."

"I gave the tickets to Zac. Our firm is also representing Sherita with her newfound wealth. She was at the firm that day meeting with one of the partners and he asked her if she was free for dinner and a play. Since then, they've been pretty hot and heavy. He's even visited her in Boston. I wondered why he rushed to take a business meeting there when we could have sent two of the junior partners. He wanted to see her. Just let her tell you. When she does, put on your acting hat and be surprised and yes, still happy for her. I haven't seen Zac this interested in a woman, well, never. They make a cute couple."

"Not as cute as us though. You know that, right?"

"Yes, baby. Never as cute you me and my beautiful lady. Now, as far as this Nathaniel stuff, I want you to know something. Let's go finish dinner because I'm starving. You had a brother on a serious work out three times!" he chuckled as they walked to the kitchen.

"How can I resist when you make my body hum the way you do?"

In the kitchen, Adrian turned the pots back on before checking the stuffed fish in the oven.

"You can't. I hope it's like that forever with us. As for your little issue, and it's a little one, I got something for him. New York has a law against what could be considered "revenge porn." Now, stick with me before you get upset. I know it wasn't porn, but his attempt to use that video to blackmail you could easily have it labeled that way. Again, lawyer here. I know how to work that. The law is about the unlawful dissemination or publication of an intimate image. That makes it a crime to share any explicit or intimate images of someone without their consent. There mores to it, which I'll share with you. The law does cover non-consensual sharing of that video. I've got a thing or two up my sleeve in dealing with him. You said he reached out to you?"

"He did; earlier today."

"Good. Tell him you'll be in New York in a few days and that you can meet with him."

"What? I don't want to meet with him!" she demanded.

"Taryn, you have to do this. I need to have you both in the same place for this to work. Send him a text and tell him to meet you at your aunt's apartment. We'll pick a time. I don't think it has sold yet."

"It hasn't."

"Good. I have more to think about around this. Do me a favor and let me handle it. I know you can handle yourself, but you have me now. We are in everything together, good and bad. You will never have to go through anything alone ever again. I love you! You love me?"

"I love you with everything in me."

"Do you trust me?"

"Adrian, I trust you with anything. I know you would never hurt me."

"You got that right. I trust you with any and everything."

"So, I'm heading back to New York?"

"Yes. You're heading back to New York with me. We're ending his reign of terror over you. No man will ever be able to have something held over you to keep you in line. Not even me. No fear. No foolishness. I don't want to delay handling him. He needs to move on to something and someone else. We can talk more about that tomorrow. Tonight, I want to enjoy being in Paris with you. Since it's about to be dark outside, I set up the table on your balcony for a nice dinner under the stars. No more talk about anything unpleasant. I never want to see you sad again. The plan is for smiles on that beautiful face forever. You with me?" Adrian asked and raised his hand for a high-five from her.

25

As his rideshare driver sped through the heavy New York traffic, Nathaniel's ringing phone had become an annoyance. He knew who was calling. His only thought was on getting to his meeting with Taryn in the apartment that was once her aunt's but is now hers. He'd stayed up most of the night excited about the fact that Taryn had finally agreed to give him the money he needs. Her giving in to his demand was exactly how he'd hoped things would turn out. He had some debts that had to be paid that his mother wouldn't cover. The biggest being one in Las Vegas. Not that he was planning to return to Sin City anytime soon, so he thought staying in New York would give him more time before his marker came due. Clearly that wasn't the case when his phone rang incessantly. Lenzino Vincentcelli wasn't going to give up on reaching him. Answering while in the car with a stranger hearing his every word wasn't his plan. He didn't have a choice. If he didn't soon respond, there was no doubt that Lenny had friends who could get to him outside of Vegas.

He looked at the driver and then turned to his phone. It rang again. Turning it off would only aggravate the man more. He pressed the green phone option and gathered himself.

"Lenny! How's it hanging?"

"I don't know because the only thing that will be hanging is you if you come up with my *money!* I loaned you a lot of cash on your mother's name. Should I go see her to get the money you owe me? You keep telling me it's coming but you know what, my bank account is still four hundred grand short. That money is growing by twenty-grand each week. If you can't pay the original amount, what makes you think you'll be able to pay me what you now owe me? Don't make me come for you. Just because you left Vegas doesn't mean I can't get to you. I want my money!"

Nathaniel shook hearing Lenny's loud, demanding tirade. The man shouted the last word so loud, the driver had to have heard it too. He braced himself to speak calmly to diffuse the situation before more threats were issued.

"Look, yes, I left Vegas. That's because the source of the money I owe you is here in New York. I'm getting it right now. Give me a few days. I'm expecting the money to be transferred to my account today. It will take a few days for it to clear because of the amount."

"Oh? How are you coming into this kind of money? What are you robbing a bank? What did you discover some rich benefactor or some rich old lady? I've seen you work your magic on the women here in Vegas. You got them flaking out and doing all kinds of things for you. I'm talking women of all ages. I don't care what you need to do. I want my money or I'm coming for you. That penthouse in New York won't keep you hidden from me. I've had guys on you since you left here. Get...my... money!"

"I hear you. Can you give me a few extra days? I'll head right back to Vegas as soon as the transaction is done. You know my girl is still there, so I'm coming back. I wouldn't just leave her."

"Stop playing with me. That woman is for the streets. She is not just yours. She's following your money too or I would have used her as leverage. You should make sure the sheets are washed after you return. The number of men she's had in and out of your suite since you've been gone is in the double digits. Look, I don't care anything about your personal life. You know I don't play about my money."

"Lenny, I promise you'll see it within seven days. I'll send you proof in a few hours. At least give me some extra time to show you that. You'll then know your portion is on the way."

"Your promises don't hold much weight these days. You need to stop smoking it, putting it up your nose and gambling recklessly with your money before you come across someone who isn't as understanding as me. If I were anyone else, they would be trying to find your body where someone would have buried it in the dessert. I'm a man of my word. Your outcome is up to you. You got me?"

Nathaniel knew Lenny was serious. Of those he owed money too, the most dangerous was him. He never should have borrowed on his family's name. Taryn didn't know it but she was about to save his life. He'd been plotting a way to get her to leave her current boyfriend and come back to him. There was a time when she hated being away from him when they were back in college. Sure, that time was years ago, but if he could do one thing, it was to get a spark out of women. That was something his mother often said that his father had a knack for. He gets his suave from him, for sure. What he didn't get from him was his business acumen.

He was a disappointment to his parents, especially when it came to his problems with drugs and gambling. They hated that he never found his footing in life. He sat up straight and fixed his slouched posture. He was about to get his life on track.

With Taryn and her millions, he could start his own company; a publishing company to rival the one his mother owned. He was also thinking about getting into the music business as a producer. He didn't have any background in it but with money, he could buy the staff and talent he wanted to have. Those high up in the music industry got all the women falling at their feet. He could handle that kind of come up in the world.

He was tired of having to beg his mother for every sent he needed to continue his lavish lifestyle. He could tell that she was tired of footing the bill. She still slid a little money his way here and there but nothing like she had been doing. He dared not even ask his father for anything. Of their three children, he was the black sheep that his father couldn't even look in the eye. While his sister and brother both graduated from college and even went as far to get their doctorates, which had them riding high in their careers, he was still floundering about from pillar to post. Soon he would show them all. Caught up in his thoughts, he didn't realize that the driver had finally pulled up in front of Taryn's building.

Exiting his rideshare and hustling into the lobby, he let the guard know that he was expected in the penthouse apartment. As the man checked, he waited. Making sure he hadn't forgotten what he needed, he checked his jacket pocket first for his checkbook. He would need that in order to provide her with his banking information to transfer the funds over to his account. He wanted to get that out of the way today.

In his other pocket was another item he couldn't wait to use. He tapped the right pocket and smiled when his fingers encountered the small box. It wasn't a ring. He was nowhere close to that. Instead, the box held four circular items. He was hoping to convince her to keep the apartment instead of selling it. He had many ideas for living in it. First, he wanted to reminisce with her on the days back when she gave her virginity to him back in those early college years. She was the most inexperienced women he'd ever been with. By now, he hoped she learned a few tricks. After all, he needed her to keep him interested while he spent her money; or should he say, *their* money.

He was escorted to the elevator.

"Thanks, bro. Looking to seeing you more often in the coming months. The lobby could use an upgrade. After I move into the building, you can let me know who to take that up with."

He started to say something when the guy looked at him as if he was an alien speaking a foreign language. Instead, the elevator door closed. His eyes caught him walking back to the front desk shaking his head from side-to-side.

The elevator rose quickly. When the doors opened, he stepped out and with confidence, he walked to the door of the apartment. Inside was his destiny. She had better play his game or he would follow-through with his threat.

Today, he would also have a little taste. One thing about Taryn was always her killer, shapely body; all natural. She was perfect in every way. He looked forward to a ride down memory lane. First, the transfer of money. He was also eyeing a nice private plane they could travel back and forth on. So much to do. Her money made it all worth it. Shaking off any apprehension, he pressed the bell.

26

Taryn shook nervously when she heard the buzzer. She knew Nathaniel was on his way up. David, the concierge on duty for the week during the day had already messaged her that he'd let Nathaniel in the elevator. He even shared with her Nathaniel's comment about the lobby needing some work once he moved into the penthouse apartment. They both laughed it off. She alerted David to what was going on, just for his awareness. In case she needed to have Nathaniel escorted out by his feet, she wanted David to be on standby to facilitate that. He told her two of the other men were also on duty and doing other tasks, but he would wrangle them together with just a sign from her either through the alert buttons throughout the penthouse or she could text him. Either way, he was ready to help if needed. Taking her time, she walked to the door and opened it slowly. On the other side stood a man she could barely stand to look at because she was disgusted by him. She couldn't believe he was the son of one of a few women she admired the most in the world. He'd fallen so far that even without spending anytime with him yet, she could see that he was on something. He tried to dart his eyes away, but she caught them. She knew what she saw.

"Come in," she said moving to the side to allow him to come in.

When he leaned forward in an attempt to hug her, she moved out of his reach.

"Oh, so it's like that?"

Taryn closed the door and walked ahead of him into the main open space of the living room. Though void of furniture, she had a reason for going into that space to talk.

"Like what?"

"I was trying to give you a hug. The last time we talked there was a lot of tension."

"Nathaniel, you accosted me outside of my building. You threatened my livelihood or to avoid that, you want ten million dollars."

"I know it seems like a lot, but for you, it can't be. That's a small drop in the bucket for you. I googled what your aunt was worth. She had, I'm sure, already put money aside for you. She bought your Paris apartment. I heard in the media that she left you like sixty million along with property and houses. This apartment alone is worth quite a few million. Don't act like that little bit I'm asking you for will hurt your pockets. Besides, I'm not trying to make this interaction between us hostile. Did you forget what we used to mean to each other? I know it's been a lot of years, but still. We had some off and on times over the years. We could rekindle some of that, you know."

"I'm involved with someone. Remember him? You threatened to ruin him by his association with me by putting that video on the internet."

"I'm just saying, he's this big attorney and all. So what? Me and you have history."

Nathaniel again moved toward her and she backed up.

"Stop coming toward me. We're not hugging or reconnecting or anything. You came here for business, right? You came to get money from me in exchange for not putting my old personal business out on the internet. You know, in the legal realm, that's called blackmail. Call it what it is; call that spade a spade. You were bold enough to threaten me. Claim this low-life move your making."

Her frustration with him was showing. At this point, Taryn didn't care. She was over him even being in her space; in the apartment that meant so much to her. He didn't deserve to be here. He didn't deserve any of her money. She didn't care how much of it she had. Not one red penny would end up in his hands.

"Aw, look at you being all strong, black and powerful Black woman. I like that. You're feistier than I remember. That's a turn-on. You know I still have a thing for you. As a couple, we could wipe out all this blackmail unpleasantry. Do you know that we could be a power couple? With fortune and the kind of fame I'm hoping to start up with the money, we could be as big as JayZ and Beyonce. I'm just saying, it's possible."

"You mean with my money something can be possible? You have decided that what I have belongs to you too? Miss me with this mess. What are you on? Drugs? Alcohol? I'm thinking drugs. You are out of your mind."

She then saw something that was making her sick to her stomach. Nathaniel's eyes were taking in her body. She could feel his creepy eyes as she wiped her hands down the sides of her black skirt which was formed to her body. Too bad her attire wasn't for him. When his eyes rose to glare at her breasts which were covered in a white, long-sleeved top that tied at her waist, she knew that it was time to put all this mess to rest.

"Look, I'm not trying to make this a volatile situation. You know you are one gorgeous woman. You're different. You're confident. I love that in a woman. Look, I'm going to let you think about what we could be together. In the meantime, what about the money. Can you transfer it today? Do we need to go to your bank to do that? I have my check book with me that has my bank routing and account number on it. It should be easy to do."

"The video? Where is it?"

"On my phone."

"Is it anywhere else? With this amount of money, I want to make sure you don't have some hidden version another place that you'll come back to me at another time for more money. This is it. What I give you today is it; nothing more."

"I only have it on my phone or in the cloud or whatever it's called."

"The original?"

"This is it."

Nathaniel reached into his pocket and took out his phone. When he reached in his other pocket to take out his checkbook, he pulled it out and a small box fell to the floor. He tried to grab it before she saw it, but her eyes were faster than his hand.

"What the..."

"I can explain that," he nervously said.

Taryn moved further away.

"You came here with what other intentions? Sex? You have really lost it."

"Hey, you never know. We were good together once."

She laughed out loud at him.

"Let me see if I have this straight. You blackmail me out of millions. You want to somehow weasel your way back into my life. Then you show up with a box of condoms in your pocket! Nathaniel, what is wrong with you? Who have you become?"

"I know what you must think of me. I'm desperate. I'm going to tell you the truth. I owe money to some really dangerous and shady guys; some Italians. I need to pay them back this week. My family won't give me money and I need it. Can we just do that and forget about what you just saw? I only have a few days to pay these guys back."

Taryn exhaled and let her shoulders drop. She was done.

"Get out, Nathaniel. Right now. Just get out."

"What? Hold up. We had a deal. I'm not leaving here without the money. I still have the video. I promise you that if you don't go to the bank with me today and transfer that money, before evening hits, I will have that video all over the internet. Don't think that I won't. That's how desperate I am right. You need to reconsider."

"And you need to step away from my woman or we're going to test if these windows are shatter-proof."

Taryn turned her head in the direction of the office where Adrian had been waiting.

"Uh. Oh, I see. The boyfriend is here to save the day. Well, you had better school your girlfriend on how I can damage her life and her reputation since I'm sure you heard everything."

"You should also remember that you know I'm a lawyer. Your entire conversation is on record. In the state of New York, it's against the law to blackmail someone with revenge porn, which, in legal terms, is exactly what this is. Since you already know I'm a lawyer, peeped this – Penal Law section 245.15 criminalizes the non-consensual sharing or publication of intimate images which includes the video of the two of you that you have. Now, the fine and penalties aren't high but if you're looking at a reputation you can ruin, think of your mother's. If and when this gets out if you stay on this path, that's what's going to happen next. Shall I assume you care enough about your mother to not drag her name through the courts with this? I plan to file a motion in court first thing tomorrow morning. That is, if you survive being this close to my woman. I already told you to back away from her."

"What? Taryn can't speak for herself?"

"In this instance, she can speak for herself along with any other aspect of her life. Today, I am here protecting MY woman from a predator such as yourself. I suggest you figure out handing over the phone with the video on it."

"Yeah, whatever. This phone is mine and so is the video. Feel free to try and pry it out of..."

Taryn was stunned when Nathaniel didn't get a chance to finish his statement. In mere seconds, Adrian had Nathaniel by the neck, lifting his body off the floor and up against the large glass window. She struggled with what to do to end the scene before her. She knew that Adrian being stronger, taller and more in shape than Nathaniel that she could hurt him. She didn't want Adrian to risk getting into trouble for physically hurting Nathaniel.

"Baby, no!" she shouted. "Don't."

Taryn could hear her words being broken up as they came over as she was on the verge of tears. She didn't have to do anything when a voice behind her spoke up.

"Adrian. It's okay. Put him down. I've got this," Eloise said coming from the office where Adrian had come from.

Taryn was happy that they had both accompanied her back to New York to confront Nathaniel. She learned a major lesson behind all of this. She finally understood that she was not in this world alone. It was Adrian who thought of the plan to have him and Eloise at the apartment, unseen, while she talked with Nathaniel. She needed is mother to hear who her son now was. Outside of Adrian's brilliance was his quick wit in the way he saw a situation play out from beginning to end before deciding if it would work. What he came up with is exactly what was happening right now. She was thankful for the man who loves her this much. She didn't want Nathaniel hurt. She only wanted him to stay out of her life. She has a man who lets her be her while still making sure that she knows he is and will be her protector in everything.

When Adrian dropped Nathaniel back down on his feet, she watched him stumble as he worked to catch his breath. Then reality set in. He noticed his mother was in the room and not in Paris where she knew he assumed she was.

"Mom? What...what are you doing here?" Nathaniel stammered out through the persistent coughs that he couldn't control after being hemmed up by his throat.

"I'm here listening to you blackmail Taryn. When she and Adrian first told me of this atrocity, I couldn't believe my ears."

Taryn moved as Eloise made her way past her to walk right up to Nathaniel. If having Adrian lift him with ease from the ground wasn't bad enough, Nathaniel's mother grabbed him by the chin and held on as she twisted it from side to side. Even though her back was to them, Taryn could still see

Eloise's face turn down into a grimace. Taryn moved next to Adrian and took his hand into hers. She could sense the fury and anger in his body. She rubbed her hand across his back to try and calm him. She felt bad for what he had to hear and endure as Nathaniel spoke to her like she belonged to him. She was overwhelmed with fear when Adrian, uncharacteristically picked Nathaniel up by his neck. She feared he would really hurt him. She was never more thankful than right now. No doubt, the window wouldn't break. She'd never seen Adrian so mad. She understood. Nathaniel was being a horrible person.

"Mom, it's not what you think," Nathaniel tried to explain.

"No? So, I didn't just overhear you blackmail Taryn for money over an old video of the two of you? You have gone off the deep end. It's a good thing I was here or Adrian would have really hurt you."

"I swear it's not what you think. I wasn't really going to release the video," Nathaniel slowly stuttered at the end of each word.

"Because you thought she was going to give you money. Insane. Absolutely *insane*. The phone. Give it to me now!" Eloise yelled while thrusting her hand out, palms up.

From the authority behind her powerful, demanding voice, Taryn realized even she shook with fear at the voice of a woman who has had enough. Nathaniel handed the phone over to his mother.

"Eloise?" Taryn questioned softly, pointing to the phone.

Eloise held a finger up pausing anything further that she may have to say.

"Are there copies of the video anywhere else other than in this phone?" Eloise asked Nathaniel. "You said something about the cloud," she added.

"No. That's it."

"Have you ever shown this to anyone else? Would this be in the hands of another living soul on this planet?"

"No, mom. I would never..."

"Save saying what you would never do. I never would have expected this version of my son before me today, yet, here we are. Getting rid of it on the phone and the cloud will make this disappear forever? No copies, no traces?" Eloise pressed.

Nathaniel dropped his head after spending the past few minutes trying to soothe his neck where Adrian's hands had been.

"No," he spoke in a low tone.

"Look at me!" she yelled right into his face.

They were so close that Nathaniel had to feel the heat come from the words that were coming out of her mouth.

"I didn't mean any of what I said," he tried to explain.

None of them were believing it.

"I don't think I have ever been this disappointed in you. You have done some crazy things and stunts over the years. This right here is lower than I thought you could ever go."

"I'm sorry."

"To whom? Me? You have to know that what you're saying is misdirected."

When Nathaniel's eyes landed on her, Taryn started to look away.

"No, baby. Look at him. He owes you an apology and a lot more for how he has terrorized you during the hardest time of your life after losing the only mother figure you have ever had."

Silence lived in the space for more than a few seconds before it was broken by Nathaniel's words. Taryn looked him in the eyes and didn't turn away.

"Taryn I'm deeply sorry for what I tried to do to you. Being desperate should have never led me here. I'm so sorry for the drama I brought into your space. Adrian, I apologize for disrespecting Taryn." Eloise handed his phone to Taryn who looked to Adrian for direction on what to do with it.

"My son Jersey is on standby waiting to hear from you. He runs one of the biggest tech firms in the country. He will help you get rid of any and every trace of the video. Passcode?" Eloise said directing her latest statement to Nathaniel.

"What? To my phone? I have personal things on there?" "Not when your brother finishes with it. Again, passcode." As he ran everything off that they would need, Taryn sighed with relief as Adrian took out his phone and captured what they needed including her son's number to get everything erased.

"Thank you, Eloise."

"If you find that you need anything else, let me know. Nathaniel will not be leaving my sight until my husband arrives in LA where we are about to fly off to in order to meet him. He's flying in from Dubai from a business meeting that he's willing to leave early in order to deal with our son. He and I will deal with him and his issues. Trust me when I say, you will never, ever hear from him again. That's my promise to you, Taryn. Nathaniel, I have a car service in front of the building. Get to it and don't move once you get in it. Oh, and there are two men waiting for you to get off of the elevator in case you think of bolting. I will be down in a minute. We have a flight to catch. Go, now!" she yelled.

Without any more words being exchanged, Nathaniel left without looking at any of them.

"I appreciate you so much for who you have always been for my aunt and for me as well. My aunt really appreciated the work and personal friendship you had over the years. I want to thank you for the opportunity you afforded me that got me to where I am today. I want to inform you today that I will be putting in notice that I'll be resigning."

Out of the side of her eye, she saw Adrian move away from the wall that he was leaning against. Not only was she shocking her boss, but she was also doing so to Adrian. She didn't have time to talk to him about the decision she'd made the night before they flew back to New York with Eloise on the same flight.

"You're quitting?" Eloise asked. "Why? Is it because of what Nathaniel tried to do to you? If so, I can guarantee that you will be able to work in peace and not come across him again at the office."

"No, no, this has nothing to do with him."

"What is it? You are one of the best on my team. If it's not him, are you unhappy? Do we need to renegotiate your contract? What can I do to get you to stay?"

"I appreciate that. It's not about being unhappy. It's about the path I want my life to go in. I have something different I want to do with my life and my career. I think this is the perfect time to make a change. I don't want to leave you or my team in a lurch. I plan to transition everything during whatever timeframe is needed. I'll make sure I complete my aunt's last novel with the company."

"Are you returning to Paris soon?"

"That is my plan. I'll reach out later today with what that plan is. I promise I will be in the office in a few days. I just need a few days to do some planning while I'm here in New York. I hope you'll understand."

Eloise nodded at her and Taryn let out a deep breath. This wasn't the perfect time to make the revelation. This was the start of the blueprint for what she wants to do. She thought about it during the entire flight. She was ready.

"I do. I hate to see you go. I know that whatever you do, it's going to be great. I can't wait to see you soar. Your aunt wanted that for you. Most of all she would have wanted this young man with you for the ride. Not only has she loved you like a daughter since forever, but I remember her telling me about him as well. Her biggest wish for you was him. I see that happened. I'm happy for you. Again, I'm sorry for what Nathaniel did. You will never have a problem out of him again. Live well, Taryn. See you around the publishing world, I take it?" Eloise said and hugged her.

"Yes, you will."

When she turned and left the apartment, Taryn's back was still to Adrian who hadn't said a word after she revealed her plan for her life. She wasn't sure she was ready to talk about it. Being in Adrian's arms is all she wanted and needed in this moment. Her nerves had her under lock and key since Adrian shared his plan with her. She didn't want anything to go wrong, and it didn't thanks to him. Before he could say anything, she turned around and raced into his arms. He held her close, whispering repeatedly how much he loved her.

"You sprung that up on me," he finally said.

"I know," she noted, snuggling closer. "Can we go down to your apartment before you have to go to the office? I'm hoping you can show me just how much you love me before you have to leave," she added.

When she tried to turn and take him by the hand to follow her, Adrian didn't move which caused her to remain planted where she stood.

"Not so fast. I think you need to say something else here."

"What? Do I? Is there something else I need to say in order for you to take my clothes off? You're so good at that," she tried to say with the voice of a seductress.

"Don't try tempting me with that sexy voice. I can take off all of your clothes with my teeth, but that's not the most important thing right now. Explain, please. What was that? You are resigning? That came out of left field."

Knowing they weren't about to leave just yet, she knew it was time to lay it all out for him.

"The idea of me resigning is only coming out of left field for you. I've been thinking about it. I thought long and hard. This was not a haphazard decision. I want to explore the idea of starting my own book publishing firm. I know it will take some time to grow, but that can't happen if I don't start. So much has happened in my life lately. I feel like I've been a participant. What I want to do is drive the bus. I want to pivot into something that I can work on and make my own. I have my aunt's unpublished novels which are not under contract for the company I work for. That means I can do what I want with them. I want to publish them. I also want to do some writing of my own. On top of that, I want to help others get published that some of these larger houses won't even touch if the writer doesn't have a large social media presence or any of the other reasons they give for not giving a new writer a chance. My aunt always had faith that I could do it. You have had faith in me that I could do it. We talked about it. You encouraged me. I want to take the time and get a game plan in place. I'm hoping that the man I love will help point me in the right direction with his knowledge and his contacts."

"Baby, I am extremely proud that you've come to this on your own. I am here for whatever you need. Are you sure you're okay after what just happened? I know it was a lot. He was a whole lot. I need to know that you're good."

"I am perfect. Because of you, that mess is behind me. He won't try barking up this tree again. Oh, one other thing I haven't shared with you yet."

"Whew! I wish there was a chair left in this apartment that I could sit on. I'm surprised the realtor hasn't staged this place yet in order to get it sold. I need to sit down. You're hitting me with thing after thing. Do I need to lay down for what's next?"

Taryn leaned up and kissed him softly on the lips.

"I want to move to New York. I plan to keep my place in Paris because I love it. It's my own getaway spot. I want to be back here for my next phase. I want to be here with you."

"Taryn, you know that nothing in this world would make me happier than you being back in New York. May I remind you that I was serious when I said that I would be wherever you are at any time. I want you to be free to live your life when and where you want. We are forever in this life together."

"I know. One of the main reasons I love you is that you have been willing, from day one, to follow my lead when it comes to how we move. I love that. You listen. You love. You give me what I now know I've been missing; the love of an amazing man who doesn't define me but who lets me be me with your unconditional love. I know there are women who say that we shouldn't change our lives for a man. I'm not doing it for you. I'm doing it for me. You are a big part of my life now. I want to have a life with you. I know how much you are willing to sacrifice for us. I want to do some of the sacrificing as well. That's why this place isn't for sale yet. I'm coming back to New York to live."

Adrian dropped her hand that he'd been holding and walked away from her. He turned and gazed out of the large window that overlooked the heart of New York City. She didn't know what to think about what was on his mind. She waited. When he turned around to face her without a smile, she didn't know what to think. Did he not want her close to him? She couldn't imagine that was the case.

"I love you. I want you. I need you. I adore you. It's your plan to move back to New York and live one floor above me? Can I offer a different option?"

She nodded as he walked back toward her, taking her hands into his.

"Yes," she uttered softly.

"Move in with me. If you're coming back this way, I would love to go to bed each night and wake up to you. Sure, we can do that from two different places, but do we need to? I have no doubt that you are my forever lady. There isn't another woman for me. I've waited a long time to feel for a woman the way I feel about you. When you went back to Paris, the way I missed you was crazy. The second I saw you in Paris, I wanted to hold onto you forever. I think we can make what we have last forever. I want to say marry me, but that I plan to do in a big, magical way. I know you don't like surprises, but you already knew that was going to come your way sooner rather than later. I didn't want to force your hand if you were going to continue living in Paris. With you coming home, the life I want is with you. If you want to wait until we're married, if you say yes, when the time comes, I'm good with that too. I love that you'll be near. As long as this decision isn't about us, but more about you and what you want."

She smiled as bright as her lips would allow.

"You already know my answer is and, on that day, will be yes. This is your show, baby. I don't even have to think hard about moving in with you. That's a solid yes from me."

The kiss that Adrian planted on her took her breath away. Still, she wanted more. How much time they spent in the heated exchange she didn't know. What she did know was that she couldn't wait to get these kinds of kisses day after day, morning noon and night.

"We have a lot to talk about. Do we sell both of our places and get a new place? Do we move in here? Into your place?"

"I don't care what we do as long as we are together. I was looking at the new construction a few blocks away. After seeing your aunt's place year after year, I have been thinking of getting a top floor apartment with two floors. We can work all that out. Enough talking. I think I have some panties to remove with my teeth and definitely my tongue!" Adrian said.

This time he raced to the door with her in tow.

"You can never threaten me with a good time. Wait? Isn't Adore coming by?"

"She is but not until after I meet with her at the law firm. She wants me to look over a new contract she received. By the time she gets to the apartment, you'll still be asleep because I plan to celebrate hard and deep over the fact that I'll get to have you every single day and night!"

Taryn put her hand over her mouth at how fast Adrian was walking toward the elevator.

"I guess I'm not the only one in heat!" she declared.

"With you around, is there another state for me to be in?"

In the elevator, when he lifted her up and placed her body against the wall for the short ride down one floor, she let him have his way, getting what he needed. She couldn't wait for a lifetime of his loving.

27

Two Years Later

"Mrs. Jarreau, your husband is on the line."

Taryn ended her call with Julianna who now worked for her at her own company, *Horneslow Publishing House*. After relocating to New York City, to start her life with Adrian, the first call she made was to Julianna to offer her a job at the company she hadn't yet started but had big plans for. That had started her on a path of slowly knocking things off her bucket list like a pro.

She patted her heart softly when her eyes landed on the large picture of her mother and aunt that Adrian had made for her as a gift on the first day that she walked into her new company as president. She was proud to have named the company after them by naming it after their maiden name.

Her bright smile was evident when she finally answered after a quick trip down memory lane. The was happy believing that she'd made both women proud.

"Baby!"

"Hey, you. Are you done for the day yet?"

"Just about. I was just running a few things by Julianna. She was letting me know how much she loves her new office."

"You're finally getting settled in, huh? If you find anything that doesn't work to your liking or suit your taste, let me know.

I can have the company come back out to make any changes you need."

"No, everything is perfect. Also, when your sister gets here in a few days, I want to take her out again for a nice dinner. She and Loren did their thing with the interior design."

"Amora hasn't stopped bragging to everyone that she led the design team for your new office space."

"She's found her place in her career. As for me being done for the day, yes. I was expecting this call from you."

"Good. I know Julianna can run things so that you can get out of there. I want some quiet, alone time with my sexy wife. This is one of three nights a month that we promised each other we would step away from work to make sure we never stop working on us."

"Adrian, we're heading out of town for two weeks. That's more than the days we promised each other. I won't complain. We've been busy for months now; you with clients and me with my clients. This time is going to be great."

"Yes, it is. No work at all. Just us doing whatever we want to do without any pressures when it comes to our jobs."

"I got you, baby. I'm on my way down. I was signing off on all the new office equipment that was delivered. There is a team here from that company getting everything hooked up and working. I'm glad we found this space because the publishing company was getting too big to be operating out of the apartment. Besides, the architect will be coming into the apartment to take measurements for the redesign so that we can move from what was your apartment that turned into our apartment the day we said our "I do's". Now that we're moving up to the penthouse, I want things to be just right."

"I get it. You can do all of that when we return. I promised you two weeks away on a vacation of your dreams and that's what I'm doing. It won't work if you're still here in New York."

"Are you going to tell me where we're going? Not that I wouldn't follow you anywhere, I need to know what to pack."

"Not on your life, baby. I know you. You cannot talk me into revealing my plans. Trust me – you will love where we're going. Don't forget, I know my baby. I'm taking you away and it's a secret until we get there."

"You plan the best surprises. I promise that I only have a couple of things left. Um, can I ask if Sherita and Zac are going with us? I'll admit that I may have overheard you talking to Zac about it the other night. You know I'm a light sleeper until you join me in bed."

She was relieved when he laughed heartily on the other end of the phone.

"You are so sneaky!" he declared.

"I swear, I didn't hear any of the plans you made."

"I guess that part doesn't have to be a secret. Yes, they are going. So are Tellum and Cheyenne Blackstone. That's all I'm going to say about it. Now, can you please come and lay one of your sweet, sexy kisses on your husband who is desperate for the touch of his woman?"

"Yes, baby. I swear, my cousin is so tight-lipped. I talked to her last night, and she didn't say anything."

"That's because, like you, she doesn't know where she's going. She also doesn't know that you and I will be coming along. We fellas planned the entire trip."

"We are the luckiest women alive!"

Signaling to her executive assistant, Antonica, Taryn pointed to what she needed her to finish up so that she could get out of the door.

"Hand it all over to your staff and let's go. I'm downstairs in the car waiting on you. We need to get to the airport."

"But, how do I know that what I packed is what I'll need? What if we're going someplace with cool weather? What if it's a place that is extremely hot? Adrian – help me out here."

"No can do. I had your assistant pack for you based on where we're going."

Taryn huffed in frustration. She really wanted to know. "So, I only got to pack my essentials while she did the rest. No fair."

"It's all fair in love, baby. Besides, if there is anything you need, you can get it where we're going. When I say surprise getaway, that's what I meant. Five-star all the way, baby."

Taryn looked up when Julianna walked into her office and started to turn around because she was on the phone, Taryn waved her inside. They needed to talk about a few more things.

"I'll be down in five minutes; I promise. I love you. I'll be right there."

"Are you ready to go celebrate your one-year wedding anniversary?"

Taryn looked at her friend with cautious curiosity.

"Do you know where he's taking me?"

Julianna held up her hands in surrender.

"No way. He told me that I couldn't hold water. He knew that you put me up to ask him to see if he would reveal it to me so that I could tell you. That man knows his wife. He's right. I would have told you," she laughed.

"Yeah, he's right. I'm going to let it go and be happy that I have a man who loves surprising me with things like trips of my dreams. He hasn't failed me on any of them."

"That man is ready to love all on his wife for two straight weeks without any interruptions."

"Whew! That's for sure," Taryn beamed.

"How many times has he begged you to get out of here?"

"You mean my vacation surprise king? A few."

"Stop keeping him waiting. You know I've got this. The best decision I made was to come and partner with you in running this publishing firm. The first book of your aunt's that we published has already garnered a contract to turn it into a movie. I sent the contract off to Adrian's firm to have it looked over. We've gotten some inquiries from actors who want to be a part of the project because of how long the book is still sitting at the top of the charts. We're ready to publish the second book in the series. This one is going to top the first. But, no more work talk for you. Your king awaits. Have a good time. The entire team will hold everything down. I'm even letting the architect in the apartment while you're gone. Trust me that I got this."

Taryn jumped up and hugged her.

"I know you've got this. I'm a workaholic, that's all."

"Not for the next two weeks you're not. I know he's the surprise king, but do you have what you need for your own surprise for him?"

Taryn danced in place and shrieked with excitement.

"My bag. Look inside," she said, pointing to it. She was too excited to pick it up herself. She was a bag of nerves.

Jules opened her bag and pulled out a small box.

"What's inside since you have it wrapped already? I swear, you and Adrian are a perfect pair. Surprises all the time."

"A cute pair of baby slippers and a white t-shirt that says, daddy-to-be."

"That's what I'm talking about! He's always coming up with nice, cute things to surprise you with. Finally, he gets his day to be surprised. You're going to make a beautiful mommy. Adrian is going to be an amazing father. I'm glad you decided to stay in New York. This is the path your life was supposed to go on. You were never meant to say goodbye to go have a life without him. You get that right?"

"Who knew this is where I would be? In love, happily married, about to have a baby and running my own company. I may not have seen it but it was always a part of my plan. I'm glad I listened not just to my heart but to friends like you, Natalie and Sherita who always have my back."

"When Adrian stepped into your life, there was never a plan for you to go back to life the way it was. Everything happens for a reason. In your case, all you had to do was believe that there would always be more hellos than there would be goodbyes. I'm so happy for you. Just go love on your man. Don't ever look back."

"And I never will. Bye girl!" she cheered.

Taryn grabbed her bag and made her way to the door.

"Oh, so you do know how to say goodbye," Julianna said while playfully patting her feet on the floor.

"I sure do. Just not to my husband; never, ever again."

Epilogue

Two More Years Later

Adrian moved throughout the Paris apartment as quietly as he could with Myles fidgeting in his arms. The toddler was making it clear that he wanted to be put down to run around.

"Son, give me a few minutes and I'll put you down. I need to keep you from running into the bedroom where mommy is asleep. I swear those little feet of yours sure can move at seventeen months old."

"Dada, down."

"I know Myles. You like to run. How could you have skipped walking and gone right to running everywhere. I know you love having daddy chase you, but wait until we get to the park. We're going out right now but first, you have to sit in your stroller. Work with me," he pleaded.

Adrian laughed at himself trying to reason with Myles who simply smiled at him, showing him his grin with eight teeth gleaming.

He hustled trying to keep him from sliding down while he gathered all he would need for their early morning walk. He promised Myles the park. If Taryn was going to get any sleep after a restless night with Myles, he was going to have to take his rambunctious son out.

When Myles finally stopped trying to get down, he resorted to cheek patting. He thought his son would have been exhausted after being up half the night. It was clear with all the excitement and gusto that he was ready to play. When he placed him in the stroller, though Myles often hated it, he seemed content knowing that being in it meant they were going for a ride. Taryn would finally get her much-needed sleep.

Two months pregnant with their second child and possibly third child, morning sickness and already swollen feet made moving around in the morning almost unbearable for her. They took the trip to Paris from New York so that he could convince her to step away from everything work related. To try and stave off the morning sickness, Taryn needed time to fully wake up into the day. Taking Myles out for a walk was his way of providing that she would be able to do that in peace. If Myles saw Taryn up and moving about, he would want her to play and focus on him.

"You know, son, I love our early mornings, but maybe you can consider giving me and your mother a few late morning risings perhaps one day a week?"

Adrian nuzzled Myles' nose before placing him in the stroller. He grabbed the bag of needful things before grabbing his keys and heading out.

"Dada?"

Adrian leaned over so that Myles could see him while they waited for the elevator.

"Yes?"

"Cookie?"

"Yes, you can have a cookie, but only one. Your mother would have a fit if she knew I was giving you sweets this early in the morning. It's a celebration, though, right?" he asked, reaching in the bag and pulling out the snack bag with four cookies in it. Myles bounced around excitedly in his seat with his little hand out.

"Dada, dada" Myles happily sang. He then used sign language that Taryn had been teaching him pretty since birth to sign that he loved him.

Adrian returned the sign back to Myles.

"Dada loves you, too."

Before the elevator door opened, one of their neighbors came out of her apartment and joined them. She has been a long-time neighbor of Taryn's when she had lived full-time in the apartment before moving back to New York years ago. They decided to keep the apartment to have as a place to escape away to that was familiar.

"Adrian! You all are here? A short visit?"

"Yes, about a month. Taryn needed a break. You know how much she loves the apartment and the Paris skyline. Besides that, I thought it would be a good idea for her to visit some of her friends here that she's been missing."

"How are you, Miss Isabel?"

"I'm wonderful. I see that you're just as handsome as ever."

She then leaned down to Myles' level who tried to hand her a piece of his cookie.

"And look at you, Myles. You are getting so big. You were a tiny thing the last time I saw you. It's always good to see you all even though it's not often. Going for a walk?"

"We are. Taryn was up late and needed her rest. Myles and I are going for a stroll and then to the park. Now that he's bigger, I want him to see some of the places his mother and I loved seeing when we dated. We started coming here more often right after we got married."

They stepped into the elevator and chatted a little more before they reached the ground level and went in two different directions. Before he got too far and his phone rang, he knew it was Taryn. He assumed she heard them leave and wanted to know where they were going without her. That was the usual conversation when he and Myles stepped out of their apartment back in New York.

"Where's my baby?" she asked.

"Which one?"

"Funny. Both of them. I woke to an empty apartment."

"How are you feeling? I left a few crackers on the nightstand. That usually helps you in the morning."

"I ate those immediately. I'm feeling good. I think this baby is going to be a girl. And then, maybe a girl and a boy. I had some sickness with Myles but with this pregnancy, it's a constant visit to the porcelain in the morning. Are the two of you out for a walk?"

"We are. We won't be gone for long. I'm going to take him over to the museum. He won't find it as interesting as I usually do, but you know how he loves a ride in the stroller where he gets to talk his talk to everyone walking by. We'll stop briefly at the park. After a few minutes on the swings, he'll probably be ready for an early morning nap by the time we get back. I hope you're going back to bed."

"I am. I miss the two of you already."

"Adore is there. She's probably still asleep."

"Yes! I'm so happy she made it. I can't believe Myles let you take him out of here. When his *DorDor* is around, he doesn't want anybody else but her."

"I wonder if he will always call her *DorDor*. I know it's because he hears you call her that. He hasn't seen her yet. You were all sound asleep when she called to let me know she had landed late. When she got to the apartment, she was wired. I stayed up with her for a few hours before I yarned for the tenth time. After checking on Myles, after he'd had a hard time staying asleep, he was sleeping soundly. I crawled back in bed. You never even knew I had ever left it. He'll see her when he gets back. Plus, you should know she'll want to talk to you when she gets up."

"Oh? Is everything okay with her?"

"It's a girlie thing that she only wants to talk to you about. She flew all the way here after I told her we would be here a month. She claimed she wanted to talk only to you and in person. She flew right out. Me and Myles being gone will give you some time to talk."

"A girlie thing? What does that mean, Adrian," she prodded.

"A professional football player is sniffing around her. I think she's into him, but she wants some sisterly advice. My sisters have always had each other but they've never had a big sister like you. I do believe they like you better than me, which wasn't an easy achievement. Have your time with her. We'll be back later. Are you going to tell her that we're possibly having twins? She and Amira won't be the only set in this family anymore."

"I didn't know if you wanted to tell your parents before telling your sisters. I would say at this point, it's more of a possibility than not. I did not carry this big with Myles this early. My last appointment showed two. Not telling anyone or claiming it yet is just me being cautious."

"Adore and Amira will be more excited than you and me. I get your caution. That means we will have two infants and a toddler. You see how they fight over Myles and who his favorite twin is. Both babies are growing good after that small bump in the road a week ago. You are two days from three months. We will soon be an instant family of five. My sisters will be excited about spending more time around to help us with them."

"Amira practically lived with us my last month of being pregnant with Myles and at least the first two months after bringing him home. I bet they will practically move in with us once the babies are born. Before you ask if I'm okay with that, yes – more than you know. I love Amira and Adore. Are we making plans for today?"

"Only if you want to."

"Are you doing any work?"

"Baby, I told you that when we are having down time outside of New York, my time belongs to you and Myles. Zac and the team can handle everything in my absence. When we are here or at the house in Lake Geneva, there is no time for work. I didn't make any plans for today just in case you wanted to just rest up."

"Is a cruise on the water too much? Adore would love that," she asked.

"It's not, if that's what you want. Myles will love it more than any of us."

"Other than that, I just want to relax with my family."

"If that's what you want, that's what we'll do."

"You know, life is going to get crazy with two new babies in the house. Are you really excited? Not only was having another baby soon after Myles in our plans, but to find that there are two of them is a lot."

"Are you serious? Damn right I am!"

"Damn right," Myles said.

"No. I shouldn't have said that. Myles just mimicked me."

Taryn laughed on the other end.

"He is his father's twin but with my hazel eyes. You know he likes to repeat after you."

"Right. Anyway, we won't be long. Sherita called last night. She and her fiancé are planning to come for a visit while we're here. She wanted to be sure that was okay with you."

"Yes! I can't wait to see her. Can you believe her and Zac are a couple who are now engaged? I mean, who would have thought?"

"I'm sad I won't be a matron of honor for her wedding like she was the maid of honor for mine."

"Well, she said pregnant or not she wanted you to play that role. You don't want to?"

"With two babies I'm going to be huge. I don't want to be a distraction at her wedding. We'll see how that goes. The wedding was planned. The pregnancy is a surprise as far as timing."

"Are you excited?" he asked.

"I'm over the moon with happiness. You know I want to have a big family. With the publishing company continuing to turn a large profit and Julianna and the team doing great work, I plan to step back some. I had struggles with my first pregnancy. I won't take chances with twins."

"That's good to hear. We have an entire lifetime together. Family is our priority and always will be."

"Is that my big brother?" Adore yelled into the phone.

"Tell her yes it's me and to stay out of my snacks," he joked.

"Whatever. Where's my Myles? I woke up and expected to hear him running around."

"Taking him out to tire him out. We'll be back soon."

"Bet. See you then. I'm going to make me and Taryn some breakfast," Adore said.

"Make enough for me."

"I got you," Adore exclaimed.

"She's off and running. Kiss my baby and keep an eye on him knack for tossing things to the ground."

"I'm all over that. I thought he was about to toss his cup like a football. Instead, he took it from me and laid back. We may not be out as long as I thought. I think he's tired. That's my boy."

"I love you even more as daddy Adrian. Myles has the best father in the world. That's why I'm excited about these babies. We could have ten and you will always love them unconditionally. Having a family has always been my dream. Losing so many people close to me had me desiring a family of my own to love and cherish. You're giving me that. I love you more each day."

"Babe, I love you too. You are my life; my world. You and Myles and soon, our new babies. You and Adore enjoy your time. I'll see you in a bit?" he asked.

There was a pause. He knew what was next. It was a sentiment that he and Taryn have come to love. Then she said it.

"Hello, my love," Taryn said.

"Hello, my baby. Always hello," he replied.

"And never goodbye," Taryn added at the end of their call.

He knew that she needed to hear him say hello. He would make sure he always said it. Always hello, never, ever goodbye.